MURDERLICIOUS

GW00646574

N.JOY

Murderlicious was a fun book to write, but all due credit should go to my long suffering husband, who's habits may have been inspirational!! Thank you for having smelly feet!

Charlie & Paige, thank you for putting up with mums writing. One day.

To my wonderful dad, thank you. Your involvement was integral to the story line, I couldn't have done it without you.

Thank you to my amazing mum for your unwavering love and support.

For the encouragement and love, thank you little Sis.

Lee Sherborne of Braddicks and Sherborne of Bideford, I can't thank you enough for the time you spent with me. Your professionalism and knowledge was second to none and proved invaluable.

Simon of Devon & Cornwall Constabulary, it was a fun experience! Thank you for not making me commit a crime and allowing me to question you!

To the Rapids Response teams that came to my rescue, thank you for your time and the medical knowledge, it was graphic!

To my friends for the missed coffees and the distracted thoughts, thank you·

Copyright © N.Joy 2018

Printed and bound by Amazon

Find out more about the author and her work @ www.nljdesigns.co.uk

ISBN 978-1-9997358-1-4

For my family & friends

Thank you for continuing to believe in me

I Loves you all   x

1

Have you ever wished that you could get away with murder?

Have you spent hours dreaming of ways to dispose of that problematic person in your life?

Louise Wilson had.

Louise and Jim loved each other. They had produced two grown-up children. They had a wonderful life but one day, over thirty years in, a carelessly discarded and rather smelly pair of shoes lead Louise to be plagued with an avalanche of daydreams, all involving an array of ways in which Louise would become a widow.

It had been a long day and the shelves of the supermarket had been decimated as the first frost had sent the locals into a buying frenzy. Six-foot-high metal cages jostled for space in the aisles as impatient shoppers pushed past them to grab the last can of soup or pint of milk. There was no one for all, it was a case of all for one with zero displays of chivalry.

Between the war on bread and races up and down the aisles the supermarket had turned into a scene from Argos on black Friday. Boxes of cereal were snatched away as quickly as Louise was restocking them. Louise Wilson was the type of person who was always busy. She was rarely idle, always doing or thinking of something, but even she despaired at the retail madness. It wasn't technically in Louise's remit, but she strived to help, and it was all hands-on deck, or risk being taken down by an over-zealous granny or a budget restricted family after a trolley full of bargains. The store was heading for bumper profits and the residents would have cupboards stocked with tins of food that would never see the inside of their oven. At least the harvest festival will have lots of produce as parents dig out the bad weather reserves, dusting off the tins bought in panic. Louise was counting down until her shift finished and she could head home.

As long as she beat her husband Jim through the front door she could get the heating on and be snuggled up in the comfort of her slippers and mammothly fluffy dressing gown catching up on *Come Dine with Me* or one of the many shows featuring the boys in blue. Whoever got there first got control of the remote control, a coveted prize. She liked to lose herself in the craziness of reality TV. The viewing proved a source of research into how to commit an undetectable murder, or rather how not to do it. The heavy oak front door of their detached house a welcome sight after the day Louise had had.

The door slammed to mark Jim's arrival, the wrath written all over his face. Louise's eyes rolled, and her heart saddened as she could sense another argument brewing. The management at Jim's work had employed an enthusiastic, and very young, executive to 'redirect' the company and they were causing ripples among the long-standing, and long-in-the-tooth team.

Sometimes it seemed to Louise that the arguments were for arguments sake. Some days it felt like he would argue that the sea wasn't blue, and that grass isn't green. Although in this neck of the woods the waters were more brown than blue, and grass was yellowing from a lack of water or over use of a mower in the long-forgotten summer season. Jim, however, always made his argument with a degree of authority.

Jim had never physically raised a hand to Louise, he probably knew that she would not hesitate to return the blow, but the mental anguish was harder to control. His mouth was just not able to resist the words flowing from his brain. It was often just little jibes, water of a ducks back to most but too Louise they were like insects, burrowing into her subconscious so they could keep reminding her of her inadequacy's when Jim wasn't around. Louise was by no means an innocent party and could be found guilty of antagonising a situation or using a condescending tongue. Jim may have the gift of the gab, perfect for his role as an employee, but he didn't use his 'shut-up' switch, a downfall for his role as a husband. Louise often thought he should have worked in construction, he was always digging himself into a hole. And, in Louise's opinion Jim should pay better attention to her, that way he would learn what was good for him, and he wouldn't end up in imaginary predicaments.

There was a lot of love there once, there still was but not in the way that Louise yearned for. She craved emotional attention whereas Jim thought that a good session in the sack was a cure for all ill feeling. There was a general difference of opinion as to what constituted a good time, but Louise had mastered the art of humouring her husband, his smile indicating that he thought it a job well done.   The glimpses of the original person that they each fell for still broke out every now and then but soon surrendered to the pressures of work and the hectic trappings of the modern world. Their appetites had changed over the decades that they had shared yet neither wanted to end the union, well, maybe a little, on occasions. Louise, a typical Taurean, was stubborn and determined to see it through, to the bitter end. Jim, who thought horoscopes were codswallop, was too lazy to put the time and effort into another woman.

Today Louise had largely escaped from the torrent of negativity, Jim to wound up to focus his efforts, instead stomping up the stairs for an early bath. Louise took the opportunity to get tea started. Straight from the freezer to the oven but after a day at work she was never going to be a masterchef. As she slid the tray of frozen chicken and chips onto the shelf she felt guilty that she hadn't loving prepared a fresh meal from scratch. Episodes of *Come Dine* flashed through her mind.

Every time she watched the contestants in their kitchens she thought to herself that she would prepare her own sauce, that she would serve up a three-course meal worthy of any Michelin stared restaurant, but life seemed to drain all passion by the time she was back home from work. On the days that she wasn't required at the supermarket there seemed a multitude of chores to complete, leaving little time or inspiration to produce a dish to rival Gordan Ramsey. Louise cooked a mean Sunday roast and her steak melted in your mouth, but it was the same old dishes time and time again. Not much variety and little spice - mainly because Louise wasn't very adventurous and wasn't a fan of hot or spicy food, southern fried was about her limit, and then she needed a jug of water.

Subconsciously this is probably why she never achieved her culinary goals, that and royally messing up with an inedible offering and having to prepare another meal. When the children lived at home there was always a reason for rushed repeated meal times; clubs, homework, immature taste buds and when the children got older and more self-sufficient Louise increased her hours at work and the dreams of being a domestic goddess stayed on the back burner.

As dinner cooked Louise returned to resume the episode that she had paused. Her frozen chicken and chips a shame on her as she watched the Lincolnshire resident prepare a main of broiled salmon with shitake mushrooms and asparagus, marinating the meat and chopping ingredients to make the accompanying sauce. The closest Louise got to a glaze was when she did the occasional roast potato in honey.

The water that pounded the bathtub as it filled was accompanied by the vibration of footsteps as Jim paced the floorboards upstairs waiting for the bath to fill.

As the timer digitally counted down on her phone Louise's mind wandered from the envious viewing of the perfectly prepared and presented chocolate fondue pudding to thoughts that she had entertained once or twice over the past decades. Bumping off her spouse.

Sometimes she just fantasied over the deed itself, other times her mind hosted an episode of *CSI*, from the murder all the way through to the disposal and evasion of justice. Today her daydream bypassed the execution and started with the disposal. All the gory bits skipped, the daydream started in the kitchen as she prepared to cook Jim's remains for her very own televised dinner party. A thigh roasted in the oven. Salt and oil smeared over the scored skin so that it crackled. Her daydream mind wondered if a human skin produced as good a crackling as a pig. Potatoes nestled against the flesh to cook in the fat. Veg was swimming in pans on the hob. There was no deconstructing of the meat but there was seasoning.

Louise talked to an imaginary camera in true *Come Dine* fashion as she pulled the bones out of the fingers and wrapped bacon around the human sausages before placing them in the oven. As they cooked she prepared a crushed pea base for her starter. The food was presented on slates, Jim hated food not served on traditional china. He'd be super perturbed to find he'd been presented on roofing tiles. Louise pushed the pea mix into cookie cutters to form a pretty shape and positioned the fingers-in-blankets on the emerald bed. She drizzled a zigzag of home-made sweet chilli sauce down the side. The guests waited in a lavishly furnished dining room that was not part of her own kitchen dinner but belonged in a magnificent stately home. Seven people were seated at a great rustic oak table all looking expectantly at the food as Louise gladly placed a slate in front of each guest.

The incessant beeping of the alarm brought her out of her daydream just as her guests were about to devour their first mouthful of Jim. Disgruntled at not knowing the outcome of her first dish Louise sulked into the kitchen to dish up her mundane meal. Her carefully prepared dream peas substituted by tinned marrow-fats pumped with radiated heat and spooned haphazardly onto the porcelain plate.

Louise shouted up the stairs that tea was ready, Jim's muffled reply confirmed that he had heard her.

Louise was already half way through her meal before Jim joined her looking refreshed and relaxed. They ate in silence, the TV providing the only conversation. As was usual Louise not only cooked but she also did the dishes. Jim thanked her for the food, as he often did, making her feel bad, briefly, about serving him up as the main course.

The remainder of the evening was spent in front of the TV before retiring to bed. Jim lost in his laptop, scrolling social media, the odd giggle escaping over someone's status update or comical photo fail. A dreamless sleep left Louise desperate to get back to her fantasy and find out how her meal was received. Would her guests give her a ten? Did human really taste like chicken? She would never know as she had a shift at work, so her daydreaming would have to wait.

2

Things had been going surprising well between the two. A whole week had passed with not a cross word, disgruntled face or snipe being exchanged on either side. A night of disturbed sleep put pay to that. It had been a long time since Louise had had to wake during the night as the children had flown the nest years previous. But, after the third rude awakening Louise's murderous scenarios were running amok. The first two times Jim's snores had been hushed by a rough push and had returned to a low rumble but the third time it took all of Louise's will power not to follow through and keep the all too real fantasy in her mind. Louise used her own body weight to propel Jim onto his side which temporarily silenced him as her mind silenced him permanently. Louise lay in bed waiting for sleep to come for her before Jim's pneumatic nose kicked into gear, again.

In her imagination Louise looked down on the open-mouthed snoring monstrosity taking up one half of the monarch proportioned bed. Fantasy Louise's blood boiled as she watched her sleeping husband. She reached down with one hand and took the pillow her head had occupied mere minutes before. Gripping her feather-filled sack tightly with both hands Louise stood above her husband, an avenging angel of dreamers. She positioned it over his open mouth, her knuckles white from the force of her grip. With arms locked at the elbows Louise smothered Jim with the pillow from Sainsbury's luxury range. In his sleep induced state Jim put up little in the way of a fight. His hands slapping and clawing helplessly at Louise's pyjama clad arms in an attempt to survive the snore ending extermination. In reality Louise would likely have lacked the strength needed to hold the pillow in place long enough but then again, a tired scorned woman would be a force to be reckoned with.

Once Jim had stopped struggling Louise relaxed, but did not relinquish the pillow, there would be no air getting back into those lungs. Her arms started to shake from the effort and the breath that she had been inadvertently holding was released in a flurry of hot air, further contaminating the crime scene with her DNA. In her mind Louise left the pillow balancing on her dead husbands face for several minutes before removing it and going back to sleep herself. To her delight the deed had been accomplished and Jim looked not gone but peaceful, in a tranquil slumber.

With a smile forming on her lips sleep came at last and took Louise on a journey that she could not recall by the time her alarm shrilly woke her, a mere four hours since she had last looked at it.

Louise sat on the edge of the bed fumbling for the clothes that had been discarded on the floor the night before. With eyes only half open, she desperately willed the clock to turn back time. Not having a time machine meant that regardless of her bodies protests Louise had to drag her carcass from her warm divan into the harsh reality of a sunless morning. The depressing weather fuelled another daydream as Louise rummaged, in the darkness of the bedroom, through her draws for clean underwear. Resentful at the broken sleep and Jim's tardiness on a morning. Louise huffed and puffed as she got ready. It was a good job they didn't live in a straw house.

Her daydream was in full swing by the time she adolescently pulled the bedroom door shut with a slam. Jim stirred but as per usual remained in his dream world. He didn't have to be at work for an hour and a half and the housework fairy would already have visited so he felt he could sleep his morning away.

Louise was irritated that she had missed so much of her own daydream. The echo of her footsteps as she stomped down the stairs breaking the spell of the fantasy just at the moment when she was delivering the death blow. Even as she rained the baseball bat down upon Jim she was aware that she was muttering to herself about of all Jim's short falls. The ferocity with which Louise wielded the bat was uncharacteristic, proof that sleep deprivation can trigger perverse reactions in even the calmest of people. Where the bat had come from she didn't know but it felt comfortable in her hand. Jim's head a large bloody ball on the floor, just like a scene from *The Walking Dead*.

Louise left most of her breakfast, stirring the increasingly soggy cereal around the bowl. She couldn't shake the miserable mood she was in. The can of Coca-Cola she guzzled with olympic speed gave Louise the sugar rush she so desperately needed to get her moving but left her burping as she closed the front door behind her. It was too heavy to slam. Her nose tingled from the coke bubble fizz and her eyes welled at the corners.

She still had a bee in her bonnet over something that was partly out of Jim's control when she left for work. No matter the sleep aids Louise had found Jim had found an equally 'valid' reason for refusing to use it. He said that nose clips "felt funny and ticked his nose", the chin straps made him "feel like a prisoner in his own head" and nasal strips made his nose "tingle" which he didn't like, the list went on. The bumpy pot-holed lane from the house to the main road should shake some sense back into her.

Louise's frustration was reinvested against the other road users. There was a tractor six cars up, so the progress was slow and the car behind was starting to grate on the little cool that Louise had left. With oncoming traffic and a line of cars there was nothing to do but chug along but the boy racer behind was unnecessarily close. Louise thought his car must be trying to start a love affair with hers, no courtship he was going straight to first base. Already coming to the end of her tether before the day had even got going Louise released a torrent of abuse at the driver, none of which he could hear. To the relief of the tail back the tractor turned off down a dirt track and the procession that had gathered behind him began to pick up the pace. Not fast enough for speedy behind as he shot around them like a bat out of hell. A near collision with an oncoming vehicle was narrowly avoided, Louise hoped he wouldn't be someone else's problem. The considerate car behind gave her the space she needed to calm down and compose herself. By the time she pulled into the staff car park at the rear of the store she had belted out some 80's power ballads and was feeling in a much better frame of mind. The sleepiness blown out with the volume of her singing.

Time went fairly quickly. Louise was kept busy with employee grievances, store policy and customer re-directing. The shift was over before she knew it. Much better than the days when the clocks seemed to taunt her by moving at a snail's pace.

The return journey was a compilation of rock and country. Louise's tone-deaf voice murdering the lyrics, but the enthusiasm of her performance would have been at home on the pyramid stage at Glastonbury. Pulling onto the drive Louise squeezed her bashed up BMW, Clarence, next to Jim's functional but unattractive, and unnamed, white van. In the garage Jim had both a Lotus Esprit and a Kawasaki ZZR600 but they only came out every now and then, and certainly not when it was raining. Though Jim denied it Louise suspected their purchase was down to a midlife crisis, Jim trying to recapture the thrills of his youth.

It took her a few minutes to locate Jim. He was in the study comparing energy prices on the internet. The man liked to think he was receiving the best deal, hated the thought that there was a discount out there that he wasn't getting.

Louise had picked up a few bits of shopping before she left work, determined her happy mood would be translated into her food. She had decided to start small, a few side dishes to accompany a well-practiced main. Cheating by buying a pre-cooked chicken Louise filled a pan with rice and brought it to the boil.

Louise's singing wouldn't win her any awards. Forgetting that nobody else could hear the music pumping out of her headphones she belted out a tune, treating the empty room to the tuneless vocalisations of another's timeless hit. It mattered little to Louise as she was in 'the zone', besides she was past caring what Jim thought of what she termed her 'quirkiness'. And, he was no Barry Manilow himself. The microwave was nuking the petit pois, which should have been pre-cooked, whilst Louise concentrated on her *Come Dine* ingredients to give the Chinese staple a little Louise flare. Not that she had followed any standard recipe. No. Louise was cooking on a trial and error theory basis. The trial being the first attempt from something she'd seen someone else preparing on TV. The error being that she should probably have followed some kind of instructions and the theory being that she liked the taste of everything that went in, so she should like the end result. The kitchen was awash with harmony, the pan bubbling, the microwave humming and the extractor fan whirling.

Louise mixed pineapple chunks and garlic into the rice. Next came several doses of pre-bottled sweet chilli sauce. Thinking it lacked something Louise diced a few spring onions and chucked them into the pan as well. Jim came in mid experimentation and rolled his eyes at Louise dancing round throwing in ingredients like a witch mixing a spell in her cauldron. Louise stuck her tongue out at Jim and blew a childish raspberry as she watched him retreat from the kitchen. To concentrate on her culinary debut Louise removed the earphones and tucked them away on top of the still warm microwave.

Chef Wilson took the mushy rice and spooned it into a small pot which she upturned and emptied onto the plate in a neat dome, topping with two prawns. Next came a pot of chilli prawns, garnished with a slice of lemon and cress. The carved chicken fanned out upon a bed of aromatic rice. Very gourmet.

Washing up the last of the dishes used in preparation Louise's mind took a stroll around Fantasyland. Louise always cleaned as she went so there were only the dinner plates left to do. There would be a fifty/fifty chance that Jim would do the remainder of the dishes and an even slimmer chance that he would do them to Louise's standard.

Louise must have scrubbed around the same pan twenty times as she chuckled at the thought running through her mind. Though her mood was now a positive one Jim wasn't to escape his doom. Her mind took a comical approach as opposed to a grisly or gruesome end. From the living room Louise could hear Jim's failed challenge of '*try not to laugh*' on YouTube as he was gripped by uncontrollable fits of laughter. Louise found the crazy antics of the internet stars making fools of themselves for five minutes of fame, or in the case of many a lifetime of ridicule, amusing but Jim took the crown for encouraging such video submissions. In her fantasy Jim was so racked with laughter that he was literally rolling round the floor, holding his sides as he took deep gulps of breath to calm himself. It was as Louise considered what a fun way it would be to go, to laugh to death, that Jim seemed to gain some semblance of control over himself. Fantasy Louise thought to herself that she wasn't going to stand for a recovery so pounced on her husband like a cat on an unsuspecting mouse. She embedded her fingertips into his sides and tickled him for all her worth. Jim's face reddened as he struggled to breathe through the cries of laughter that escaped him. The plea to his wife to "Stop, stop, I can't catch my breath" fell on deaf ears. Louise only ramped up the intensity and delivered the killer strike by means of a giant raspberry being blown upon his hairy belly. A trick that would always have the children doubled up with glee when they were little. Jim lay on the living room carpet, quite dead but with a smile still on his face.

With half her mind still in her daydream and the other back in reality Louise shouted to Jim that tea was ready. Stepping down into the dining area Louise served the food. The couple always sat in the same seats. Always had done, even since the children were little.

They chatted over the meal about nothing much; the weather, the news, a quip or two about the antics of the supermarkets customers and a comment or two about a new office romance at Jim's place of employment. The potential for juicy gossip lost on an uninterested Jim.

As suspected Jim washed his own plate then retreated to his study leaving Louise to entertain herself.

She watched some catch-up TV before taking her glass of wine upstairs for a hot bath. The bathroom was as steamed as a sauna by the time Louise had filled the tub to its limit. Louise always washed her hair and body as soon as she got in, so she could just chill in the hot bubbly water. With a towel wrapped around her head like a turban Louise lay back in the tub, the bubbles persevering her modesty. A glass of red wine in one hand a book in the other.

Louise lost herself to the tale of a female murderess wreaking havoc through the streets of Whitechapel in Victorian London. What if Jack was a Jill proposed the novel?

A toasty Louise slipped from the bathroom straight into the bed she shared with her husband, the electric blanket making the duvet a sandwich of warmth, Louise the willing filling.

3

Frank and Ellen were both coming home for Sunday lunch, so Louise had been cleaning the house like a woman possessed all day Saturday. Not that their house was dirty, but they certainly wouldn't be scored a ten on *Four in a Bed*. After today, and for a week or so, you'd be able to run your finger over any picture frame or the top of the door and not a speck of dust would be found. Louise even got up on the worktop and scrubbed down the top of the kitchen cupboards.

Jim went to visit his mum for the day, 'to get out from under Louise's feet' he'd say but they both knew it was to avoid being dragged into the great clean. Jim's dad had fallen victim to a heart attack in his early sixties, cruelly just a few days short of his retirement. Poor Mary, his loyal and devoted wife had never recovered from the loss. They were one of those couples 'still in-love' after over forty years together. In the past decade she had faded away, her spirit and heart buried with Johnathan Wilson, leaving behind an empty shell. Effectively Jim lost both parents on that fateful day. Mary had lost the will to live, but Jim couldn't be with her all the time and they'd agreed that they couldn't look after her at home either, they both worked. They needed to think about long term care but the twice daily visits from carers would have to be sufficient for now. Jim never talked about his feelings but his visits to Mary continued to cause him anguish, yet Louise knew that Jim would tell her if and when he was ready to talk about it.

Jim was the type of man who would clean what he could see, skirt around the edges and be back in front of the TV before the adverts finished. Louise was marginally better. She did at least dust off the units and the ornaments every now and then. Even if she did just hold them down to prevent knocking them off instead of removing them.

The windows had been stripped bare, the chairs sat naked of coverings and the washing machine was going ten to the dozen, in direct competition with the tumble-dryer. The carpets had been vacuumed to within an inch of their lives and you could skate across the laminate flooring. Scented candles were lit in every room and the polished surfaces reflected mirror images of their surroundings. The house gleamed. Knowing that Louise had been exhausting herself all day Jim phoned through the offer of a take-away for tea. Louise was happy to sit back and wait for the food to be brought home knowing that she wouldn't have to do any dishes, just a bit of recycling. Jim wasn't being as kind-hearted as he appeared, junk food was reserved for when he wanted a break from Louise's cooking. Also, a secret burger could be eaten on the drive home and Louise would never know.

She scoffed down the fast food in record time, famished from the exertion to leave the house spic and span. Jim wondered at Louise sometimes for he knew the children would pay as much attention to the state of the house as they did growing up in it, anybody would think that royalty were coming. Louise whacked on the TV whilst she waited, her body cooling as she relaxed. She didn't smell too sweet but had planned a long hot bubble bath with a glass of wine and her book. She couldn't wait to find out how the killer took down her first victim. The scented candles would have to work their magic to disguise Louise's o'natural odour.

Before she retired to her bath and bed Louise fired up a bit of the old charm and graced Jim with a treat that was generally reserved for birthdays and other special occasions. Jim was pacified and peaceful for the remainder of the evening. Satisfied with a job well done Louise went to sleep happy in the knowledge that it was just the cooking to contend with tomorrow. That and the feeling of longing that the children always stirred in her when they came home. Not they were children anymore, but they'd always be Louise's babies. As much as Louise relished the freedom to come and go and do what she pleased she secretly pined for the noisy hectic days of having growing kids in the house. Jim did not.

Though Louise liked to pick fault with Jim she had plenty of her own. Louise could go from calm to crazed in sixty seconds over silly little matters but to her they were annoyances that could be avoided if Jim just did as he was told. Or just left things alone. Or stopped breathing, the choice was his. One of her many pet hates was Jim never putting away his shoes, or anything for that matter but shoes were one of her top five reasons for wanting to bludgeon Jim to death on a regular basis. Louise spent the kids youth saying 'there's no shoes rack in the living room' but Jim still couldn't manage to put them away.

Every morning there they'd be, abandoned and smelly in the middle of the living room. He couldn't even be bothered to put them in a corner, just flicked them off like an insolent child. They weren't the result of spontaneous human combustion either. No, he'd be let off for that and it would be a natural cause so no courts, judges or inmates. It did happen, she'd read reports, no accelerant, no explanation, no suspect. And no such luck for Louise.

Louise fluffed and straightened all the cushions on the sofa and put away the dishes from the night before. She picked up Jim's shoes for the zillionth time. Holding her dearly beloved's offending footwear at arm's length Louise imagined what death by shoe would be like. She'd heard of woman in killer heels, balancing on branded spikes, feet shaped like Barbie dolls but that wasn't how her fantasy played out. Louise manufactured a scenario where instead of hurling his shoes in the general direction of the shoe rack she took one in each hand and marched upstairs.

In a rhythmic motion Louise slapped Jim repeatedly across the face, from right to left until his cheeks were red from being beat and he lay unconscious in the bed they shared. Louise herself owned no girly style of shoe but her fantasy had produced a single lace in design stiletto that was as pointed in the toe as it was in the heel. Louise gripped the shoe in her right hand, her fingers running over the name Jimmy Choo which was etched into the sole. She rained down blows whilst informing Jim that "Shoes. Go. In. The. Shoe. Rack."

Blood splattered onto the headboard, stained the milk white pillow cases and camouflaged against the scarlet Poppies of the bed spread. Jim's face was punctured with circular holes, the shoes holding up surprising well to the battering. Worth every penny of their four hundred pounds plus price tag. Poor old Jim didn't have time to react. He went from asleep to unconscious to dead. Fantasy Louise was quite exhausted by the time the stiletto was lodged into Jim's neck. It stopped the arterial bleed which spurted over Louise's side of the king size when the shoe was removed. Louise hastily plugged the hole with the shoe, a designer bung.

Louise mused that her fantasy self would have been a few pounds lighter and with skin that was a bit tighter but instead of a perfectly formed Louise she got the real Louise, wrinkly skin, saggy boobs and hair dragged into an un-brushed ponytail.

The smell of polish persistently lingered in the air. The windows had steamed up as vegetables bubbled on the hob. Louise set the table, humming to herself. She always had a time table, so nothing was left to chance though she had perfected her roast over many years. Despite this, her veg tended to be over boiled but she didn't eat her greens anyway and nobody ever complained. She was a salad girl, had been since she left home and was no longer forced to eat vegetables.

True to form Jim slept the morning away, emerging ten minutes before their youngest, Ellen, arrived - on time. The eldest, Frank, arrived with just moments to spare, his long-term girlfriend hanging uncomfortably off his arm. Louise silently cursing her son and his entourage as she plated the carefully prepared roast. Louise always made too much, which was just as well. Ellen had inherited Louise's thoughtfulness, and both had Jim's height with the eldest sharing his fondness for his bed too. Louise was happy, just glad to have the family under the same roof.

Everyone chatted away as spoons scrapped against the dishes in the carvery style   serving, Louise chipping in from the sink as she washed up the pots and pans. Jim's eyes were screaming "just leave them women". It had become habit, to be the last to sit down. Part of Louise's martyrdom Jim would inform anyone willing to listen. The succulent beef was a tempting shade of pink inside. The home-made Yorkshires had exploded into misshapen but tasty batter mountains. The vegetables made for a colourful centre piece. Her dinner was ready to go with mushrooms and tomatoes substituted for veg and the potatoes on Louise's plate were chipped not roasted. Neither would her food be drowning in gravy, unlike the others.

After all these years Louise had never considered death by drowning in gravy, death by chocolate pudding had been invented, as such, but what about drowning in melted chocolate? Louise pondered this quickly as she finished the dishes whilst waiting for everyone to be take their helpings. The fantasy was a quick one with Louise deciding that if anyone was going to drown in chocolate it would be her. A warm cocoa sea, she'd sink with a full belly, yummy.

Satisfied silence fell as the food was savoured and devoured. An occasional compliment, sibling jibe or joke was uttered through mouthfuls of food.

Contented bellies waddled down to the living room to chill in front of the box as their dinner went down. Ellen stayed behind to help with clearing the table and give her mum a hand with the remainder of the dishes. Ellen could usually be relied upon to provide assistance. Frank was always quick to escape and shirk any responsibility, like father like son.

A classic *Carry On* was playing on the screen when the girls brought coffee to the deserters. Jim was already sat in his chair, his eyes closing as he prepared for his afternoon nap. Frank was nodding off but the vice like grip his girlfriend had on his knee kept him from drifting off to sleep. The film had already started, Louise sitting down just as Barbara Windsor's bra pings across the campsite. Sniggers went up around the room. She had seen it so many times but still found it amusing. It was her type of wit, finding humour in another's misfortune.

Despite not being there she liked to recall the story of Ellen falling of her bike into a patch of brambles. Not funny in itself but the images she conjured as she was told of the incident were very amusing and made her chuckle. Jim had taken the kids on a local trail, the six-year-old Ellen had only learnt to ride two weeks previous so was on her maiden voyage. She was wobbly and lacked the confidence of her older brother. Louise didn't 'do' bikes, didn't see the point in the two wheeled contraptions, unless they had fairings and were fitted with a 1000cc engine. With Frank zooming off ahead on his BMX Jim was caught between the fast and the slow. Apparently, Ellen had stopped pedalling and gravity took over. Before Jim had even braked she was down.

An hour or so after the meal had been eaten the playing cards were out and a game of pontoon, or twenty-one as Ellen had always called it, was underway. Jim had spent years trying to convert them to poker, but the others liked the easy simplicity of pontoon, no rules, just counting up to twenty-one, with the added excitement of going bust.

The afternoon flew by. The Wilson offspring, who had no prior engagements, were feed sandwiches when they failed to depart before tea time. They took their leave in the early evening. To Louise the house felt empty without the love and laughter of the whole family living in permanent residence. It was just an echo of what was.

A massaging shower topped off a wonderful day. Louise was asleep almost as soon as her head hit the pillow. A deep dreamless sleep followed, one that Jim failed to penetrate with his snores, or his death.

4

Another few weeks of mundane routines slipped by. The weather was starting to improve, the evenings drawing out. For Louise, it just made her feel guilty that she wasn't making the most of the daylight hours. Getting out there, maybe doing a bit of running. She did like to curl up on the sofa under her teddy blanket, the wind howling down the chimney breast and rumbling around the fitted gas fire that had replaced the glorious open fire that had once heated the room. It had been installed before Louise and Jim had bought the place, to keep up with modernisation. It was something that they had always intended to deal with but had never got around to it. Both were in rare agreement that having the original log fire, as opposed to the glass fronted imitation log fire, would be beautiful, and for Jim add value to the property. There was always a reason not to. The kids were too young and may burn themselves, a tree branch may fall out and burn down the house, the house would be smoky. The only time they had got as far as pricing the renovation the washing machine broke and needed replacing so that swallowed took precedence. Always a reason.

Heat was a bone of contention in the Wilson household. Louise was always cold. She often wore her hat indoors and her dressing gowns were constant fluffy hugs, her face and hands being the only flesh regularly exposed. Jim on the other hand had a central heating system off the scale. His skin was normally hot to the touch and he spent the summer months shirtless, just like one of the werewolves from *Twilight*, though for Louise the view was a bought and paid for hairy beer belly and not the sculpted abs of the Hollywood hunks. At times Louise warmed herself up on Jim but that led to other ideas. She used to sneak up on Frank when he was a boy and warm her chilly hands on his torso, but Frank was too big for that now, and lived too far away to be his mother's heater. There was no medical reason to Louise's chilled temperature, her circulation was fine, and she was active. She even took a coat on a family holiday to Florida and wore it. Jim thought she was just cold blooded sometimes, she could certainly be cold towards him.

Jim didn't even need to be present to trigger one of Louise's murder scenarios. Any number of minor annoyances would have Jim at the centre of a deadly scene in which he had no hope of survival. Today it was the act of a noisy cement mixer that was relentlessly churning that had Louise chomping at the bit to strangle someone. Though it was the workman who deserved the imagined punishment, it was Jim who got it.

The murder itself was skipped, Louise coming in with Jim already dead. His head and torso inside the cement mixer, his legs spinning like helicopter blades as the machine rotated. Fantasy Louise stifled a giggle as one of Jim's shoes was propelled over the fence. Bloodied tools lay strewn across the garden, a hammer abandoned upon the low wall dripping droplets of blood onto the flower bed below. Louise didn't know how Jim came to be inside the mixer but figured that the state of the tools would indicate he was assaulted with them before being drowned in cement. Jim rarely received a burial in Louise's daydreams but today he was given his own tomb. A conveniently dug oblong hole, 2×4 meters was waiting, into which the concrete was to be poured to make a patio. With a plop Jim and the cement slid from the mixer into the pre-constructed deathbed. The one shoed Jim lay like a rag doll in the dirt, half covered in cementy gunk, a screwdriver sticking out of his temple. Blood had mingled with the cement to form an attractive shade of pink.

Louise expertly filled the mixer with more sand and water, worthy of any builder, though in reality she would have no idea on the ratios, or what she was even doing. The pictures she had hung held testament to the fact that the patio would not be levelled evenly.

Louise sat in her imaginary kitchen with a cup of hot chocolate, brimming with whipped cream and looked out at the garden. The cement mixer droned on, the birds tweeted, and the sun shone. She had started to level out the concrete with a trowel but there wasn't enough mixture yet to hide him. Jim's bottom and screwdriver skewered head still partly visible. Burying a victim under the patio was such a cliché but it didn't stop Louise from conjuring it.

The fantasy jumped to a completed and somehow perfectly level patio, not a lump or bump could be found, much to Louise's surprise. Louise smiled to herself as she positioned a potted plant and a large garden ornament, her own secret headstone to decorate Jim's grave.

The house that she shared with Jim was not the home of the patio, that was some made-up property from her subconscious. It had a modest walled garden whereas theirs was a sprawling lawn of manicured grass that backed onto a woodland, separated only by a picturesque stream.

When the kids were small Jim had erected a fence, at Louise's demand, to prevent the children from falling into the babbling brook. He wasn't happy about it, moaning over Louise's neurotic fear of the children drowning but he did it anyway. She'd seen it happen on *Casualty,* so it could happen, the same way that she always held back from scaffolding lorries, just in case the pole shot off and impaled her through the windscreen. It could happen. In fact, there were thousands of prosecutions every year due to unsafe loads being transported on our roads.

Louise pre-empted Franks inquisitive nature at every turn, plug socket protects, rounded corners, stair gates, alarms. Jim often half expected to come home and find Frank wrapped in cotton wool or bubble wrap. In Louise's defence Frank was an extremely accident probe child. If there was a way to injure himself in a padded room, Frank would find it. His sister didn't fare much better, come to that neither did Louise.

Their clumsiness had defiantly been inherited from their mother. Spatial awareness and Louise didn't mix, and she often misjudged the size of her own rear end when navigating gaps. Louise was rarely without a bruise somewhere on her body from having walked into something. She had sported every range and size at some point, even the classic black eye which was obtained from classically walking into a door. It really did happen. The door had partly closed, she turned around and whack. Where she had left an open doorway there was now a 6.6 x 2 plank of wood that fared much better than her face. It was a lovely shiner that drew attention and misplaced gossip for over a week from the school mums. At the time, Jim received some unwarranted coldness from people who thought he had hit Louise but those that knew them, and mattered, were fully aware of Louise's tendency to commit unintentional self-inflicted injuries. From all the trips to A&E and the regular bandages, plasters and bruises Louise was often perplexed that social services had not come calling. In some ways she wished they had, to know that the system worked. It was easy to understand how over stretched the organisation was and how those highlighted cases slipped through the net.

Many an argument had been had over the first decade of being a parent on how best to keep their offspring safe and healthy. Their views differed wildly. Jim was old school with what won't kill them will make them stronger whereas Louise was more oriented to the yummy mummy way of thinking. No matter the protection Louise put in place Frank always found a way around it. They were on first name terms with the receptionists at the local A&E department and Frank had been x-rayed that many times he was probably radioactive. Ellen wasn't much less accidental, but Louise had learnt over time what needed professional attention and what she could patch up herself.

Thinking of killing Jim off wasn't a new concept and for every whine about Louise's overreaction to a potential life-threatening possibility she would visualise it happening to Jim, to serve him right for doubting that it could happen, proving her right that it could.

Louise was always on high alert in proximity to water. She had heard the tales of children left unattended around pools or lakes and drowning. Her own children were tweens before they were allowed to have a shower without her being present, just in-case they slipped, banged their head and drowned. If she had to leave for any reason the door would be jammed open, better that the child got a bit cold than the door being locked preventing her from rescuing them. An unlikely scenario but she had seen it happen once on TV. 'People could drown in an inch of water don't you know', she'd say to Jim. To the outside world Louise was up-beat and jolly but inwardly she was a neurotic, insecure worrier.

5

Back in the days when Frank and Ellen were small the Wilsons would spend hours walking the local trails. Frank running off ahead dressed as a superhero fighting imaginary baddies with a stick, Ellen happily trundling along pushing a buggy containing one of her many cuddly toys. Louise often found herself thinking about the past when she was unaccompanied. Her moments recapturing the past were frequently triggered by an incident in the present. People would think her mad if they saw her smile or giggle to herself over a bittersweet moment from her history when she was sitting all alone. One such memory, that involved an enchanted family holiday in the Cotswold was sadistically hilarious but could have been deadly.

The ground was still wet from the downpour the previous night, but the day was crystal clear blue skies and not a cloud in sight. Frank was dressed as Spiderman, throwing invisible webs at pretend bad guys as Jim ran along beside him, defending Frank with his imaginary shield. The girls pulled up the rear, singing nursery rhymes to the plush elephant that had been brought along for the trip, it's trunk flapping up and down like it was dancing as Ellen pushed it along the bumpy trail. In the one second that Louise had taken her attention off Ellen to shout to the boys it happened. It unfolded in slow motion, Louise unable to stop Ellen from falling. Out of the whole path Ellen had found the one route that contained a deep pothole that was camouflaged as an innocent looking puddle. Ellen tripped, and face planted the puddle. Her head submerged with an almighty splash, her arms outstretched in front of her, her hands still clinging to the buggy. The elephant was launched into the air as Ellen came crashing down. Louise was there in a flash yanking Ellen upwards by the waistband of her pink dungarees, the sodden child and buggy moving skyward in unison. Despite the shock and tears Louise had to prise the handlebar from Ellen's tiny fingers so that she could assess her injuries. The dirty water was dripping off of Ellen's face, mixing with her tears. She was more concerned that her elephant was dirty than the cut on her knee, or nearly drowning. Louise held her daughter until she had calmed down, her own heart beating against her chest as her mind played out the worst-case scenario.

Jim always dismissed his wives 'what if's'. Jim loved Louise, but she did drive him crazy and she was forever over-reacting or chastising him. It was her own fault, taking on too much and spreading herself too thin, being there for everyone. When they were first together she was devoted to him, had eyes only for her Jimbo, but work and then kids came along, and he had to share her. The heart of gold that captured Jim's was the quality in her that caused him the most sorrow.

It was a subdued journey home, Ellen had fallen asleep in her car seat and Frank had been distracted with a chocolate bar and a Spiderman comic. Louise was still smarting over Jim's lack of concern that his offspring nearly drowned and allowed her mind to wander as the scenery shot past in a green blur. She engineered a scenario where it was Jim face down in a puddle and not little Ellen.

Back when both Jim and the kids were younger it was common for Jim to head off to the pub with friends once a week though they only stayed for a few beers, so he came home relatively sober, with the exception of a few occasions when he would roll in gone one, noisy and unsteady on his feet. Louise imagined Jim, in an inebriated state, staggering home from the pub though the woods at the back of their house. He fell backwards as he tried unsuccessfully to climb the fence that protected the children from meeting a watery end. The moon light shone through the trees and illuminated Jim. Louise saw him hit his head on a protruding branch. Dazed Jim lands in the water. The ice-cold stream caused him to cough and splutter. Louise had no hand in Jim's demise, she was an astral spectator watching a play unfold.

Jim crawled from the stream, water lapping at his arms and legs as the feeble current attempted to pull him down stream. He lay on his side on the stony bank to catch his breath, his teeth chattering, his fingers turning numb as the night air bite into his wet flesh. The alcohol and physical exertion worked in harmony to induce sleep. Jim closed his eyes for a few moments, intending only to gather enough energy to make it over the fence to his nice warm bed. In the fantasy Jim never made it home. In his slumber his face slipped into a puddle of surface water that had gathered in a natural crevice created by stones. The puddle was shallow, just deep enough to swallow Jim's nose and mouth, filling his lungs with water with every breath he took. Jim's limp body lay exposed in the morning light, water licking at his shoes and pooling around his face, the sun's rays penetrating the canopy of trees and shining upon Jim's lifeless corpse.

The fantasy eased Louise's mood. The tension in the car began to evaporate with Louise visibly relaxing into the journey, her serotonin levels increasing with every mile closer to home.

Jim's nail bitten fingers made removing the plug socket protectors as much a challenge for him as it was for either child. He was often heard muttering that he couldn't use the socket he wanted because of the bloody flush protector Louise had placed in every socket that was accessible to the children, and most people aged up to fourteen. Children could climb Jim would be told. Besides Louise seemed to be able to lever them out whenever she needed to plug in an appliance so didn't see Jim's problem.

With Jim concentrating on the road and Frank concentrating on removing every last trace of chocolate from the wrapper and his fingers Louise let her mind take her on another jaunt.

Louise couldn't help but chuckle at the image her mind had conjured. In true comic book style Louise pictured Jim as a cartoon character with one finger sticking out of a plug socket. His body shocked in the shape of a star. His skeleton framed against a black silhouette of his body, his hair spiked in the classic electrocution style. His body vibrated from the currents running through it and his voice shook with a ghostly moan.

Louise passed her giggles off as recalling the dramatic turn of events with the humour that hindsight can afford a situation. She did like to recall it later for the comic factor it did have, along with the bramble bike incident.

6

Jim had just got a new phone, the third one in less than a year. There was nothing wrong with the first two, but it was his thing to have the latest android technology. To Louise a phone was used to call or text people, but Jim liked it all singing and dancing, metaphorically speaking as a singing and dancing phone would be Jim's idea of a nightmare. Jim was like a little boy at Christmas. He was positively buzzing, his face a picture of excitement. It lifted Louise to see her husband so animated but even this turned negative. All the good points of his new communication device turned into the basis on which to launch an attack on other manufactures, who up to this point had clearly gone out of their way to produce products that did not met Jim's specifications. To him it seemed that they had deliberately made phones with his pet hates at the top of their list of pros. Finally, a phone that lived up to his expectations. Anybody would think he was trying to be a rep for the company he was that determined to sell Louise the same phone. As he talked about the durability of his new toy Louise began to wonder how durable it would be if she used it to bludgeon him to death.

Would the phone break before his skull?

Louise chuckled inwardly as her brain began to visualise a factory full of husbands being employed as crash test dummies in the industry of mobile telecommunications. One was being used as a baseball bat to beat the phone. It produced quite a humorous image of a skinny woman in a lab coat, hair tied back in a pony-tail and black rimmed glasses framing her focused face. Holding a man by his legs she repeatedly beat the phone. It took all of Louise's concentration not to burst out laughing at the physically impossible task. It would have been fitting to an episode of *Tom and Jerry*.

Not all the tests caused direct harm to the unfortunate husbands, many were conducted to scrutinize the viability of the applications, the speed of the programmes as well as the clarity of the screen and information. Rows of harassed looking men stood in election style booths, mobile phones in hand, as they were issued tasks to conduct by a matronly looking technician with a cane and stern expression. They had messages to send and reply too, games to complete and applications to use as they battled against time limits and lab assistants hurling elemental conditions at them. Above each booth a white coated woman sat upon a rigging and randomly assaulted each test subject with simulated rain and sunlight to see how the device and user faired. Their thumbs were going ten to the dozen, some even had wisps of smoke emanating from their opposable digits due to texting at a rate of nots, a frazzled look plastered across their faces.

Some with tasks complete rubbed their thumbs, bemused that the digital generation used the technology with such ease and grace. Two identical Jim's were testing the ability to effectively operate the phone whilst stood on a shaking platform. Another was walking a designated path whilst texting one handed, a steaming take-away coffee cup occupying the other. Two more Jim's walked a more perilous obstacle course where they were required to dodge obstacles, avoid the pitfalls of doggy dodo and uneven pavements whilst using the mobile phone. Sound proof glass isolation booths were erected to test the clarity of the speakers.

Louise scoffed in blind acceptance that every horizontal test subject was a Jim. A row of CAT scanners lined one wall, giant polos at the head of the beds. Upon which each Jim had two mobile phones strapped to their heads so any damage from the radioactive waves transmitted to the cranial cortex could be accessed with regular trips into the scanner.

Jim wasn't the only husband in the factory – there were twenty odd Jim's being tested on but there were also multiple clones of her dear friends cheating spouse along with unidentifiable males conjured from faces that Louise had probably passed in the street or seen on TV.

The drop test bay was a comical display of husbands being pushed off platforms at varying heights, mobile phones hidden in trouser or jacket pockets. A bevy of lab technicians clustered around the fallen husbands each one examining the impairment caused to the phone. They congregated at a stainless steel work station to compare data on the damage caused in each fall. The husbands were left to be swept away by a cleaner in blue overalls operating a mini bulldozer.

A conveyor belt washing line of miserable wet men circled tanks of tap, sea, river and muddy water, each containing a submerged fella in an attempt to test the buoyancy and water absorbency of the phone.

Having finished with the manufactures testing Louise considered choking Jim with the phone. She wondered if the new slim line look would be streamlined enough to shove it down his throat. It wasn't. Louise pinched his nose so that he opened his mouth, but the phone got wedged at the back of his jaw. Drool dripped down his chin from where he had salivated around the rubber case that protected the phone from accidental damage. No amount of pushing would lodge it further down, but it obstructed the airway enough to cause Jim to fight for breath and ultimately expire.

7

Other than the untimely death of her husband Louise's thoughts were usually occupied by chocolate. Louise had been fuelled with cocoa since 1975 and she wasn't about to stop. She was a bog standard just chocolate kind of girl, milk not white but occasionally dark, after all it contained iron so was healthy, in a way that was perfectly valid in Louise's mind. She didn't like her smooth rich indulgence to be tainted with bits of candy or fruit, except orange, mint was also a complimenting flavour.

Easter was by far her desired seasonal holiday, not for any religious implications but for the mounds of tantalising foiled wrapped confectionery. Louise had attended Sunday school as a child and celebrated the holiday with the Christian participants without question until she was old enough to form her own opinions when she concluded that chocolate was more of a draw than a fanciful tale of rebirth and devotion. She was literally like a kid in a candy store when perusing all the shiny packaging. She was instantly drawn to her favourite brand with at least one egg making it into her trolley every shopping trip. Louise always felt a little guilty for buying her first, of many, packets of mini eggs during the first week of January, but it was ultimately the supermarkets fault for stocking them so early. Louise's will power around chocolate was not very strong. It was practically none existent. If Louise chose a way to go it would be death by chocolate. She could drown in a sea of melted chocolate, be crushed by a gigantic slab or pass away from coco poisoning. The tasty possibilities were endless.

With Christmas barely over Louise was secretly glad that the supermarkets pushed consumerism so heavily she knew that she could start stockpiling her glorious Easter eggs within the month. Her unbeatable record had been set at thirty-two in one year. She had challenged it many times but never beaten it. The year of the thirty-two eggs had been achievable, in the most part, to the closing down of an outlet that slashed the price on their stock, keeping Louise in chocolate until October. Jim didn't have a sweet tooth, he liked his deserts and the odd packet of sweets, but chocolate never held a grip over Jim like it did Louise. If she was completely honest she was probably addicted to the delicious brown offerings and she got anxious when her supplies were running low.

Louise couldn't pin point where her fascination for Easter eggs had come from and she couldn't explain what attracted her to them, but they felt so right to hold, nestling snuggly in the palm of her hand, regardless of size. She liked wild birds. They just gave her a warm fuzzy happy feeling. Perhaps they reminded her of her childhood, of the happy memories she had of Easter egg hunts, the joy of finding the brightly coloured foiled eggs hiding in a bush outside or balancing on top of a book on the shelf. As a child she would try to bite around the design printed directly onto the chocolate, often a bunny, she still did, her goal was to not break the image, a much harder feat with adult incisors than delicate milk teeth.

It was so distracting sat in a stuffy boring staff meeting at work hearing about targets and product arrangement when she knew that just behind the doors was a delightful selection of eggs that filled a whole aisle. Enticing and fattening up the population. She very nearly licked her lips just thinking about the chocolatey delights, the same way she would sometimes smile whilst thinking of something funny that nobody else was privy to, feeling self-conscious that she had been observed conversing with her own thoughts.

As her line manager droned on she could almost smell the sweet taste escaping the outer packaging. She tried to distract herself, her imagination began to wonder what everyone else thought about during the meetings or if they were focused on the task at hand. Louise suspected that her unmarried momma's boy jobs-worth boss probably dreamt about sales figures and profit margins whilst Skyla's beautifully pretty blonde head was filled with pink fluffy unicorns and marshmallows. Joe, the warehouse manager, was football obsessed and would slip in a footy analogy at any possible opportunity, so Louise pictured him having his own fantasy. One where jobs worth's head is the ball and Joe is scoring the winning goal. A powerful left foot booted the football head into the back of the net at break neck speed eliciting a cheerful roar from the crowd.

She was glad of the new self-service check outs, no need to feel ashamed as a colleague scanned her groceries, consisting of unhealthy ready meals, crisps and chocolate, a student's dream. In her defence, she bought her fruit and veg from the local greengrocer and her meat came from the towns butcher, so she shouldn't have anything to feel bad about but no matter how much Louise denied caring what others thought about her she did. All the years of bullying had taken a toll on her, outwardly she had risen above it but internally she was still the insecure girl of her childhood wanting to fit in but dancing around the edge of accepted popularity.

8

Louise and Jim tried to get away for a break once a year or so. Sometimes they would take a whole weeks' vacation other times they would go for a weekend getaway.

They had been on some wonderful holidays over the years, exhausting family ones when they needed a holiday to recover from the holiday. There were romantic city breaks filled with culture and sex and holidays shared with extended family and friends filled with laughter and memories.

Louise normally handled all the details from the booking to the packing, Jim having half a say in the destination. This was another matter that they could barely agree upon, Jim favouring all-inclusive packages whereas Louise liked to get out there and explore. She couldn't stand to travel to foreign locations and be cooped up in a resort. Why travel all that way to sit by the hotel pool or beach she would ask Jim. Louise couldn't justify saying she had been to a country where all she had seen was the airport and a bit of scenery on the way to their accommodation. Louise liked to visit local shops, take in art galleries, museums and cemeteries, a little morbid but she found them peaceful and beautiful. Louise loved exhibitions but always found something different to Jim fascinating. Most visits consisted of Jim's monotonous droll ringing around the halls as he read the captions aloud, Louise's exasperated expression taunting her, reflected back through the glass cabinets, the kids eyes pleading with her to make him stop. She would milk her hard-earned getaway for every last penny's worth of experience. For someone so frugal as Jim Louise never quite grasped why Jim didn't want to cram in as much as possible for his buck.

Though it was no surprise to Louise that Jim would be the last up, would drag his heels getting dressed and draw out eating breakfast she still secretly hoped that every holiday would be different, and that Jim would embrace it, but he never did. Ten am was the optimal time for Jim to rise, any amount of pushing and nagging beforehand would result in childish evil glares and grunts, several rounds of coffee drunk at a snail's pace and then an extended trip to the bathroom rendering the family abandoned without their driver. Louise too kind hearted to leave him behind no matter how many times she threatened to do it. The few times she had ventured out on her own Jim seemed to sense her disappearance and was on the phone enquiring over her whereabouts, afraid he was missing out on something.

It drove her to distraction, all that money just to spend the morning in a hotel room waiting for lazy to get up. She had learnt that two arguing children worked well as an alarm clock and got Jim moving if only to get them outside to be shouted at. By default, mornings were always a source of stress for Louise and boredom for the children in the early days. As the children got older Frank became as hard to get up as Jim so the girls would go down for breakfast and then off out to take in some sights before the boys joined them. A book kept Louise company when it was just her and Jim or when she was waiting for the children to wake. She had read many a page sat in the bathroom or hiding behind the curtains knowing that the florescent room lights would wake the other occupants before they had planned, and the day would reduce to tantrums and tears before it had even started. As a parent Louise had learnt to pick her battles. Jim had not, and they were often on opposing sides. She tried not to expel energy on the skirmishes when there was a war to be won.

Jim had exceeded Louise's expectations on a few occasions, the best being a weekend away to Bath, just the two of them, for her thirtieth birthday. He had organized the hotel as well as the childcare, it was a wonderful weekend and they came back acting like loved up teenagers. It didn't last but they knew they were capable of it.

9

Louise had arranged a two-night mid-week stay in London for her forty-fifth birthday. Jim really didn't like the capital. it was busy and costly, and Jim felt fear hanging in the air, a climate of distrust and worry that extremists could launch an attack at any time. He begrudgingly agreed to accompany his wife. Jim had no choice but to be up on time as Louise had reserved seats on the early train. She didn't expect Jim to navigate the congested rounds around the city and the train would conveniently deliver them directly into the hubbub and mayhem of Paddington station.

The reason that Louise had selected London was, not to annoy Jim, but to attend a travelling exhibition of Roy Lichtenstein's work. She loved art, adored the National and Tate Britain galleries. She'd been quite crafty in the past in orchestrating trips that 'happened to pass' one of favourite locations. To Louise it was both emotional and magical to gaze upon the original works of such revered artists as Van Gogh, Michelangelo, Degas, the list went on. Louise's heart beat with excitement of just being in the same room as the famous *Sunflowers* and she had to wipe away at the tears that always came when she looked upon Millais's depiction of a floating Ophelia. Much smaller than she remembered it to be from her childhood but none-the-less as moving. Louise could lose hours staring at the intricate patterns of her submerged dress, at the delicate details of the flowers and the realistic features in her deathly face and hands. Her lifeless eyes a premonition of the true life tragedy unfolding, somehow making the painting seem all the more real. Jim didn't see the point in art. Not all of it was an offence to the eye but it wasn't practical or functional. As far as Jim was concerned it served no purpose, yet he was happy to pass judgement on what he deemed 'so called art'.

Lichtenstein's pop art was a stark contrast to the fine art of masters such as Rossetti or Constable, not that Jim cared for any media or movement. Louise was able to bore Jim as easily on the subject as he did her over technology. Jim sat in the desolate concrete expanse that formed the lower level of the unimpressive Tate Modern building whilst Louise took in the colourful display of original works and learnt about the artist made famous for colouring with dots.

Jim really didn't like the London, it was too busy, too hot, too rude and too expensive. However, Jim really did love his wife, and if she'd taken her sister he'd have a heart attack when the credit card bill came. It was a change of scenery. Not one he would have chosen but he was looking forward to eating and drinking well, the only benefit to using public transport, which he hated.

A browse through the gallery shop did nothing to inspire Louise to make a purchase. She flicked through the books and admired the prints, but she had a collection of literature at home and no wall space for a postcard let alone a picture. Besides it would only cause Jim's face to distort in an expression of confusion and disgust when he walked past it anyway.

Jim and Louise had a wonderful evening, they dined in a traditional family run Italian restaurant. The authentic accents and décor combined with the delicious aroma made it seem like they were holidaying in Italy, a glance at the grey London skyline was a stark reminder that they were not. The attentive waiter brought copious amounts of wine and beer to the table as Louise and Jim reminisced over the past. Louise secretly missing the craziness that children inevitably bring in their wake. As unadventurous as ever Louise had ordered a Hawaii pizza and Jim ordered the Lombata D'Agnello. The paper-thin pizza base was crisped to perfection, the cheese and pineapple a melted field of yellow over a bed of cherry red tomatoes. Louise knew that her IBS would not treat her kindly for her indulgence, but it would be worth it. Jim tucked into his marinated lamb with culinary finesse, not a drop of the perfumed sauce graced the lily-white table cloth, though a few dribbles did try making a break for freedom over his chin, only to be foiled by an eager wipe of his thumb.

By the time the meal had been consumed and Louise was sucking on the customary after dinner mint they were both glassy-eyed and slightly slurring their speech. Jim holding it together more convincingly than Louise, after all he'd had more practice. Giggling like school children they wobbled hand-in-hand back to their lodgings. It was lucky that their hotel was on the same street, so they didn't have to stumble far. Louise always wore sturdy boots but that didn't mean she was any less clumsy and alcohol only served to highlight her uncoordinated gait.

The planned night of passion fizzled into a drunken farce. Louise's frequent trips to the loo were an anti-climax for Jim who fell asleep in the luxurious embrace of the fabric that covered the four-poster bed waiting for her.

For Louise it was an unsettled night, her IBS had woken her again around four in the morning and kept her from drifting back to sleep until gone five. She was finally taken on a dream-induced journey as London began to wake and stir around her, the thick curtains and triple-glazed windows keeping the world outside muted.

Louise woke with a smile on her face, her dream still in the fore-front of her mind. She shuffled out of bed as delicately as she could manage considering the pounding headache that was starting to beat against her skull. Feeling a little queasy Louise headed to the bathroom. She sat on the toilet and rested her head against the cold porcelain of the sink and closed her eyes. Glimpses of the dream she had recently departed filled her thoughts as a slide-show of the fantasy played out.

It was one of the strangest backdrops to a fantasy that Louise could recall, very Monty Python in its approach and set in the style of a traditional circus. The two main characters were the Wilsons but rather changed in appearance. Louise, much to her terror was dressed as a clown, her worst nightmare. Though it wasn't an evil Pennywise rendition of a clown it was no less disturbing to Louise. She wore the classic orange afro wig which framed a painted face with an over-sized suit, tie and gigantic shoes. The outfit was completed with a huge plastic flower which Louise was sure squirted water and a pillar-box red nose that she was sure would honk if it were squeezed. Thankfully the scene moved to a dog wearing a ruffled collar and a pointed hat balancing on a plank of wood that was balancing on a large colourful ball. All to the applause of an audience made up of multiple Louise's, all donning different outfits.

Next random circus imagery swam in and out of view in a short cinema reel film before freezing framing on a figure. The figure was Jim preparing for the grand finale. He was much rounder in the belly than he was in reality, and at least a foot shorter. He wore an unflattering metallic blue stretchy jumpsuit with white stars, a matching open-face helmet and aviator googles. He smiled and waved at the audience before clown Louise lead him to the cannon. There was a lot of exaggerated hand gestures and tom-foolery whilst Jim was comically manoeuvred backwards into the barrel. With a last wave at the crowd Jim prepared to be fired into the air as clown Louise gleefully skipped to the rear of the military machinery with a flaming torch. With a countdown of "3, 2, 1" clown Louise lit the fuse. There was a puff of black smoke and a theatrical bang. The scene followed Jim as he shot from the cannon in an arch across a crudely painted backdrop of a bright but cloudy day. As Louise watched his descent the net that would catch Jim came into view, but Jim's trajectory saw him bypass the net and head towards the psychedelic patterned floor in no man's land behind the net. Jim landed with a splat. An aerial view showed Jim, the human cannon ball, face down on the ground, arms and legs spread out forming the shape of a star. The crowd responded with rapturous applause and a chorus of "HURRAY".

Louise's stomach was still a bit touch and go but she felt better, the brass band in her head being slowly beaten back by the paracetamol she had washed down with the remnants of a bottle of cola. Louise could hear Jim's snores despite the door being shut. She crept back into the dimly lit room and retrieved a few pillows from the bed and the extra blanket from the cupboard and took up residence in the bath until Jim woke. The cushioned tub made for an ideal reading nook. Louise could read content in the knowledge that Jim would not be woken by the light nor the gentle turn of pages. Usually Louise would be chomping at the bit to get going, to not waist a second but she was satisfied to snuggle, to lose herself on a journey into the past that was no creation of her own.

It was midday before Jim was in a fit state to be seen in public. Feeling that dragging Jim to another gallery would be pushing for an argument Louise suggested they head to Camden Town to wander around the markets. Jim was unusually agreeable, putting up little resistance. They grabbed a pasty from a tube station vendor as they passed through and ate it as they strolled along the canal. Louise enjoyed window shopping but could muster no real interest in making any purchases, even the Dr Marten boots raised only a slight pang of desire. His appetite had got the better of him and by mid-afternoon Jim was tucking into a Big Mac and fries. Louise had a small cheeseburger, no gherkin, to satisfy her rumbling tummy. It wasn't a good idea.

Flagging, they returned to the hotel for a late afternoon siesta, planning to head back out and grab a filling supper. Jim dozed while Louise resumed her book, rapidly becoming immersed in the intriguing text. This time the bath was full of hot bubbly water.

10

The Wilsons headed out onto the busy streets and made their way to Covent Garden. The square was packed with a vibrant array of people from camera tooting tourists to groups of teens interspaced with well-dressed couples who mixed amongst the families as the homeless huddled in disused doorways. Street performers were situated at intervals, a petite young woman in a red dress sung like an angle outside the Disney store and a blue man frozen mid-pose silently beside the Jubilee Market Hall.

Neither Louise nor Jim were partially feeling the ambience after last night, so they headed back to the hotel where they had a non-descript meal in the on-site restaurant. They stopped off in the bar for a night cap. Jim bought a bottle of plonk from the bar and they retired to their room to pick up where they had left things the previous evening.

Louise was up early and keen to make the most of the time they had left in the capital. By seven-thirty she was noisily packing the suitcase and 'accidently' left the bathroom door open when she took a shower. To her 'surprise' when she exited Jim was sat up in bed. His face said he was not amused at the wake-up call. Jim sulked into the bathroom bringing flashbacks of Frank's teenage tantrums. Another hotel room antic, and one she had to tolerate daily at home, was Jim's nasal clearing duties. At least he only went to work behind closed doors. Louise just wished there was a closed door between them when he did it. It was one of Jim's habits that belonged on the playground, and, she'd tell him it was not an after dinner sport. Louise would be left with a crick in her neck from turning away from her revolting husband. It was never a quick retrieval. Jim's pinkie would be up there mining for minutes, the inspection always making Louise gag if she dared to turn around at the wrong time. Even Jared couldn't keep up with Jim's award winning efforts, and Louise had experienced him try on more than one occasion. She often wondered if one day Jim's brains would fall out. She'd been waiting for his head to cave in, but it never happened, and she was disappointed at the childhood lies she'd been told.

The breakfast buffet placated Jim and the conversation moved on from "how is your sausage?" to a discussion about what to do before they headed home. Full from the all-you-can eat buffet Louise stashed a couple of the apples in her pocket for later.

With suitcases in tow Jim and Louise's choices of destination had been reduced. They could head across London and stow the luggage at the station before venturing out again but that seemed such a waste of the time they had left. Alternatively, they could drag the cases around with them as they did some last-minute site seeing. Jim, not one to be rushed, chose the latter option.

The hotel was situated on Rood Lane, long rebuilt following the great fire of London that raised the whole area to the ground, back in 1666. They had 'done' the monument on family trip once, never again, so they admired the structure from the afar before setting off on their pilgrimage back to Paddington station.

They traced the path of the Thames the best they could, making detours when they encountered buildings which encroached on the riverbank. They weaved through the streets, round groups of tourists, keeping the murky tide of the waterway in view. Louise had a shocking sense of direction and one wrong turn down a street could render them lost or in an undesirable location.

Louise and Jim crossed the Thames at Waterloo Bridge. They stopped for a few minutes mid-way across to look at the city landscape as it curved into the distance with the bend of the river. Though Louise enjoyed the sight she was nervous to be standing on the bridge and gladfully moved on with a quickened pace.

Louise had always loved Southbank. She was happy to be amazed by the street performers, in awe of their energetic or entertaining routines. Jim indulged his wife's insistence on watching them and posing for a photo. It was a battle he had fought and lost too many times to know when he was beat. Louise thought it was the payment she always gave that irked him.

This part of London had always been a constant in their family trips to the congested city, the kids loved the outdoor climbing park and it generally had a 'happy vibe'. The London Eye dominated the landscape. It gave Louise a shudder when they walked near it. Imagine if it came off the base and trundled away down the pavement. Louise had a brief flash of a cartoon London Eye squashing tourists and performers as it rolled adjacent to the river, the victims stuck to the wheel spinning helplessly around. Louise couldn't help inwardly chuckling at the image, yet, at the same time feeling slightly ashamed.

Louise grabbed them both some lunch from one of the street vendors while Jim waited with the suitcases. Jim was grateful for the rest; the walk had taken them a good two hours. They decided to jump on the tube for the rest of the journey and hang around in Paddington while they waited for the train.

Louise noticed a Big Issue seller sitting quietly hopeful just down the road from the station entrance. He reminded Louise of Father Christmas, well a Santa that had been lost and forgotten like an unwanted toy. She was always drawn to the ones that didn't shout at her, she avoided those. Louise started to approach the man when Jim pulled her back.

"What are you doing?" Jim demanded.

"Buying a Big Issue, what does it look like?" snapped Louise.

"Why."

"Because I want to."

"Whatever." sulked Jim. Eye daggers flew at Jim as he turned his back.

The seller looked genuinely astonished to see a customer. Gappy yellow teeth emerged through his stained beard as Louise greeted him and asked him how he was.

"Umm......ok." stammered the aged businessman.

Louise handed over the fee for the magazine, and an extra pound just because Jim would hate it and bid him farewell.

Louise matched Jim's look of disgust with a smug smile as they walked towards the station, an aghast Jim following his wife's lead.

The wait for the locomotive was excruciatingly painful as always. The Wilsons sat, and people watched, one eye on the information board dreading the moment their train went from on-time to delayed. Bored, Louise headed off to get a drink, Jim was sulking so didn't want one. Louise made a bee-line for the Caffè Nero booth that stood at the far end of the station and ordered her usual hot chocolate, cream and sprinkles no marshmallows. The barista took longer to make the drinks than Louise had anticipated and by the time Louise had received her order her train was ready to board. Louise had to jog down the platform, lapping up the burning liquid that seeped past the thick dairy topping and through the disposable lid. Splashes dripped over her coat despite Louise's attempts to keep the drink as level as possible in one hand whilst manoeuvring an uncooperative suitcase through a grappling crowd with the other. The challenge was made harder by trying to make sure her bouncing bosom didn't off-set her balance, or a rogue boob didn't make a break for freedom and knock her drink or collide with a fellow traveller.

Luckily Louise had reserved seats and Jim had already located them, fending off potential seat stealers with constant "this seat is taken, my wife is coming". Louise battled her way through the carriage to her husband, her beloved drink cradled like a new-born baby. She was quiet puffed out by the time she had made it to her designated seat. Louise handed what remained of the chocolatey goodness to Jim for safekeeping as she battled to secure her case in the overheard storage.

The train was packed. Every seat was taken, and the aisles were crammed with people swaying with the motion of the carriage. Thankfully many departed at Reading which made the air more breathable and Louise didn't feel so trapped. No more stranger's bums in her face for the remainder of the journey.

Louise relaxed with her book. Jim sat staring at the screen of his tablet, earphones muting the movie he was watching.

Jim removed his earphones long enough to use the facilities but before he could shut out the world on his return he noticed a look in Louise's eye. It usually meant she was formulating a wicked plan or was about to say something that would embarrass him. Jim had been ignorant to the noise in the carriage so wasn't aware of the rather loud conversation that had been happening over a mobile phone in the seat directly behind them for the last few stops. At that moment the woman repeatedly said, "hello, hello, can you hear me... hello, can you hear me..." into the handset.

"Yes thank you, we can hear you." Louise giggled, a little too loudly, in reply.

She was amused though Jim shot her a look, disgusted at her immaturity. Louise felt like she'd been chastised like a naughty school girl, which only served to make it more amusing. Louise returned to her book and Jim to his tablet until the train pulled up at their stop.

The movie had lightened Jim's mood by the time they reached their station and the car journey home was a pleasant one.

11

Louise was a homebody. She loved nothing more than pottering around the house. She was one step away from being a recluse, the need to work dragging her from her comfortable abode.

The house was already only accessible via a lane and stood in its own plot of land but for Louise that was company enough. It wasn't that Louise was anti-social, well maybe a little, she was just content in her own company, didn't crave the constant attention and drama of others.

If she lived in the idyllic thatched cottage in the middle of nowhere, that she visited sometimes in her dreams, she was sure that the lifestyle of a hermit would be one she would adopt. With delivery company's two-a-penny and anything you could wish for available for purchase over the internet the life of a hermit could be easily achieved with minimal human contact.

It was Louise's maternal nature that lead to Jim's laziness. When they first meet he was an independent young man, living the life of a bachelor then along comes

Louise, the personification of a homely Goddess, and Jim's domesticated manner slipped back into teenage boy mood, never to entirely recover to that of a fully-fledged organised adult.

They say that opposites attract, and Louise and Jim were polar opposites. Jim was an anti-drug and smoking extrovert whereas Louise was an artistic introvert smoker. As many do with the trappings of young love Louise sacrificed her identify to fit into a more acceptable mould that Jim would fall in love with.

When they were younger the differences in their opinions and tastes just added to the whole package of the relationship, passionate discussions and animated conversions but now the differences of opinions caused irritations and intolerance.

Life was just one long round of Louise placing an item, Jim moving it and Louise moving back whilst muttering phrases such as "if I wanted it there I'd have put it there" whilst stabbing Jim with her eyes or giving him the finger from behind a wall. Often Jim wasn't even in the house when Louise cursed him.

It was a wonder that the Wilsons were even a couple sometimes. They differed in their taste of music, tv shows, parenting skills, ideas of cleanliness and organisation, holiday destinations, political stances and definitely what constituted hoarding.

Jim, at home, liked the minimalist approach. On the rare occasions that Louise had visited him at his place of work it was chaotic and disorganised, much like his underwear draw. Louise loved to express herself if the place she loved the most, her home. Louise adored art, books and her possessions. She took a lot of pleasure in being surrounded by her stuff. Louise was certainly Madonna's material girl, and she never denied she liked things. Louise was by no means greedy, she didn't have 'stuff' because she could, she had it because she liked it, or it held a memory that was easily jogged by the visual prompts happily displayed on surfaces and walls around the house.

The children's art still lined the insides of the kitchen cupboard doors, Louise's way of displaying more without drawing Jim's attention to it, and their more recognisable sculptures still stood proudly on the shelves. One glance could transport Louise back in time and nostalgia would wash over her.

If they calculated their net worth to the family income over the decades, then Jim's breadwinner position would secure him success. Hence, by default the majority of their worldly goods should belong to Jim but to Louise it was her stuff, her property, she owned them, they were hers. She'd take half of it to the grave with her if she could.

Every room contained at least one potted plant and as many books as she could cram into the available space, with the exception of the bathroom as the paper tended to get damp. Collections clustered in groups were dotted around the house. To her they reflected elements of her personality, of her life, her beliefs and her Louiseness. To Jim it was a collection of tat that had taken over his home like poison ivy. It was a point that they would never see eye-to-eye on, besides Jim never dusted anyway so Louise didn't see what harm were they causing him? Jim had no reason to dislike the assortments gathered in shrines, but he did. Louise was right, they didn't cause him any physical pain, and they don't come to life to torment him, but he'd rather not see them. They just weren't to his taste.

The kids had taken after Louise, their childhood bedrooms an explosion of their growing personalities, their own homes a modest version, taking on the joining of two individuals.

If Louise could sneak in a new item and get it installed before Jim saw it, he would likely not take it down, that would be too much effort. He would protest and moan, but Louise just weathered the storm while admiring her new addition. Besides they were insignificant purchases that filled the house and walls but did no real damage to the bank account. Large purchases were always made together, it was like a referendum, each side stating its case, the benefits and pledges. Jim was mostly given free reign of the technical side of operations such as TVs and phones and was granted purchases without authorisation providing they matched or exceed their current one. Jim did not control the TV package, just what the package was shown on.

12

The time had come for a new sofa. The Wilsons were to replace the raggedy family sofa from the children's youth for it was stained and thread bear from years of abuse. It had been repeatedly flopped on, jumped on, spilt on and scratched by the cats. It had lost its bounce and comfiness.

Jim voted leather, Louise voted material.

Then there was the decision of getting the same size and style or feng shui the room to accommodate a different design and if so do they go corner or reclining, two- seater or three, with or without a matching armchair.

It would be a bank holiday of negations, tantrums and arguments as the sales staff tried to impart their wisdom as to the sofa that would best suit the needs of people they met five minutes ago. The usual sales brought out the hordes, some serious buyers, others window shopping as the obituary bank holiday rain had kept them away from the beaches and parks. There were harassed parents trying to placate bored children and remind them that the sales assistances frowned upon bed bouncing and loved up newlyweds buying their first settee together, the store was packed.

Jim had always campaigned for a leather sofa but never won. Louise gave the argument that nobody wants to have to rip their own skin painfully off the leather when they get up. She had sat on friend's sofas and any exposed skin would stick to the glossy covering resulting in a tender removal and unsightly red marks. Jim's point that it was easy to maintain and wipe clean was a valid one and Louise didn't often display bear skin, even in the summer, but even so – "ouch or not happening" in Louise's opinion.

Jim had done his research by googling the styles and prices in advance of their trip to the national chain store, armed with the competitors deals. Jim hated the thought that he may miss out on a saving. Louise, lacking the confidence to challenge the price tag, secretly respected Jim for his tenacity but was outwardly embarrassed by his bartering technique.

Louise had a rough idea of what she wanted, she'd seen it on one of the design programmes on the reality channels that she loved. Louise's ideal sofa was raised off the floor on polished oak feet and the plush silver fabric was trimmed with black. Thick foam cushions padded the surround and the back was high enough to sink into. She could imagine the soft material against her skin as she cuddled up to watch the TV, with a cushion that bounced back when sat on and arm rests that were not pitted with claw marks.

In reality, the picture was far more comfortable and squidgy than the sofa actually turned out to be. Louise had visualised sinking into a fabric heaven but was greeted by a sofa that was intolerant on her ample rear end with a rigid feel that the mounds of cushions cunningly disguised from a distance.

After much toing and froing Jim succumbed to his wife's wishes and they ordered a large three-seater corner sofa, not the same one that Louise had found on-line, but it was in a two-tone black and grey with a plumage of cushions, to be delivered in six weeks' time.

After Jim's torturous defeat he sought solace in food. The shopping complex that housed the sofa store was home to a bevy of food outlets ranging from high end burger joints to the family take out franchises. Louise knew she reigned victorious so allowed Jim the small victory of choosing where they would eat. Jim wasn't one to cut off his own nose to spite his face where money was concerned so opted for a venue that would suit them both.

Still smarting a little from the honed sales tactics Jim led Louise though the golden arches, a table opening up between a family with three rowdy boys, now all sugared up from their happy meals and carbonated drinks and a couple whose tray was piled so high, the contents of which could have fed a small army. Not wanting to fill the car with the lingering aroma the Wilsons reluctantly took up position at the vacant table, hoping that soon enough the family would inflict their uncontrollable volume-challenged offspring on some other unsuspecting member of the public. By the time that Louise had returned to the table with the order balanced on a tray the family had departed. Regrettably an equally challenging teenage duo filled the space, swooping into the empty seats like vultures on recently expired prey.

Louise munched the thin salted fries three at a time, a watered-down coke nestled in a pool of condensation as water droplets cascaded in a race to the bottom. The spice on the chicken was enough to force Louise to take a mouthful of drink after every other bite or so which left her feeling bloated, but fed. Jim was more experimental in his food choices, wrapping his chops around a seasonal burger, the sauce and melted cheese dripping down his chin.

The Wilsons were on their way again within thirty minutes, Jim's wallet lighter and Louise's weight heavier than when they left the house that morning.

Jim was at work when the new sofa arrived. Within fifteen minutes it had been deposited in the living room and the old one removed, heading off to an unknown destination. Louise's burly delivery men consisted of a larger than life character and a gentleman close to retirement, Louise prayed that he didn't keel over under the weight of the settee, but he possessed a strength that was camouflaged by his years. She could hear the truck carefully rumbling back down the lane, untamed branches scrapping at the top as it squeezed its way back to civilisation. Mrs Henderson's manicured hedgerow was an unfortunate casualty of the Wilsons modernisation.

By the time Jim got home Louise had settled into her half of the lavish new couch, an impression of her bum already starting to form when she got up to make Jim his tea.

13

Louise often looked back on her life, seeing how far she had come, how some things had changed, how some had not and imagining what could have been had she chosen differently.

Louise had no intention of altering her situation, but she couldn't help thinking about the 'what if's' that life tended to throw up. So many decisions could have led her down different paths, some of which may have led back to where she is now, but others would have taken her in another direction.

Growing up Louise had set her heart on becoming a firefighter, she had outgrown her childhood ambitions of becoming a horse or a princess and found a realistic career.

Unfortunately, life had conspired against her and she was too short to join the brigade by the time she was old enough. Her life of fitness and fire extinguished in a heartbeat. Louise had no backup plan, a half-hearted letter to the police force was meet with rejection and her career as an author was stunted after several rejections crushed her sprit. Had Louise followed her passions with conviction she may well have achieved great things, headed a team of officers or written best-selling novels, been the next Sherlock Holmes or Terry Pratchett. She had no foresight at school to plan for failure so ended up at a factory, mind-numbingly capping bottles as they passed on a conveyor belt, the line manger a Hitler of the assembly floor. Becoming a wife and a mother was the greatest job that Louise had ever had, though she selfishly wanted something that was just hers, that she could excel in, so she forged ahead in retail.

Jim had never been paternal, hadn't been that bothered about carrying on the family name, but Louise had worn him down and they had started a family-. With one of each, both happy and healthy, Louise should have been content, but she had always wanted a big family. "Just come off the pill" her friends had told her over and over again when she had moaned to them that Jim didn't want any-more children, however Louise could not deceive Jim like that.

She may have been guilty of many things, but she was loyal and liked to stand on the moral high ground whenever she could. She made no secret of the fact that she spent most of Ellen's adolescence in a state of broodiness. Ellen was such a well-behaved child Louise would have loved to have had more, she didn't see it has triple the trouble, just triple the love but Jim didn't see it that way. Jim was unsure what to do with a little person, but he did take himself off for the chop for fear that another little Frank or little Ellen would enter the Wilson household.

Louise was never one for foreign shores, she had never been bitten by the travel bug, but she wondered what it would have been like to see the world. What adventures she would have had and the people she would have meet. The fantasy didn't extend to how she could afford to fund the international adventures. There was backpacking through New Zealand and Australia, a road trip from Mexico to Canada encompassing all fifty-one states of the U S of A, a pilgrimage through the holy lands and a cultural tour of Europe ending in humanitarian work in Africa. One day, maybe.

Louise had always had an eye for the men, appreciated a handsome face and a good sense of humour. She wasn't what most would consider popular or beautiful, but she had a certain quality that meant she was rarely without an offer of company. Jim was caught often enough making cheeky comments or coping a look as a pretty lady passed, when he thought no one knew, after all Jim was a red-blooded male.

Jim didn't consider any alternatives, he was content with his lot. Though Louise was sure that he must occasionally consider swapping his wife for a younger, thinner and more attractive model that would hang off his every word and worship the ground he walked on. Most woman fantasise about ridiculously sculpted adonises, rippling pecks under golden tanned skin, unrealistically good looking with honed features and gleaming white teeth. Louise's fantasies were murderlicious rather than delicious. They made her feel good in the same way running your hands down a muscular chest would. They allowed her to daydream her frustrations away, and not be hauled in front of the judge on a murder charge.

As she stood in the kitchen deciding what to prepare for tea she couldn't help pondering that one question, what if she had gone to university and pursued a career within the field of forensics. It was one of the biggest regrets she had. Would she have been a renowned specialist, or would she have simply progressed to a small town police officer where murders happened once in a blue moon?

Louise must have been so engrossed in the destiny that was lost to her that she paid little attention to the meal she was preparing. As a result of her culinary negligence she almost accomplished killing Jim, for real.

She had not filleted the haddock as thoroughly as she should have when preparing Jim's fish cakes. She knew this when Jim suddenly jumped up from the table, eyes wide and hands desperately clutching at this throat. After a fleeting moment of pure panic, when Louise's brain was temporarily suspended of all rational thought, her first aid instincts kicked in.

All protocol went out the window as Louise found herself leaping into action. She closed her eyes to recall a mental image of the chocking vest that had been used on the training course a few months previous. Louise slapped Jim firmly on the upper back several times in an attempt to dislodge the bone, but Jim's face was beginning to turn a troubling shade of crimson. Changing position Louise felt Jim's torso for the end of his ribs before thrusting her balled fist into his chest. Her actions seemed to send the bone in the correct direction, but it was not yet free. Jim's eyes bulged from their sockets and Louise's heart was starting to beat out a frantic background rhyme to accompany the drama. Louise returned to delivering back blows, the second of which forced Jim to cough and the offending bone was deposited on the table. Jim took several deep breaths, forcing air back into his lungs. Louise was as shaken as Jim, thankful the ordeal was over and relived that she had not actually killed her husband.

It came as a slight surprise to Louise that when she thought she might lose Jim an icy sensation gripped her insides. She knew in that moment that, no matter what, she did love him completely and really did not want to be without him, regardless of what her subconscious would have her believe.

After Jim's breathing returned to normal Louise's guilt began to fade a little. She had not intended to harm him. However, she couldn't help thinking what would have happened if she hadn't dislodged the bone and Jim had really died.

Would the coroner have treated it like the accident it was, or would she find herself in the middle of homicide investigation, proving her innocence? With no history of domestic incidents, a respectable house and stable finances the death would probably be treated as an unfortunate accident. The post mortem would find the fish bone was the cause for the obstruction of his airways, the position of the bruises explained away as failed life-saving attempts. Louise would be sufficiently traumatised by the accidental death that she wouldn't need to feign being the grieving wife. She thought that once the initial shock had worn off and she had accepted the loss, a funeral would be held followed by a period of mourning. Jim's ashes would be scattered, and Louise would have to move on with the rest of her life. She visualised a future as a widow.

The life insurance policy would pay off what little remained on their mortgage leaving a very sizable amount for Louise. A lump sum would be given to Frank and Ellen, their rightful share in their fathers' assets.

Though Louise wished no dishonour on Jim's memory she did not visualise a life of celibacy and pondered how she would meet a new fella. Times had moved on since she met Jim, the world was now in a digital era with people meeting primarily in cyber space rather than in the same space.

Louise wasn't very good with computers, with anything electrical really, she left that type of stuff to Jim. She knew how to shop, could just about manage her email and Facebook account, but the technical stuff was beyond her capability. Her new man would have to be able to do gadgety stuff, and cook and clean and be romantic, and handsome with a fit body would be nice too. Louise would set-up an on-line dating profile and see what matches were out there. Plan B was to get out into the wide world, dust off her flirtatious side and ignite the chemistry in person.

Jim was grumpy for days following his near-death experience. Though Jim wasn't one to hold a grudge, that was one of Louise's flaws, he did not hold back with little remarks of his time being numbered with Louise trying to kill him. Louise was sure it was all in jest but there were moments where she wished the bone had finished Jim off. He viewed every meal for the remainder of the week with suspicion, cutting up the food into such tiny pieces a baby bird would have been able to eat it.

Jim's real brush with death had provided Louise with a stockpile of imagery to fuel her daydreams. In one she was trying to shake the bone out of him. In a gravity defying manoeuvre, she held Jim upside down, her arms wrapped around his waist as she shook him. Jim must have felt like a human ketchup bottle. In another surgeon Louise stood over her patient extracting the bone with shining steel instruments.

14

The choking incident would be a long-lived episode in the Wilson household. Jim had stopped dissecting his meals but continued to make curious glances at his plate for the next few weeks. For Louise, it made her more irritable with Jim. They'd need new plates by the end of the month if Jim didn't stop scrapping his cutlery across the porcelain, so were his efforts to ensure that his meals were hazard free. Jim was acting was if he feared the bone had been intentional and that Louise would again try to bump him off.

Every now and again Jim would turn up unannounced at the supermarket and they would do a joint shop. Louise was always saying that if Jim didn't like what she bought then he could go shopping himself, he was, after all, a grown man and perfectly capable. Jim's version was to meet Louise after work and subject her to a drawn-out tour of her place of work.

Jim was still going on about the fish and not buying anything that could kill him, so he had come to vet the purchases. Louise wished that the fish had been a murder weapon.

In principal Louise didn't mind sharing the chore of grocery shopping but with Jim it took so long. It was a reflection that he wasn't the main shopper as he didn't know where items were located so he had to painstakingly walk up and down every aisle, looking at almost every product. It was torture for Louise, and much more expensive at the checkout. It reminded her of when she used to have to drag the kids along - the constant requests for this or that and always an over spend, anything for a peaceful life. Louise found herself tidying the shelves, not her department, but out of habit and pride. It's not that she had planned a career in retail, but it should see her through until retirement and she always did her best, no matter the situation.

By the time they had reached the deli counter, home to the murderous fish, Louise had started to lose the will to live. She would have completed the shop and been home by now.

Jim stood staring at the clear fronted freezers, deliberating what he fancied. Louise had already scoured the cabinets for what she needed, and it was in the trolley, slowly dripping condensation onto the floor as Jim 'ummed and ahhed', his taste buds leading his choices.

As Louise stood in the frozen aisle her mind drifted into a daydream, her eyes hypnotised by the crystallised patterns made by the frost gathered on the corners of the see-through doors.

Selecting a lamb shank, Louise removed the meat from the packaging and gripped the bone firmly in her right hand. Jim was leaning into one of the chest freezers, presenting a perfect opportunity for Louise. Without hesitation, she brought the leg of frozen lamb down onto Jim's skull with the force of a skilled lumberjack. There was a distinctive crack as the ice-cold slab of meat connected with the back of Jim's head. He slummed onto bags of frozen veg, picked at the height of freshness. They cushioned Jim, preventing him from slipping head first into an icy coffin. The choice of weapon was ironic as lamb was Jim's favourite meat.

Jim's lifeless corpse gave way to gravity and his body fell to the floor, a smear of blood running down the glass fronted freezer. The shoppers went about their business, casually stepping over Jim's silent body to reach the veg needed for their Sunday roasts.

Louise was brought back to reality by Jim tapping her arm, saying "come on love, you were away with the fairies". Louise obligingly followed Jim, doing a double-take as she walked past the bags of veg, the tiniest hint of a smile teasing at her lips.

Louise couldn't remember the last time she had done a shop that didn't contain chocolate. This shop was no different, with the exception that she had a six-foot conscience tutting as the items were scanned and bagged.

Jim, to be fair, rarely mentioned Louise's figure. He was always calling her "sexy" and "beautiful", not that Louise considered herself either. The trouble was Jim didn't need to raise any issue about her weight as any previous, seemingly innocent, comment he made was lodged in the anti-Jim memory bank, to be recalled and used against him whenever the opportunity arose. "Not exactly a stick figure yourself" were the words that had doomed Jim, never to be forgiven and forever to be used as ammunition.

The primary reason Louise hadn't given up chocolate is because she didn't want to. She'd lose weight and save money, but she wasn't obese or poor - yet. She loved the chocolatey taste that lingered on her tongue after the block had melted into her system. Louise had an addictive personality but had managed to ditch the cigarettes years ago, happy to rid of the unpleasant cost and smell as well as the health implications but she wasn't relinquishing her admiration of cocoa. She knew her limits. For Louise, there was nothing more satisfying than the snap that biting into refrigerated chocolate made. Cold chocolate was the best.

Louise did yoga to keep the excess weight at bay. It afforded her a small level of fitness but it's main purpose was to work off Louise's sweet tooth. It was also an hour out the house twice a week. Louise hated the thought of going, and sometimes hated the instructor, but she was not ignorant of the fact that she needed to go. Most sessions she was exhaling when she should have been inhaling, up when she should have been down and facing left when the rest of the class were facing right but she was nothing if not persistent. She was rarely in time with a single step and often left the class sweating like a pig but feeling pumped and energised. She didn't like the aching legs the next day but, like drinkers and hangovers, she went back for more.

Louise had tried, over the years, to convince Jim of the benefits of getting fit but Jim was no gym buff and getting him out of his arm chair on an evening could prove trickier than an undercover operation to infiltrate the cartel.

Louise supposed it didn't really matter, neither of them were going anywhere, she'd invested far too much time in her husband, not that she had done a very good job at moulding him into the perfect helpful and attentive spouse. Jim still had too much freedom and will-power to be classified as under-the-thumb, but he did occasionally toe the line and play the dutiful husband, especially at family gatherings.

Jim's fear of being poisoned to death had done nothing to improve his culinary skills. Louise remained the head chef though Jim had morphed into the world's harshest food critic, he made Jay Rayner seem like an angel. Jim was sensible enough not to pull a Gordon Ramsey and criticise Louise directly whilst the cooking took place as he couldn't be sure he wouldn't get a hot pan or sharp knife thrown in his direction.

Louise knew she was no Nigella Lawson, but she did try, on the most part. Jim's idea of cooking however was popping out for a take-away. The kids used to love it when Louise was on lates as they knew that they would be getting fish & chips or a McDonalds for their tea.

The only item to have escaped the fatal ridicule was Louise's pouched egg. She had learnt the skill after watching an eager host on TV prepare a breakfast fit for a king. How it avoided scrutiny was beyond Louise's comprehension, what with the risk of salmonella. Louise even received compliments from Jim that they were "poached to perfection". Despite the compliment Louise couldn't help herself imagining poking Jim in the eye with a fork. What would poached eye be like she thought to herself? Probably like eating a mussel or an oyster she silently concluded, yuk.

Despite the opinions of outsiders, Jim couldn't be considered brow-beaten, despite his repeated refrains that Louise was naggy or bossy. He put in his two-penance worth, Louise just chose to ignore him on the most part. They had made it through several decades in this manner, Louise knowing that she really wore the trousers, she just let Jim play dress-up.

Jim's comments were starting to really grate on Louise's nerves and the thought of actually poisoning him briefly crossed her mind. To avoid a manslaughter charge Louise went to stay with her sister for a few days. It would give Jim some space and make him appreciate what he had and allow Louise to calm down a bit.

Louise didn't admit to Jim that she was fleeing him for a short period, she made up an excuse that Fran needed her, and she was living up to her sibling duties.

15

Fran lived up North. It wasn't a journey that Louise looked forward to, but it was one she had done countless times.

As she headed out of the scenic South the landscape gave way to miles of tarmacked motorways and industrial units before the greens of the Yorkshire Dales signalled that Louise's journey was nearly at an end.

Hours of power ballads and high-speed driving rendered Louise quite favourable towards Jim by the time she pulled into the driveway of her sisters isolated cottage. It had been a good run, the usual hold up as she approached the major cities on route but otherwise it had been plain sailing. She'd been out paced by a few Audis, Beamers and supped-up Fords but held her own whilst avoiding any cameras or unmarked patrol cars as she weaved her way between lorries and cautionary drivers.

As was a customary family tradition Louise sent a text to Jim to inform him of her safe arrival. She'd normally let the kids know she had arrived without incident at her destination, but it was a last-minute trip and the children didn't even know that she had gone, and Louise was confident she would be back before either were any the wiser.

Louise texted Jim *'Here safe, speak soon xxx'*. Within thirty minutes his reply came – *'Say Hi to Franny. C u soon sexy xxxxx'*, which was received with irritation as Louise knew that Fran detested her brother-in-law's nickname for her which would lead to an anti-Jim rant if Louise relayed the message in its entirety.

She didn't, nor did Louise tell her sister to truthful purpose of her visit.

The two middle-aged women headed to the local pub for a meal and a catch-up over a bottle of wine. An open fire warmed the old stone building, the light from the flames shining a glowing reflection onto the polished brass work that hung from the rafters.

Despite the distance the sisters were very close, they spoke weekly on the phone and holidayed together. Louise and Fran hadn't always got on as well as they did now. Growing up, Fran was the annoying little sister who followed Louise around, copied what she did and got Louise into repeated trouble, whether she was to blame or not, though it was more often than not Louise's fault. Fran had gone on to university, to pursue a career in costal conservation whereas Louise followed her heart into a relationship with Jim. Fran had always liked the beach whereas Louise preferred the rock pools, to her the beach was an unfortunate by product of living near the sea. The sisters reconnected when Fran returned with a Doctorate in marine biology, their hometown on the South coast a fabulous opportunity for Fran to put into practice her education. With a great career under her belt Fran became a wildlife crusader, campaigning for safer waterways. Louise resented Fran for following her dream, for putting herself first but she would never admit it to her little sister, she would barely admit it to herself. When Fran had moved away to start a new life in Yorkshire, it had caused some tension, placed a strain on the sibling bond but Louise got over it and again they were as close as two peas in a pod.

Louise hadn't always fantasied about killing Jim, they had been a loved-up couple once. The honeymoon period was long over but they had a family together, a house together, their lives had been intertwined for a lifetime. Too untangle them would be like separating Siamese-twins, one may thrive but the other would face an uncertain future without their better half.

It was actually a rare occurrence that Jim and Louise spent the night apart, even as the kids got older and needed them less. Louise had visualised spa weekends away with the girls or drunken boy's weekends away for Jim, but they never materialised.

Louise found people to be so fickle sometimes. Everyone was happy to be involved at the planning stage but when it came to committing, to parting with money, that's when people got flaky, when the excuses came.

The thing that Louise liked most about being away from Jim, apart from not having to put up with his less-than-happy tone and his smelly feet, she could handle the not-so-sweet aroma of her own feet, was having the bed to herself. Luxury.

The taxi dropped the inebriated ladies back at Fran's. Within twenty minutes of wobbling through the front door Louise was snuggled down in bed, a cosy dreamless sleep took her through the night.

The next morning Louise woke to a thumping headache and her mouth felt like she'd licked a fox. Louise had never been much of a drinker, for her the good company, good food and good ale resulted in a bad hangover. Fran breezed into the kitchen, on top of the world. Louise secretly wondered if she still might be a bit tipsy from the night before. John was in the kitchen preparing breakfast. John was the reason that Fran had moved hundreds of miles away from her family. Louise wanted to hate the guy for taking away her sister but in all honestly John was a great man. He loved Fran unconditionally, was thoughtful and kind, in fact he was the male version of Fran, they were destined to unite as one. Louise could see why they had found each other, and she didn't begrudge her sister some happiness, even if it did leave an envious stamp on Louise, one that she would never admit to, but was there none-the-less. An abusive husband left Fran a wreck, a shell of her former self. She was as emotionally and financially devastated as the ship wrecks she encountered on her dives, just an empty shell on display. John had given Fran back her smile, for which Louise would be eternally grateful, she just hated that they lived so far away. That was the one compromise that John wouldn't make so Fran happily upped sticks and followed her soulmate.

The smoky smell of bacon wafted from the kitchen to assault Louise's senses and send her running from the room. As she ran the alcohol from last night seemed to churn in her stomach, urging her on. Although she looked and felt as rough as a badgers arse her body was hanging onto any and all fluids.

Once she had composed herself an ashen-faced Louise poked her head around the kitchen door.

Louise was greeted with jovial "good mornings" from the happy couple. She replied with less enthusiasm, liking how she felt to the backside of local wildlife. John couldn't contain his reply and just about got out "and you look it" between cheeky giggles. Louise knew it was only in jest so didn't take offence. Besides, Louise would have to admit that she hadn't yet braved looking in the mirror that morning for fear of what she would find staring back at her. It wasn't uncommon for Louise to go days without gazing upon her own reflection, she'd never been vain and found that looking at herself only served to highlight her inadequacies. She wasn't averse to a quick glance, just to make sure she was relatively presentable but didn't spend hours preening herself before stepping out the door.

Fran and John were sat at the rustic table, enjoying a fry-up and chatting about the days plans. Louise declined Johns prepared breakfast and instead opted for a slice of toast and a cup of black coffee, which John mustered up with a sympathetic smile.

The sisters spent a few days together, taking in the sights and visiting the moors. They enjoyed recreating scenes from Bronte classics, Louise's broody Heathcliff a contrast to Fran's over-acted Cathy. Years of adulthood dripped away as they ran around like school girls, just content to be in each other's company, knowing that the inevitable return to the South beaconed Louise. She did have a job to return too, and so did Fran. Fran was self-employed so was moderately more flexible than Louise who had been phoning in sick with a fake cough for the past couple of shifts.

Louise's suitcase was packed and, in the hall, ready for her departure. John had prepared a leaving lunch. The sisters sat in the conservatory and looked out at the spacious landscaped gardens as they ate the ploughman's style dinner that had been attentively prepared for them. John was not hanging around, he had errands to run and jobs to complete, so he said his goodbyes, departing with a peck on the cheek for Louise and a lingering, lust filled kiss on the lips for his true love.

The women were treated with an exceptional view to accompany their lunch. Birds of all varieties frequented the lush green garden, bees buzzed throughout the lavender bushes and the occasional squirrel committed theft from the bird table.

By far the best view was that of the twenty-something gardener who had been tasked with clearing up after a recent storm. As the property backed onto a small forestry the garden was littered with broken branches, it looked like a botanical massacre had taken place.

For a short time, Louise was lost in her own thoughts as she watched the topless gardener load fallen branches into the wood chipper. His biceps bulged and tickled Louise's fancy as she followed the contours of his chiselled torso. Louise didn't feel guilty as it was only window shopping, a bit of eye candy, the role of a builder reversed, just without the wolf-whistling.

As Louise watched the gardener she couldn't help thinking that she hadn't considered this yet as a form of disposal for a body. In her mind's eye, the murder had already taken place, she just needed to dispose of the body.

She deliberated if she would be able to get Jim's whole body in or if she would have to chop it up with an axe before feeding it into the wood chipper. Louise decided that it would depend on the type of chipper she had access too. The one that the gardener was using would need the body to be chopped up which would be messy and time consuming. If she used one with a lower shoot she thought she'd be able to manage to drag Jim's body into it, then he would be disposed of in one go. Either way she imaginarily scrutinised his body being sucked into the chipper and watched as a rainbow of red and green sprayed out the other end. In another twist on the gardener from hell she imagined Jim accidently falling into the chipper, tripping on one of the fallen branches and, losing his balance, falling into the machine, head first, debris and Jim spraying out the end of the machine.

Louise did sometimes feel guilty over her fantasies, particularly when Jim was having a romantic moment, but she had never acted on them, never needed to, it was more fun to kill him over and over again. If she did it in reality it would literally be a once-in-a-lifetime experience and she had no intention of spending the remainder of her life behind bars, for anyone.

Louise and Jim had been a couple for so long that if Louise had done Jim in when they'd first met she could have been out in half the time, she should know, she'd done the calculations. The length of the sentence would depend on the circumstances and she was hopeful she could convince the judge and jury of her innocence and remorse. If she was accused of premediated murder, without the use a firearm or explosive she could receive a sentence of approximately twenty-five years but would have been released after only twelve and half years. Louise hated guns and would probably only blow herself up so was sure that she would have found another way, securing herself just half a century punishment. The good old British justice system required only half the sentence to be served in prison whilst the remainder would be spent out in the community, only the threat of being recalled keeping them on the straight and narrow. Unless she got an unforgiving and vengeful judge who slapped her with a full life sentence.

Louise had concluded that manslaughter was the way to go, if any. The law offers more freedom to the magistrates, giving the judge the opportunity to impose a community sentence, a suspended imprisonment or a custodial sentence. Louise was positive that her demure manner would not be assessed as dangerous and the passionate murder of one individual would not constitute as a hazard to the general population. Louise had watched enough C.S.I and Silent Witness to have a small understanding of the forensic evidence that can seal a killer's fate. If she could not lie herself out of the conviction then she would have sought a plea deal, with the judge likely to reduce the sentence by up to a third, dependant on how quickly Louise surrendered her innocence. To Louise it was irrelevant anyway as she had zero intention of acting on her fantasies. That's why they were fantasies, just musings, daydreams.

it was almost midday by the time Louise had faffed around and said a drawn-out tearful goodbye to her beloved sister. She decided that she would make a bit of headway then stop for a quick bite in the services, if she stayed any longer at her sisters she might never go home.

A toilet break and an over-priced sandwich later Louise was heading down the country, making great time. As she drove she washed away the taste of the processed food with a carbonated bottle of Coco-cola. The result of eating on the run was Louise belching between songs, a burping chorus of backing vocals, conduct that would normally have been meet with tuts and expressions of disgust from Jim. The travel was the only thing that kept Louise from regularly turning up on her sisters' doorstep, from doing a lot actually. If she was even in the tiniest bit technically minded, then she would have put her determination into building a teleportation device. She would be unstoppable with one of those, popping up all over the world in the blink of an eye. Between singing and thinking about what she would do with her teleportation machine the journey was over before she knew it. She could visit the seven wonders of the world in a day, have a tour of the pyramids in an afternoon or pop over to Hollywood and stalk a star for a morning.

It was still daylight when she pulled into the drive, in fact she'd made such good time that Jim wasn't even home from work yet.

The house was little changed when she returned, her lack of notice meant that Jim had been unable to wangle any time of work, so the devastation was at a minimum. There was a build-up of washing at the foot of the machine and in the bowl, but Louise could hardly fault Jim as she hadn't announced her departure and had also returned home unannounced. Jim had played the role of dutiful husband well, allowing his wife the time to spend with Fran without complaint, no doubt relishing the short-lived peace and freedom at home.

Louise tore through the house with the duster and vacuum, sorted the post, most of which went straight into the recycling, put on a wash and filled the sink with hot soapy water. By the time Jim came home there was a food cooking in the oven, the dishes were drying on the drainer, the clothes were on spin in the dryer and Louise was catching up on her soaps.

The Wilsons had a lovely evening together, chatting like long-lost friends, ending the night in bed.

16

As Louise had been calling in sick to work, whilst away at Frans, her return would have to be convincing. A very late night and early start would render her looking sorry for herself, dark bags under her eyes highlighting her naturally pale skin.

Louise smiled awkwardly at the colleagues who asked after her health, said they were happy she was back. They were genuine as Louise was a kindly person to work alongside, fair yet authoritative when she needed to be.

The day dragged by tortuously, the second hand on the clock mocking Louise as it moved in slow motion. In contrast, her lunch break was over in the blink of an eye, the scent of onion lingering on her breath. Louise was so keen to get home that she almost got herself a speeding fine.

An hour after being home and Louise wished that she was still at work.

She had made a shocking discovery in the conservatory that left her blood boiling. She was furious with what she found. If Jim had been home then Louise probably would have killed him, she was so angry she could feel the vein in her neck throb as she ground her teeth together.

In her absence Jim had been busier than it first appeared on Louise's return.

It took her a few minutes to detect what was amiss. The conservatory was rarely used, it was stifling hot in the summer and an icebox in the winter, so it was more of a store room and thoroughfare to the back garden. It was here that the butchery had been committed.

On first a glance there was nothing missing, nothing had been moved, which was intentional on Jim's part, his attempt to remain undetected in his crime. Unfortunately for Jim Louise lived by the motto *'a place for everything and everything in its place'* which was Jim's downfall, he'd failed to stand up an ornament he'd knocked over.

The room was marginally brighter than it had been which caused Louise to cast her eyes towards the ceiling which is when she noticed what Jim had done. It took all her self-control not to call or send him a string of angry emoji's. She would instead brood on it until Jim came home then give it to him with both barrels. It was lucky for Jim that they did not own a shotgun.

A brief image of Louise as the ultimate eco-warrior flashed across her mind. She was stood, dressed more as Lara Croft than Charlie Dimmock, in the hallway, awaiting her prey. An oversized gun, held with both hands, pointed at the door. The remnants of plants at her feet, scattered across the floor like the ashes of the dead. "This is for them" warrior Louise screamed as Jim crossed the threshold, pulling the trigger and blasting him back through the doorway in which he had just entered.

Louise had needed to calm down, to walk away. She returned to the conservatory with worried expectancy akin to a student awaiting their exam results. She desperately hoped that in her frustration the damage was an optical illusion, not as bad as it looked. On closer inspection, this turned out not to be the case, the damage was far worse than Louise had originally anticipated.

Louise wasn't a confident person, she internally struggled with most aspects of life, but she did pride herself on her green fingers. Her method was mainly to let Mother Nature work her magic, especially outside, but she did occasionally prune the house plants. She as incredibly proud of the magnificent Ficuses that lined one wall of the conservatory, a living wallpaper. The luscious specimens stood eight foot-high, the top branches curved owing to having reached the ceiling but resolved to keep growing. They were Louise's pride and joy. Each over twenty years old, arriving as new saps, lost in the pots that held them.

Louise was loathed to admit that the plants were slightly unruly, but it was part of their charm as far as she was concerned. Jim had mentioned on many occasions that they needed chopping back, reigning in, only to be meet with a vicious determination from Louise that the plants remain untouched. Louise wasn't passionate about a lot of things anymore, but her plants were like her babies, something to be nurtured and cared for now her own children had flown the nest, and plants didn't answer back.

Louise found it hard to take compliments, always sought a double meaning in any praise but she basked in the glory of the admiration given to her plants. Guests complimented their beauty, were in awe at their outstanding size. It gave Louise a buzz when people revered her handy work, pleased her to the core that she had something of envy to others.

Two rubber figs stood like sentinels, protecting the more temperamental weeping fig. The two identical plants were grown from cuttings, loving nursed by Louise into the glorious horticultural masterpieces that they were, that is before Louise unknowingly abandoned them to Jim's callous mercy.

It turned out that Jim had lopped off about two foot from the top of all three spectacular specimens. The branches that once trailed across the rafters were now missing, cut down in their prime. Little care had been taken, Louise could see where branches had been ripped from the trunk, wood splintered where once proud arms were held aloft, supporting the gigantous sized foliage. Jim had forensically cleaned the conservatory to detract from the crime, not a stray leaf was found to alert Louise to the heinous slaughter.

The snaking cheese plant that resided in the furthest corner had escaped the massacre. This only served to fuel Louise's anger as it was the plant she liked the least and, although she would have been pissed off, would have recovered from its destruction far quicker than her beloved figs.

To say that Louise was angry was an understatement, she was fuming, spitting feathers, the world couldn't bring down enough condemnation and hellfire upon Jim at the very moment. If there was ever a chance that Louise would carry out one of her fantasies this was it.

She was so livid with Jim for going behind her back that she got as far as dragging the suitcase back out of the loft. In half a mind whether or not to pack it.

Jim was taken slightly aback at the force of the Louise's wrath. He knew that she would be upset but hadn't grasped the depth of affection she had for the plants.

Jim knew when to beat a hasty retreat and slithered off to the pub for a few hours in an attempt to let Louise calm down and gain some composure over the situation. Tears stung Louise's eyes as she was transported back to when Frank was a small boy with a head of fine untouched hair that framed his face like a helmet. Jim had taken Frank out for the day and had had Franks head shaved, Louise was crucified when they returned. Her angelic little boy looked like a mini thug, his amazing flowing flocks a stunted spiky mess on his head. Seeing the plants scalped brought it all back and Louise was reminded of the crushing hurt that she had felt at Jim's betrayal.

Louise did nothing to rein in the ferocity with which she attacked Jim in her fantasy. Louise wielded the axe with the tenacity of a woodcutter. Off came one arm, followed in quick succession by the other arm and then Jim's legs before chopping off his head. Louise was confronted with a dismembered Jim, blood oozing from the severed limbs onto the polished hardwood flooring. Louise retired to the kitchen for a cuppa, exhausted from the effort used to slice through bone, a trail of bloody footprints leading from the murder scene. Refreshed, Louise returned to the body, it couldn't stay where it was, a scarlet heap of flesh, she would need to get rid of it. She couldn't visibly put it out with the food waste and she really didn't fancy eating him.

She couldn't logically call the police and say it was an accident, after all she'd chopped him up. She couldn't dump it in the stream as it would be discovered, and it wasn't deep enough to keep a body hidden. She could put bits into the rubbish but if a seagull tore through one of the bin bags and exposed a limb then she would be busted. She would have to bury the remains. She could reintern the pieces in the plant pots then Jim would fertilise the plants that had been the cause of his death. Jim was a big man so had to be spread throughout the homestead, a bit here, a bit there. But not in the veggie patch, Louise didn't want to pull a carrot in ten years' time and find part of Jim clinging to it, she'd heard many a tale of long lost rings making a reappearance years after being lost whilst gardening.

The bloodied clothes that she had removed from Jim, they don't biodegrade quickly, her own stained attire and the soaked towels that she used to clean up the evidence where burnt in the chiminea. Flames ignited the material, with the help of some gasoline. Louise sat on a garden chair and watched the evidence disintegrate into a pile of ash, a glass of wine in hand, a book in the other. She thought toasting marshmallows would be a bit tasteless, given the circumstances of the blaze.

Louise was so angry and wound up that by evening she was suffering with an exceptionally bad irritable bowel attack. Louise had been managing the condition for years, rarely experiencing more than mild discomfort these days. Prior to first being diagnosed Jim and Louise had researched all the possibles, from bowel cancer to celiac disease but the doctor had labelled her with an idiosyncratic irritable bowel, stress and fatty foods the main culprits for causing an episode.

Jim found Louise rolling around the floor in agony, clutching her stomach and whimpering in pain. There was little Jim could do for his wife when she was in the middle of a debilitating cramp. He usually slept in one of the spare bedrooms so that Louise could fitfully rest and have the freedom to use the en-suite without disturbing Jim. Not that she would have cared on this occasion as he was the cause, but she did usually feel awful for disturbing Jim's sleep. Jim was devastated at how useless he felt when his wife was ill, there was nothing he could do to ease the pain and Louise was an awful patient, she had a tendency to wallow in her own self-pity.

Louise woke late, having fallen into a restless slumber as dawn began to break. She was startled to realise the time and jumped out of bed in a panic to find a note pinned to the door. With some trepidation, she read the note: *'called in sick for you, have a good day, Love you   xxxxxxx'*

A surge of guilt at Jim's concern and thoughtfulness washed over her but was quickly replaced with annoyance. Jim would not be forgiven that quickly or easily.

17

Jim wasn't very romantic, but he knew how to act when he was in the dog house. He came home from work ladened down with a floral display of guilt and a box of luxurious Belgian chocolates. A cliché he knew, but it went some way to thawing the frosty atmosphere. What would have worked quicker would have been to grovel, to beg for forgiveness and apologise profusely but Jim refused to apologise as he stood by his decision to scale back the atrocious light eaters in the conservatory. A small slither of hatred still clung to Louise's heart when she thought of the deforestation and how Jim could so coldheartedly destroy something that Louise loved so much, but he did have form.

To his credit, Jim supported Louise through her diagnosis of IBS. He held her hand and comforted her whilst the doctors were in the investigative stages. He talked to her kindly when she'd played doctor and internet searched her symptoms, had reassured her that what she had found were probably worst-case scenarios. Jim was always positive in Louise's presence, dismissing her concerns with sympathy and empathy he had rarely shown before or since. Jim remained strong throughout the early days of Louise getting ill but, owing to his unemotional manner, it came over to Louise that she was an inconvenience, that she was deliberately making herself ill. The family were Jim's unwitting saviour, breaking any confidence he held them in and pointing out to Louise how worried Jim actually was. He was putting on a brave face but secretly he was terrified that his wife would be taken from him, and he was powerless to prevent it.

Louise tried to remember this as often as she could, always did when promoted by an IBS 'do' as she called them, but the intensity of the pain paled everything else in comparison. Louise wasn't a good patient, she was best left on her own to come through it. Jim was the cause of a lot of Louise's stress so ultimately, in Louise's eyes, it is Jim's fault she was ill.

Louise accepted the flowers and chocolates gracefully but inside was still bubbling with fury, the chocolate yet to work its magic and redeem Jim of his failed horticultural skills. Every bite of delicious handcrafted chocolate softened Louise, by the end of the week she had mellowed enough to hold a civil conversation with her long-term spouse.

It was a tense week in the Wilson household. The last time Jim was on tenterhooks was when they were waiting for Ellen's university placements to come through. Frank had somewhat stumbled into his, applying late, not really bothered if he was accepted or not but for Ellen, she had placed her whole future on a positive reply from her first choice. She had been accepted but it was a tortuous wait while she opened the envelope, Jim was sure he could feel himself sprout grey hairs in the process.

Jim tentatively tested the waters by attempting to instigate a romantic liaison in the bedroom. He was successful. Louise hadn't forgiven Jim, but she had decided to try to forget the best she could, his sins had been put on the back burner, to be used as ammunition if and when it was needed.

The pair had a beautiful night, Louise falling asleep with endorphins running through her system, numbing all remaining traces of the cramps brought on by her medical condition.

Louise opened her eyes and stretched, Jim was lying peacefully beside her. She leaned across her dormant husband and stirred him to life with a kiss.

They were making love as the early morning rays of sunshine shone through the brakes in the blinds, Louise on top, riding Jim like a gymkhana pony. Just as Louise began to feel the sensual stirrings of climax Jim's eyes widened, he took a gulping breath and fainted. Perplexed by the series of events Louise tried rocking her hubby back to consciousness but when this didn't work she dismounted and proceeded to prod him with her index finger. After a minute or so of prodding and gentle encouragement Jim hadn't moved.

Now starting to panic, Louise ran for the phone to call the emergency services. Her attempts at CPR failing to revive her man, his member the only organ with blood still coursing through it.

She dialled 999. The rapturous laughter that meet Louise when describing her husband's lifeless state didn't seem to register to Louise. Her imagery was so vivid, but on closer inspection the scene was a poor imitation of reality, revealing that Louise was in fact asleep.

Dream Louise solemnly lead the police officers upstairs to where Jim lay, the sheet covering his modestly but unable to disguise the obvious evidence of their encounter It looked like a poorly constructed tent with feet poking out of one end and a smiling face out of the other.

Louise indicated to where Jim lay in the master bedroom, which was followed almost instantly with stifled giggles and the exclamation "we've got a stiff ...... literally!".

Paramedics announced their arrival by shouting up the stairs, they were beaconed to the calamitous turn of events by their emergency colleagues. Louise hung in the doorway watching the professionals check Jim's vital signs and prepare his body for removal. The bedroom resembled a landscape painting, streaks of green and blue canvased around a snow tipped mountain. Jim's corpse was escorted from the house to a chorus of "what a way to go", "lucky chap" and "well, at least he went with a smile on his face". There was no investigation, no post mortem, no coroner's report, just a dead body who'd expired, probably from a heart attack, due to strenuous physical activity. A verdict of natural causes was recorded.

Louise was unwillingly dragged from sleep the following morning by the shriek of her alarm. Avoiding the temptation to hit the snooze button Louise dragged herself out of bed. She moved sluggishly around the bathroom and forced herself out of the door and into the car for work. She felt like she'd run a marathon. Her attacks did knock the stuffing out of her, but she was normally up and moving at classic Louise pace by now. Her get up and go had got up and gone.

A few strong coffee's and a grievance procedure to attended as a representative for a colleague soon shook off the cobwebs and got Louise focused. Louise found that she was lacking the usual guilt that followed one of Jim's murders, presumably due to the loving way that he passed over.

The clock ticked at a painfully slow rate. A couple of times Louise could have sworn that it had gone backwards, but eventually the hands were at opposing angles signalling the end of her shift. Louise had never been happier to see the dazzling lights of the supermarket fade into the distance in her rear-view mirror as she hurtled home.

The house was empty when Louise got there, so she kicked off her shoes and headed straight to the living room. When Jim walked through the door Louise was in her dressing gown and slippers, catching up on *Come Dine with Me*. Jim came in just as the third contestant gave their score, placing the prospective winner in second place.

"What's for tea?" inquired Jim.

"whatever the Chinese cooks for us." came Louise's nonchalant reply. "I'll have duck and special fired rice thank you".

With raised eyebrows Jim obediently retrieved the menu, placed the order and went out to get it. Not that he had much of a choice as Louise had made it quite clear that she had no intention of doing it. For Jim, he could comply, cook his own food or go hungry. He had no intention of rivalling Jamie Oliver, was peckish after a day at work and was keen to make amends with his wife. The remainders of the Chinese were placed in the fridge and Louise headed to bed for an early night. She'd had a long week and was quite exhausted by last night's dream sex.

18

Although Louise was part of the senior team she was seen by her colleagues as one of them. The representative for the masses, the one who would fight the cause of the casual workers, the season temps, those too afraid to cause a fuss or be noticed by the big bosses. And as a result, Louise often found herself listening to her colleagues' gripes and groans.

Many were placated with a few kind motherly words, others just needed encouragement that they were on the right path, or not complete loons and others needed a firmer hand to curb destructive tendencies that would lead them down a path that Louise did not want to see them tread.

One worker in particular saw Louise as an unofficial agony aunt, coming to her with all her life's problems. And she had a lot. The poor woman's existence was like a soap opera, jumping from one disaster to the next. It was beggar's belief how she got herself into some of the situations and Louise was beyond any clue on how to help her. It was exhausting just keeping up with who was who and who had done what. Annie was a large character with ill-fitting clothes and greasy hair, but she was a lovely woman, she had a true salt of the earth charm. She lived on the council estate across the road from the supermarket, had five different kids by as many different fathers but she had a heart of gold, would take anyone in. She'd give her last penny if it meant that someone didn't go without which is why Louise always had time for her. No matter what else was happening at work Louise would make sure that Annie knew she was there if she was needed, and she often was, if only as a sympathetic adult ear.

It wasn't just Annie that came to Louise with her problems, many of the ground floor staff did, it didn't matter on gender, Louise was a pal to all, a point of advice on marital woes to financial crisis.

Louise was outwardly a very positive person, all smiles and bubbliness, a friend to everyone. She had a reputation for making people feel better about themselves. She was considered by her friends and colleagues to be happy individual, which was often the case, but her happiness hid a multitude of feelings, ones of inadequacy, fear, worry. She just didn't project it onto the outside world, kept it all bottled up inside, Jim bearing the brunt of any irritations or frustrations. Louise belonged to the school of thought of if you don't laugh you'll cry. She did care what people thought and would fester over misinterpreted looks or remarks but had learnt to be her own person regardless.

Though Louise was friendly and approachable she didn't really like people all that much, wasn't really a people person. Content in her own company she didn't need to seek reassurances, had her own unique dress sense and a moral backbone to support her convictions. It was a trait that she had had since childhood, friends disclosed troubling feelings, colleagues shared titbits worthy of whistleblowing, yet her kids were always rather elusive with their problems. Franks junior conquests remaining largely unknown to Louise, not that any mother really wanted to know the ins and outs of their children's love lives. After a chat with Louise most people left feeling lighter, chipper, problem free. Louise found that most people wanted something to satisfy their own agenda. She was a sounding board for friends and relatives, asked for advice, dumped upon, but the gossip could be good, not that she discussed it with anyone, sometimes the cat if she needed to share. Louise didn't mind so much, found it flattering in a way but sometimes the problems discussed ended up running amok in her mind. She couldn't stop thinking about them, feeling that she should step in whereas if she uninformed she could continue in blissful ignorance as opposed to facing situations that had nothing initially to do with her.

It surprised Louise at the true nature of people sometimes, those that looked composed on the surface were a chaotic mess of insecurity and disorganisation and there were some that looked like their lives were about to unravel at any moment, yet they passed through life without a care. She knew from her un-appointed position of therapist that even if a person appeared happy and positive on the surface if you slice through a layer you'd be surprised how dark they are underneath. And in Louise's experience those classified bad, written off by society, could be capable of redeeming behaviour.

The look of Annie's face told Louise that today was going to be a long day, that something of some importance had happened. Looking more exhausted than normal, her eyes glazed over from lack of sleep. Annie pulled Louise to one side and proceed to tell her about the incident that had happened on the estate the night before.

A suspected dealer, the local residents basing their diagnosis on the sheer volume of foot traffic through the house, had been attacked and the house ransacked. The estate had been crawling with police officers, sirens echoing into the night. Annie's youngest too afraid to sleep, the older ones to intrigued with what was happening to sleep. Poor Annie, who turned up for her shift come rain or shine, hell or high water, looked dead on her feet. She emotionally recalled the events that lead to her zombie like appearance, never considering calling in sick.

During the assault on the alleged dealers house, two doors down from Annie's three bedroomed flat, it was looted, the windows smashed, and his pets released. Owing to the fact that he was the owner of a fearsome Doberman and had in his possession a Burmese python and a ten-foot boa constrictor known as Lucy the local residents were held hostage in their own homes while police attempted to track down the menagerie of potentially lethal animals let loose on the estate.

Lucy, the escaped snake, had caused panic within the occupants of Bull Heights as she was known for her temper. She had been used on more than one occasion to scare victims or frighten neighbours into keeping quiet about the activities that went on behind the reinforced steel door. Annie's youngest took heed of the story that it had once eaten a child and would happily munch on another should she get the opportunity. It was the early hours before the sirens stopped, and the hammering ceased. Annie had managed to convince her youngest that every creak he heard was not the snake coming to eat him, she had even had to tape the letterbox shut, just in case.

Louise embraced Annie, a comforting hug that the woman melted into, just needing to be held, fatigued from reliving the trauma of the previous evening. Louise sent her for an extended tea break, covering her till duties. Louise scanned the customers shopping as it trundled down the conveyor belt, conscious to give them the time to pack each item instead of whizzing it through and causing a jam. Some cashiers would play a devilish game to see how quickly they could make a customer pack.

A comical version of what had occurred at Bull Heights played out in Louise's mind. Snakes the size of buses slithering around the estate, peeking into windows in search of prey. Though Jim had no reason to be in Louise's fantasy he popped up, dressed in a suit of armour made from baking trays and sauce pans, a lone avenger ready to battle to oversized serpent. His wooden spoon weapons were no defence against the cunning strength of the skilled reptile. Circling Jim like a desert rat the predator prepared to make its move. Jim managed a sharp knock to the snake's skull as it struck out the bite him. Dazed, it shook its dustbin sized head and rounded on Jim for another try. This time the snake used its superior size to position its body around Jim, circling like a whirlpool of slithering scales. The boa constrictor started to squeeze the life from Jim, it's rippled skin tightening around Louise's heroic husband, the pressure becoming so immense that Jim's eyeballs popped out and rolled along the ground.

Despite herself, a small giggle escaped Louise's lips, making the customer give her a cursory glare as she packed the remainder of her shopping into the five pence carriers reluctantly supplied by the supermarket chain. Louise offered a redundant apology with the assurance that she had just remembered something funny she had seen the night before on TV.

The Wilsons were both trying very hard to stay on each other's good side, putting in extra effort, listening to what the other had to say and actually taking some of it in. They held meaningful conversations over glasses of wine and kissed each other because they wanted to and not because one or the other felt they needed to. Jim even put his smelly socks in the wash instead of waiting for them to grow legs and walk themselves to the washing machine.

Louise's generosity of spirit goaded Jim but at the same time her devotion to others was part of what made the woman that Jim fell in love with. She had a knack for making people feel better about themselves and could always manage to get the kids to smile. Not great at jokes because she could never remember the punch line, that was Jim's department, but she had an animated personality. A natural mother figure she attracted lost or confused souls the way lavender attracts bees.

As the pair hadn't had an argument, disagreement or dig at each other for the best part of a month Louise decided to book the murder mystery weekend she'd seen advertised in the local paper, determined to make the most of their new-found truce but risk upsetting the apple cart.

It was one of those coach packages, frequented mostly by the elder generation, but Louise noticed it each year and had always fancied it. She missed the board game nights that they used to have when the kids still lived at home. Louise was a Cluedo champion, wanted to try her hand at a live role play version, Jim her reluctant guest.

19

Every week the local paper advertised coach destinations, the old fogey brigade page as Jim referred to it, as the itinerary was usually designed for the more discerned and mature palate. Louise had previously been tempted by the Christmas market trips to Copenhagen or Prague but had got no further than a discussion with herself as to the pros and cons. She could have gone with her mother but didn't like to intrude. Though she was quite advanced in years Louise's mum was always off doing something with her circle of friends, which was wider and more fun than Louise's carefully selected friendship group.

It was the third week running that Louise had noticed the advert for a murder mystery weekend. Feeling like fate was trying to play a part Louise went on the website to look at the outing in more detail, check out the Ts & Cs. It was something Louise had always fancied, a real-life game of Cluedo.

Set in a secret location on the outskirts of Windsor guests will be delivered by coach to the undisclosed destination where they will spend the night followed by the main event, where a team of actors will perform an interactive investigation, accumulating in a gourmet five course banquet. A second night will be spent at the 'crime scene' followed by breakfast before guests are returned home via the coach that brought them.

No matter how enthusiastically Louise presented the idea to Jim he showed zero desire in joining her. Louise suggested the idea to Ellen who was too busy to accompany her mum and Louise very briefly entertained the idea of going alone but wasn't going to play the role of Billy No Mates so shelved the idea.

Fate was definitely playing a part in getting Louise to the weekend as her mother had an invitation for her when she popped round for her Thursday evening chat. Though Louise's mum, Joan, was heading rapidly towards her nineties she was furiously independent, still lived in her own home and drove her own car, just. One of her mum's posse had been taken ill so her place at the weekend was up for grabs, it had been offered around the group with no takers, so Louise was the last hope. Not expecting her daughter to say yes Joan was pleasantly surprised at the enthusiasm Louise showed. With plans made all Louise had to do was secure the weekend off work. With her award-winning smile and banked hours her boss always said yes, despite her recent bout of 'sickness'.

Jim wasn't best pleased that his wife was deserting him again, but he had been offered the opportunity to go so Louise felt no inclination of remorse at leaving him behind. The nearest collection point was about fifty miles away, so Louise picked up her mum as well as the two other ladies and they headed off to meet the coach and the other guests from this end of the country.

The journey was surprising loud, old time swing music played through the speakers. Louise was aghast at the ruckus a coach load of senior citizens could produce, they could have given a bus full of teenagers a run for their money.

The destination was a beautiful manor house that had been converted into a luxury hotel. Set in several acres of woodland the isolated property was the perfect setting. The reception desk in the entrance hall was sympathetically installed to be in keeping   with the original features and charm of the house, complimenting the sweeping staircase that branched off into the East and West wings, leading guests to their bedrooms.

Louise huddled in the hall with the rest of the coach party, in awe of her surroundings. Ornate Georgian furniture was positioned strategically to show off its magnificent splendour, beautiful paintings covered the walls and gleaming ornaments stood proudly on polished surfaces.

They were checked in by a charismatic plump lady in her early fifties who seemed to be genuinely enjoying her employment and then directed to a handsome young gentleman who carried their cases and escorted them to their rooms. Louise felt a bit guilty following the bellboy, she was used to lugging around the cases, it felt a bit alien somebody doing it for her. Mother and daughter had been placed in adjoining rooms.

The formal activities didn't start until the following day, so the guests had the freedom to enjoy the hotel and surrounding area at their leisure. Louise left her mum in the company of her friends, a spot by the open log fire recently vacated calling to her. Louise sunk into the antique chair, a content sigh escaping her lips. Leaving her jumper on the arm, a claim that she was returning, Louise went to the bar and ordered a large rose spritzer. She chose a novel from one of the bookcases she passed on her return journey, looked over at her mum to check she wasn't being missed, she wasn't, and settled down. The proximity to the fire close enough to keep her toasty warm but far enough away that she wasn't in danger of singeing her hair.

There was a sense of anticipation in the air at breakfast, a mixture of excitement and uncertainty at the unknown. In terms of experience they were all virgins on the murder mystery scene, a few had done some theatre in the past, nobody was quite sure what to expect.

At nine am the guests were given the lowdown on what would be happening and how they would be involved. Every card had a unisex bio on it, giving the participants key areas to help them act out the character, one card will inform the player that they are the killer. They were to find a quiet place to study their temporary persona and regroup at ten. Everyone was given a sealed envelope and scurried off in various directions to digest their new identity.

Louise's character was a twenty-five-year-old chef and was at the hotel for a job interview. She was not the killer. Louise felt like she was under suspicion the second she re-joined the party. Previously kindly looking individuals had morphed into super sleuths, poker faces set in stern expressions. Louise felt a little intimidated.

The guests were directed to pretend to go about the 'daily business' of their character whilst events played out, the event actors mingling, keeping the scenario going by playing key roles in the drama, waiting for the perfect moment to stage the murder.

Nervously Louise began to 'introduce' herself to the other guests and got to know the characters they were playing, mentally noting anything of interest, giving away as little about her own role as she could in her answers, but enough to be fair. After the initial flurry of conversation, the pace slowed, the inexperienced audience nervously waiting for the murder to happen.

Louise sat in a chair in the longue, watching the silver haired suspects acting out their characters. Her mind began to wonder, what if Jim had come? The daydream jumped to Jim, lying dead on the floor of the dining room, Louise looked down at the bloody candlestick in her hand. She had no idea what Jim had done to deserve such a fate. Louise felt her heart quicken, despite herself a slither of panic rippled through her and in a moment of madness she devised a plan to frame one of the other guests.

She crept to the door, peeking stealthily into the deserted hallway. She tiptoed back to her room and placed the candlestick on the bedside table. Composing herself she retrieved a metal nail file and crept into the hallway. She listened at the doorways of the adjoining rooms, all was quiet. Using the file to break into her chosen room Louise edged her way into the suite, Hollywood style, a mirror image of her own. The occupant was fast asleep fully clothed, spread eagle on the bed. Louise could detect the scent of whiskey the closer she got. Satisfied that alcohol would render her second victim of the night senseless for a while she returned to her own room, retrieved the murder weapon, having already wiped it clean of her fingerprints with antibacterial gel. She tentatively lifted the unsuspecting innocents right hand and slipped the slender stem of the candlestick under his palm. He stirred as Louise leased his hand, causing the candlestick to roll off the bed. Louise froze, waiting for him to wake up and find a strange woman in his room. The bang that Louise expected was only a dull thud, the plush carpet cushioning the impact. Sleep retaining its hold on the unfortunate drunk. Saying a silent pray Louise exited the room, checking the coast was clear, she slipped unseen back into her own room.

Before Louise found out if her diabolically wicked plan succeed she was startled out of her fantasy by the cries of "murder, murder". The game had been unfolding around her, the murder had been committed, the search for the killer was on. One of the actors lay 'dead' in a chair in the dining room, a plastic knife held in place, fake blood dripping carefully from the 'wound', his tongue hanging out of his open mouth. Each guest came to gawp at the victim, some taking notes, others cunningly weighing up the circumstances.

Lunch was announced while the hotel 'took care of the rather unpleasant incident'. The open buffet was a hit though the atmosphere was not as friendly as the previous evening. People sat in silence as they thought about the crime and tried to piece together evidence, think of questions to challenge the other players, most eager to catch the killer.

Louise sat with her mum, attempting to glean some information that might help but Joan had always been competitive and wouldn't give her daughter any advantages, she even marked Louise as a possible suspect due to her fictional career as a chef.

"Cheers Mum." said Louise

"Well you could be darling, chefs are good with knifes." replied Joan cheerfully.

The role-play continued, guests asking each other questions, trying to establish whereabouts and alibis. Louise had already discounted several from their MO's but still had an unacceptable number of possible suspects. An hours' worth of interrogation and eaves dropping left Louise with three suspects.

She was approaching one of her suspects, a woman that she recognised from the coach journey, when a blood curdling scream stopped her in her tracks. Following the source of the commotion Louise found herself in the midst of a real-life crime scene. At the bottom of the staircase lay the body of one of the guests, blood pooling onto the tiled flooring. The majority of the party had gathered in the entrance hall, surrounding their fallen comrade. Most of the woman were crying, the men in a state of shock. The flustered actors and staff rushing around performing CPR and ushering the guests into the function room.

Gallons of tea was brought round the shaking ensemble, the staff desperate to avoid any further deaths through heart attacks or shock. Louise comforted her mother. The unfortunate chap wasn't part of their coach party, but Joan had been on several excursions with him over the years. The stark reminder that mortality was only a borrowed concept, could be taken from them at any time had put a damper on the event.

Before long sirens heralded the arrival of the emergency services, the gravel churned up as the vehicles rushed to their assistance.

Trying her hand at a little C.S.I Louise started her own investigation, keen to solve this murder now the mystery murderer had been forgotten in the tragic circumstances. In the guise of a sympathetic ear she sat with the guests, listening to tales how they knew the deceased and where they were at the time of death, offering a caring cuddle or words of support.

Paramedics took over the attempts to save the gentleman's life while the police officers spread out amongst the party to establish a timeline of events and determine if they were investigating a homicide or an accident.

Louise attached herself to one officer in particular, a handsome bearded copper with seductive blue eyes. She showed him her notes and pointed out who she had spoken to so far. The officer diplomatically thanked Louise for her diligence and tried to continue the investigation, unaided. Louise hovered in the background, interrupting with facts she had deduced herself and quizzing him on operational procedure. The officer kept his composure, but his tone and body language were starting to indicate that Louise was getting on his nerves. To appease his budding apprentice the officer recorded Louise's findings on his tablet, thanking her yet again for her assistance before politely yet sternly informing her that any suspects would be taken to the station for questioning where they have the facility to record any disclosures. Louise was oblivious to the fact she was becoming a nuisance, she felt important assisting the police with their enquiries but was coming close to being arrested for interfering with a police investigation. Her clear criminal record remained intact as the investigation was wrapped up when the organisers produced a series of photos of the event that captured the unwitting victim falling to his death. There was nobody in the vicinity but a puddle of water on which the gentlemen slipped to his doom. The coroner would record a verdict of accidental death, case closed.

Nobody could get hold of the coach company, so they had to wait for the scheduled pick up. A few had called relatives to come and retrieve them from the horror, but most had to stay at the hotel that night. The banquet, the pinnacle of the event failed to be the joyous meal that everyone had anticipated, instead it was like the last supper, a mournful tone in the room. Some of the more optimistic of the generation turned the meal into a mini memorial, reminiscing about past outings, those that knew him personally regaling tales of a charismatic and caring individual.

Breakfast was subdued. The dining room was only half full, many opting to stay in their rooms until the coaches turned up to take them home.

The camaraderie atmosphere on the way up as distinctly lacking on the way back. Where before there was chatter and laughter there was now silence, fellow travellers lost in their own thoughts, distracting themselves by the landscape that whizzed past in a blur.

Louise had never been so glad to see Jim, throwing her arms around him when she stepped over her own threshold, the experience of the past 24 hours evaporating now she was safe in her own home.

20

Louise was a strong and dependable character who loved her family and friends with a fierce loyalty, but she had the constitution of a plate of jelly when it came to being frightened. She considered herself one of the jumpiest people she knew and could be scared by a leaf falling at the wrong time. Sometimes she'd merely squeak, other times it would be a full-blown horror movie scream, eyes wide in terror, twisted jazz hands flapping about beside her face. Louise enjoyed the adrenaline rush caused each time, finding it funny once her heart had returned to a normal rhythm, amused at the silliness of jumping out of her skin.

It was a family tradition to scare each other. Nobody had to put in much effort to get Louise to yell in fright. Half the time they weren't even intending to scare her, all they had to do was just come unnoticed into a room, and they'd be pealing Louise off the ceiling. There was no guilty conscience, she would just become so involved in whatever she was doing that she hadn't factored the appearance of another so when they came into her view point it took a moment for her brain to register who, or what it was, filling the split seconds before with some warped nightmarish vision.

Louise herself took some kind of perverse pleasure in scaring her family, the boys in particular. Recalling some of the especially good scares made Louise chuckle to herself. It was a little of her darkness coming to the surface, a balance to the light that usually shone so bright to the outside world. On more than one occasion she would notice them coming, hide behind a door then jump out on them with a "raaa" or a "boo". It was all taken in good jest though Jim sometimes acted like she was trying to scare him to death. Louise was known to jump at her own reflection. On this occasion she'd come out of the shower, her mind pondering life's little mysteries. The bedroom door was open at such an angle that her own image was reflected in the bathroom mirror from the mirror lined wardrobe door in her room. Catching herself in her peripheral vision her heart skipped a beat thinking there was an intruder in the house. Using her foot to kick open the door she searched the bathroom, then the spare room and her bedroom before reassuring herself she was alone. Laughing at her own stupidity Louise carried on with the household chores. Short of using her naked body to terrorise an intruder she was armed with only her wit and ample bosom. The experience had put her in a funny, mischievous mood.

The plan had already formulated in Louise's mind as Jim pulled onto the driveway, she would crouch behind the wooden front door and jump out on him. She fleetingly considered nipping upstairs and throwing on the lingerie that Jim liked and shouting "surprise" but decided that time wouldn't allow her to pull it off, so she went for the bog-standard scare that she had perfected over the years, and it was more satisfying.

As the footsteps crunched on the gravel Louise got into position, giddy with excitement, supressing a laugh with a wide toothy grin. She let Jim take a few steps inside before making her move. "RAAAAA" she screamed like a banshee jumping up like a jack in the box. Jim physically left the floor, only just holding onto his bowels. He lost his composure, less than amused at his wife's childish antics.

"For fucks sake Louise, how old are you?" he retorted, stomping off to the study to wallow in his own miserableness.

Louise had to stifle giggles whilst preparing tea, careful not to get caught revealing in Jim's displeasure, thoroughly amused with herself. Louise went through the routine of heating up frozen food for an unimaginative tea that she could have done in the dark, allowing her mind to wander, posing an alternative ending to Jim's fright night.

Jim came through the door, Deja-vu style, and Louise jumped out like a recoiled snake. But, instead of a telling off, Jim clutched at his chest and left arm, his eyes wide, mouth agasp, the hairs on his arms and the back of his neck standing to attention. Fantasy Jim had been scared to death. The natural cause of a heart attack would be recorded, his death attributed to his nervous system shutting down, from a severer over-load. Could the police proceed with a prosecution for scaring someone to death Louise wondered? Fantasy Louise was ashamed of her behaviour and bereft at her husband keeling over, his heart giving out like an old man.

The sadness that crept in was soon usurped by the daydream progressing to Jim's heart giving out in various scenarios – there was the fire work spectacular, the explosions setting of a series of internal bombs that stopped his heart. The sudden heart failure caused when a balloon was unexpectedly popped next to his ear was another way to go. Louise's daydream accumulating in Jim's arachnophobia setting the scene for death by spider. A hairy specimen dropping from a web, it's front legs probing Jim's open mouth as he screamed in terror.

There was a Stoney silence at the dinner table that night, Louise gave a feigned apology to smooth over Jim's ruffled feathers, but they went to sleep without saying more than a few words to each other.

Halloween was Louise's favourite seasonal holiday. She'd loved witches, ghosts and ghouls since she was a little girl. She wanted to be a witch in her teens, had bought books on spells and charms and tried to start a coven. She had a dark little soul that was almost corrupted but the slither of light that ran through its core reigned supreme. Magic fascinated her, and the dead had never really bothered her. In fact, she quite fancied working for a funeral director. She had even seen a dead body, up close and personal, they just looked like they were asleep having passed peacefully away, none the wiser. The only thing she wasn't keen on were the zombies, she didn't do zombies, with all the fake blood but she'd got better over the years with it. And the spiders, she tolerated them, was the arachnid catcher at home but wasn't a fan of the eight-legged foes.

Louise was like a kid in a candy store when the Halloween decorations went out for sale at work. Her mischievous streak would always find its way out at this time of year, the temptation to set off all the dancing singing skeletons too much to resist. An a-cappella chorus of *Time Warp* could be heard across the store after Louise had been in the aisle, merchandise testing she'd say. When the kids were little she had once set a load of singing mechanical Santa's lose in a garden centre, activating and releasing them to waddle amongst the customers.

Louise was happy to admit that she was a part of Pottermore, had a love for all things Hogwarts. She had seen the films countless times, lost herself in the whimsical pages of the novels on more than one occasion and wished that she had her own real wand. The fun she would have. Her years may be advancing but she was young at heart. As she went about her duties she noticed two children duelling with wands, still in the packaging, mini versions of Harry and Ron. If she ever found a genie in a bottle she'd wish for magic, the trouble is she'd probably be a bit vengeful with it. She could picture herself moving offending vehicles off the road with a wave of her hand, inflating the bottom cheeks of skinny Skyla or forcing people to walk or talk in amusing ways. It was a nice escape to believe in magic, to believe that there were people in the world who possessed the ancient knowledge. Jim loved to debunk illusions and tricks whereas Louise was more than content to have faith that it was all real. Life could be so mundane and boring, what was the harm in a make-believe fantasy, she wasn't hurting anyone, unlike if she did really possess power, that might be a slightly different story.

Louise couldn't help herself thinking about what she would do with a magic wand. Once all fantasises about household chores doing themselves, transporting herself to faraway lands and back again in a blink of an eye and magically producing a huge pile of gold had evaporated her thoughts turned to using the wand as a weapon, to dispose of Jim in an ingenious manner.

With a gentle flick of her wrist, the wand held expertly in her hand, she could cast a spell which would turn Jim into a small animal, such as a worm, and watch as he gets devoured by a feathered adversary. She could turn him into a frog and release him in the stream at the bottom of the garden. Another swish of the wand saw her turn Jim into someone else, give him the sculpted face and body of a Greek God. Another sent him scattering across the universe in a billion sparkling pieces, a meteor shower of Jim particles. The last spell she cast was to turn Jim into the tabby cat she had always wanted, just like her favourite witch, Mildred Hubble. But, Jim cat was mean, he scratched and hissed so she booked him into a cattery, using a false name to conceal her identity and never collected him.

Louise's thought's blackened as the sky turned dark with rain clouds, the wand she was holding was replaced with a wax doll. An effigy of Jim, his hair crudely pushed in clumps onto the dolls head, a representation of his work uniform etched into the wax. As Louise whispered some made-up foreign voodoo spell she pushed pins into the poppet, imagining Jim yelling in pain, his body replicating every move made on the doll. A slight snigger snorted out her nose when she pictured Jim's body being thrown around as if an invisible giants hand was shaking the life from him, a possessed display of levitation to the innocent bystander.

The atmosphere in the Wilson household had heated up, the chilly temperature that had been evident for the past few days had been ignited in a united display of forgiveness. A mutual desire to bring about peace and goodwill to all men as the season of giving was fast approaching, and both the kids had announced that they'd be coming home for Christmas, invited or not.

The skeletons and bats still held pole position over Santa but as soon as the little monsters had been on their travels to con candy out of innocent home owners the tide would turn with Santa and his merry band of helpers infiltrating every corner of the world, until Auld Land Syne beckoned in the approach to Easter.

21

Louise was a very organised person but one spanner in the works and her carefully laid plans could be thrown into a tizzy. Jim was usually that spanner.

Since embarking on a grown-up family orientated lifestyle Louise had planned Christmas with military precision, accommodating relatives, time scales and diets to provide a festive wonderland for all involved. There were lists galore strewn around the house - quest lists, present lists, shopping lists. Every year she out-did herself, spending hours scouring the internet for unique gifts. Outwardly Louise gave the impression that she wasn't that bothered by Yule time but secretly she enjoyed that happiness of the season, the sparkles, the joyous atmosphere, and the preparation. Mostly the preparation and the feeling of accomplishment looking at the piles of neatly wrapped presents and beautifully written cards.

The family Christmas tree was on its last legs, one side was practically bare, several branches were hanging on with tape, but it held so many memories of Christmases gone by that Louise didn't have the heart to replace it whilst Jim tried to ignore the fact that Christmas was even happening. The decorations might be perfectly spaced and arranged with the meticulousness of an interior designer, but it wasn't the same, it lacked that haphazard enchantment that only came from the excitement of little-ones.

All Louise received in response to her hard work, turning the house into a modest version of Santa's grotto, was a grunt from Jim and raised eyebrows. *Bah Humbug* was the theme of Christmas, as far as Jim was concerned. For Jim it was nothing more than an over-hyped, commercialised holiday when he was forced to be polite to long-distanced relatives and get up at an ungodly hour to watch the kids tear into presents he didn't want to buy them.

As Louise added the finishing touches, a sprinkling of glitter here, a garland of tinsel there her mind began to wander.

The scene was set, a vibrant green Christmas tree stood in the centre of the room, colourful lights twinkling in the branches between glossy baubles and presents wrapped with ribbon stacked methodically around the base of the tree. All expect one that lay unwrapped on the floor, the box opened, and the contents removed. The present, supposedly destined for Frank, had contained a futuristic shrink ray gun and Louise had it pointed directly at a grumbling Jim. Using both hands to steady her aim, and with little provocation, she pulled the trigger. A blue tinged taser of electrical rays shot out the end of the gun and fused with Jim, the air around him shimmering as his body mass waivered in the science fiction beam. Louise's arms shook with the power it took to minimise the atoms that made up Jim, annoying her further that she couldn't control her bat wing arms from vibrating.

A six-inch-high Jim sat wide eyed on his seat that was now a fabric field surrounding him, the cosy arms a patterned mountain, the distance to the ground a perilous drop. As the gigantous Louise moved in on her prey Jim considered fleeing but he had nowhere to go, the cushion was like a boulder. He briefly considered leaping of the chair and hoping for the best but if the fall didn't kill him it would render him even more helpless in the face of his assassin. Poor fantasy Jim was like a mouse trapped by a cat, stalked and hunted, it was only a matter of time before he was caught. But Jim was to suffer a far worse fate than being a cat's dinner.

Louise's mind had concocted the ultimate punishment for a Grinch, to be turned into a fairy and mounted on top of the tree, overseeing the festivities. And that is where Jim ended up, an undignified end to a scrooge. Louise allowed herself a giggle as she topped the tree with the traditional family star, Jim ignorant to the alternative tree topper he had become.

To Louise the temperature was as much a part of the Christmas feel as the tinsel and food. She loved a cold crisp morning, it made her feel Christmassy and she could justify turning up the heating.

Louise thrived on the hustle and bustle of family life and felt redundant when she wasn't needed. It was alien for her to relax and she'd had to learn to take time for herself. As much as she pined for the kids, suffered in silence with empty nest syndrome, she couldn't deny that having grown-up children had its advantages.

Even after successfully raising two productive children Louise often felt guilty indulging herself, her greatest pleasure being reading by candlelight, it conjured magical images of tranquillity and peace.

Jim came home from work to find Louise cosied in her chair, thick house socks and a teddy blanket keeping her warm. A glass of wine stood on the table, droplets of condensation cascading down the curved glass, racing to the bottom as quickly as the bubbles raced to the top. The romantic notion of reading by citric coloured flames was outweighed by the harsh realities of reading by candlelight. The flicker of the flame was an annoyance, it was like driving through a forest on a sunny day, so Louise often reverted to turning on the table lamp. It still looked like a scene from *Country Life* magazine.

What Louise wanted most of all, had wanted since seeing it in an edition of *Woman & Home*, or some other such lifestyle magazine in the doctor's surgery, was her very own book snug. She had the perfect alcove at home picked out, had organised the shelves countless times in her head. She had even colour matched fabric with paint, so it would be warm and welcoming. She had wanted Jim to build her a snug, she'd dropped enough hints, left magazines strategically placed, the open pages displaying happy women enjoying their snugs. Ellen had even told Jim directly that Louise wanted a snug, but she was still waiting. She'd even tried over the years to construct a snug by rearranging the furniture, but it always looked like it had been constructed by a bunch of children, an uneven den to hide away from the world in. Louise had flirted with the idea of properly building it herself but her D.I.Y creations were prone to looking like they had been cobbled together in Frankenstein's laboratory. They were functional but not pretty, and she wanted her snug to be pretty. For now, the Christmas tree stood in the space that should have contained Louise's snug.

Louise had a backup plan, if she couldn't have her snug then she'd have a shed. With the snug Jim had simply ignored Louise's hints but with the shed he'd put his foot down and said "no". They had a shared shed he'd rationalised, but Louise wanted a pretty shed, a girly white shed with windows. A shed that wasn't full of dirty tools but full of lovely feminine things like flowers and cushions. A shed that she could make into her own personal writing or art space. She'd seen pictures in magazines so knew that she could order one to her specifications and have it delivered and assembled for a fee. The more Jim said no the more she wanted it. He'd had a choice, snug or shed.

Louise made the purchase on the theory that out of sight meant out of mind and Jim would be less inclined to do anything about its removal as it was outside. As long as she was crafty with the delivery date and Jim wasn't home to refuse it then the shed would be hers. If Jim gave her a hard time about it she'd hide his body beneath it, use the excuse that he'd left her for defying him as the reason for his disappearance. The tension from Jim was palpable when he discovered the shed, four days later. He hesitantly accepted the arrival with a modicum of grace, at least it wasn't inside the house and hopefully he would get some peace while Louise was using it. Jim hated that his wife had gone behind his back but when she had her heart set on something she usually found a way to get it. Another quality that Jim both adored and reviled with equal measure, Louise drove him crazy.

The scent of spiced apple fragranced every room, gingerbread men congregated on baking trays in the kitchen and a Christmas cd sang to itself in the living room. Ellen was the first back home, arriving just after lunch, trailing a broken heart and full suitcase behind her.

Louise was only halfway through the saga that had ended Ellen's relationship when Frank arrived, bringing in his wake another dilemma, a very pregnant girlfriend. Would there be a real-life nativity thought Louise?

Jim thought he'd walked into a pantomime arriving home, later than expected, to a daughter in tears, a son pampering to a stranger that looked like they'd swallowed a beach ball, a tea left to go cold and a disenchanted wife, the anticipated homecoming of the Wilson children in shambles.

Louise couldn't deny that her initial impression of Trinity was not as positive as it could have been, and she chastised herself for stereotyping the girl. She knew she admired the courage it took to stand out from the crowd, to challenge perceptions. It wasn't the poor girls fault that Louise's meticulously planned homecoming was in tatters. Louise thought that she was coping relatively well under the circumstances, hoping that the minute slip in her positive exterior had gone un-noticed and welcomed the unexpected guest with open arms.

Admittedly the young lady, Trinity, or Triny as Frank referred to her, looked rough. She was tattooed and pierced from head to toe but when she spoke she had the voice of an angel. It was alien to what Louise had anticipated, her exterior a decorated shell that did not do justice to the sweet and caring centre that exposed itself over the coming festivities, especially considering she had to contend with a 10-stone ball of blubbering Ellen that would burst into tears at the drop of a hat.

When quizzed alone, as to the what the's and when the's etc of his predicament Frank had the good grace to look sheepish at his lack of communication. Louise couldn't help feeling a little hurt that her son hadn't let them know sooner. It was their first grandchild, it was a big deal, however she wasn't sure how she felt about being a grandmother in her forties, her very late forties but still her forties.

Frank started at the beginning. "I've known Triny for years Mum, we mixed in the same circles on and off since I moved to Basingstoke. We got together about a year ago…."

Louise's eyebrows raised so high they nearly fell off her face, but Frank placated her with "Let me finish. So, it was about a year ago, it was so intense…" Frank paused, looking reminiscent for a moment before continuing.

"It was full on for months, we lived for each other. I was so in love I was considering proposing, had even looked at a few rings." Louise couldn't help the excited squeal that escaped her, her fingers involuntarily spasming in response, Frank raised his eyebrows and continued. "But then she started acting funny. She was snappy and irritable. God, I didn't know what to do, no matter what I did or said she'd just flip at me. We had a massive row about some stupid thing…" Frank let out a defeated sigh

"...something about always leaving clothes on the floor, oh I don't know what it was about."

Louise tried not to side with Trinity and smile at her son's misfortune but the irony of father like son wasn't lost on her though Frank didn't register a response.

"So, what happened next?" Urged Louise "As there must be more to explain Mary over there". Louise's eyes frantically pointed in Trinity's direction.

"She stormed out and didn't come back, she stopped answering my calls and texts."

"So, you lived together?" interrogated Louise, trying to calm the annoyance that she was starting to feel with her son for failing to keep her up-dated.

"We didn't back then, Triny had her own place with a mate but she practically lived at mine. I was going to tell you about her Mum," pleaded Frank "honest, but then it all went wrong so there didn't seem much point." Frank looked down. Continuing he said, "We saw each other sporadically over the next few months, stayed in contact by text, you know what I'm like mum."

Louise looked sympathetically at Frank, placing her hand on his arm to comfort him. Louise waited for Frank to resume his tale of true love.

"She asked me to meet her. I went thinking that she was going to end it all but instead she told me she was pregnant. For a while I doubted I was the father, but she insists I am. You know you brought me up right mum so we're giving it a go. We've living together too." Frank looked to his mum for support and confirmation that he was doing the right thing. Frank looked like he did as a teenager, agonising over his approach to girls.

"But I still don't understand why you didn't let us know Frank" replied Louise, the sorrow creeping into her tone.

"It didn't seem right to call with the news, we wanted to tell you in person, but work was so busy. Besides I wasn't sure how to tell you, I thought it might give dad heart attack."

Wishful thinking thought Louise to herself, "We know now," said Louise, embracing Frank in hug "Off you go and get her settled, see you in the morning. I'll deal with your dad, love you."

"Love you too mum, it's good to be home." replied Frank, kissing his mum on her forehead before retrieving Trinity and heading off to his old bedroom, the stairs creaking under his footsteps.

Louise sniggered at a flashback to the daydream when Jim expired due to a super steamy sex session, but Louise had to admit that if anything could give Jim a heart attack it would probably be the birth of a grandchild and the impending babysitting responsibilities.

The conversation, in the privacy of their bedroom, started off, predictably, with Jim unable to contain his opinion any longer.

"Did you see the tattoos? She must have had more pricks than a prostitute."

"My God Jim, did you even talk to the girl? She was perfectly lovely." retorted Louise.

With no evidence to defend his claim atheist Jim replied with "don't take the lords name in vain Darling".

"Like hell are you religious Jim. And besides, how many times, you should never judge a book by its cover," was the cliched phrase that Louise stated as her closing defence for Trinity. So true in many circumstances in life, people being the easiest target to justify the statement and Jim had always been very judgmental on first impressions. The rumblings from Jim continued but Louise chose to ignore them, a placating "a-huh" and "umm" thrown in occasionally.

Though Louise was guilty herself of basing her opinions an initial gut impression she was more flexible in her approach, accepting the queerness of folk as a quality not a detriment. She applied this principle to many aspects of her life, from food to fashion and its exactly how Louise choose the books to read. The titles helped but it was the look of the spine that had Louise sliding a book from its itemised placing on the shelves. The library was always the first port of call when discovering a new voice. Disappointment would set in when the cover looked tantalising to find that the blurb made the offering seem mundane and boring. She was disillusioned with people sometimes on the same principle, they looked happy and exciting, but the reality was arrogant or tedious. Charity shops were a good one too, worth a try, a small cost to take a punt on an author, and if the book was bad it goes back. Unfortunately, this principle couldn't be applied to people, they had to be treated with respect and diplomacy, you can't take them back for a refund or exchange.

Even if Louise had got her snug there'd be no chance of using it, with a heart to heal and a grandchild to prepare for, any '*me*' time that Louise had planned for the foreseeable future would be spent full of nappies and first dates.

Having placed a stocking outside each door, her hoarding saving the day as she had a spare stocking as well as gifts to fill it. Louise went to sleep with thoughts of Santa and sugarplums running through her head. Her Yule wish granted, her family all under the same roof, and that family was expanding. Christmas day was filled with laughter, and tears from Ellen, the meat was succulent and tasty, the crackers corny. By three pm the presents had been opened and only two out of the five were still awake. Jim, Frank and Triny were asleep in front of the TV. Ellen was getting steadily drunker and Louise was clearing the table of the remains of the gastronormous dinner, ready for round two, a buffet of finger food and desserts.

22

With the season of good will over, new year's resolutions already broken, and all illusions of a prosperous future forgotten the general population had returned to their antagonistic selves. The kids had returned to their prospective lives leaving the house empty and Louise testy. She often had a post-Christmas come down, all the organisation and happiness of the festivities over, her attention again on the mundanity of life.

Louise had been in an off mood most of January, she was dutifully worried about Ellen's happiness, who had directed her loneliness into being an auntie to a baby that seemed intent on staying firmly in its mother's womb. Perhaps it was the imminent change in the role of mother to grandmother that had Louise on edge or perhaps she was entering that period of her life, the big M. Either way Louise's tolerance for the human race was dwindling at a rapid rate, she was finding that people where driving her balmy, more than normal. At work both staff and customers came across as rude, an inflated sense of self-importance driving their actions. Something inside Louise snapped, her patience stolen by Santa's elves. Louise didn't know if all the years of seeing knock-down prices after shelling out a small fortune a month prior had caused her displeasure, but she felt angry at the establishments for encouraging you into debt every December, and the population for buying into it. It was all Louise could do not bite back at those that confided in aunt Louise and scream in their faces 'I don't care, sort yourself out', but it wasn't in her nature. She just grinned through it and listened politely. Louise felt that humans were very anal in their behaviour, she was no exception. They had preferred patterns and internal codes of conduct that seemed to drive or justify their behaviour. Louise herself was guilty of possessing several of these traits, one of which was borderline, if not already over the fence OCD.

At the supermarket she had a preferred place to park, one that she had secretly designated as her own personal space. She always parked there but if she found another car occupying the space it left her feeling quite perturbed. And today her space was taken. She almost cried which was a rarity for Louise unless her heart strings were being tugged. Another bugbear for Louise was people sitting in her favourite spot in the staff room or during meetings. Louise was as obsessed as Alice's white rabbit about time keeping, she was one of the first on-site and she always lived by the rule that being early was better than being late. Jim would be late his is own funeral. Louise tolerated it, she had little choice, but found the invasion of her spot highly irritating. It was hers, she'd found it and claimed it unofficially as her own. It was the same with cups and pens at work. "Louise won't mind" she knew they'd say, but Louise did mind.

"Where's my pen?" Louise demanded of the room.

Her answer was a resounding silence from the staff unlucky enough to be on a break. "Pens can't just grow legs and walk off." Louise muttered aloud as she left the room, on a mission to track down the kidnapped biro, "if I find the culprit I'm going to use their eye socket as a pen holder." she said under her breath, concerned glances following the out of character Mrs Wilson. The older she got the more this trait imbedded itself, but it started back in the days when she ferried the kids to their clubs, it was the newcomers who needed to educated not to participate in this practice. The words of her own grandmother echoed through her mind, ignorance breeds ignorance.

As a veteran martial arts parent Frank had attended the club for six years before his sister took up the mantle as the families' ninja. Ellen had excelled, the only female black belt for years at the club that had sporadic membership, possibly owing to the constant change of owners as well as premises but the Wilsons had weathered all the storms. It was here that Louise began to develop her righteous tendencies. As one of the clubs longest spectating parents Louise felt she had earned the right to sit, unchallenged, in a space of her own choosing, and it was the same space in each venue. As the years rolled on her lenience of the newbie parents man-handing her daughters equipment and the carefully placed attrite, that had been used as a seat saver when she left the building, diminished rapidly. In her eyes the decade she had spent supporting the club trumped the few weeks of attendance from the seat stealers. On one occasion she nearly lost the plot and turned samurai herself. Having come back from her ritual hot chocolate purchase, her treat for spending an hour in a room full of screaming mat slapping children, she found that she had been reduced to half her original seating preparation. With an exaggerated display of rearrangement, she squeezed her ample rear end in to the remaining gap with much nasal huffing which had the desired result. The parent in question found somewhere else to sit for the duration of their time at the club.

As much as it pained her Louise was the first to admit that she was a material girl. She loved stuff, rejoiced in the kindred spirit of a fellow collector. She'd always been a collector, ever since she could remember she'd fixated on a subject or style and collected it. Jim had a minimalistic attitude towards most aspects of life, including displaying his feelings, yet his private areas, his study and beside table, were cluttered and overflowing. She didn't know why she liked things, but they made her happy, made her feel secure. Maybe she had an addictive personality or was attracted to the chaotic nature of collections. She viewed them as art, gems pulling the viewers vision in each and every direction.

Another life mantra that Louise used was 'a place for everything and everything in its place', and Louise knew when an object was out of place. She hated it when Jim moved her stuff, even if he only changed the orientation of an item. Louise would move it back, with a grumble that went something like 'if I wanted it there I'd put it there' followed by a brief daydream on how she could kill him with the said object.

If Louise relocated an item at home then it was like training a new puppy to pee in the litter tray, Jim took weeks to grasp the new home of whatever Louise had moved or introduced. It was a trait of Louise's that Jim didn't favour but it wasn't costly. Many of his acquaintances had a hit to the wallet with their spouses heading on a shopping spree to increase their mood, Louise moved furniture around. Jim never knew quite what he might come home to.

Jim was getting on Louise's nerves no less than her complaining colleagues and customers and no less than he normally did, but her idiot-meter was at an all-time low. It took Jim less effort than normal to bring on one of Louise's fantasies. Never mind long sightedness, Jim had long hearingness. Louise never could fathom how he could hear a mutter two rooms away with the TV on, yet he had trouble listening to a face to face conversation. It was an inherited skill that he had passed on to Frank, though he had a watered-down strain of the affliction.

Another characteristic of Jim's that drove Louise to distraction was Jim's ability to start a conversation and then walk out of the room whilst still talking. He'd sometimes shut the door after himself yet still expect Louise to respond, it drove her bananas. It was Jim's way to justify and absolve his guiltiness when an argument would inevitably ensue with Louise denying that Jim had told her something he insisted he did. He knew the words had left his mouth, whether or not they reached the recipient was beyond his control, but he was justified he'd told Louise.

Louise was happy to indulge the daydream, anything to escape the reality of January. It started as a light-hearted remedy to Jim's hearing issue, a simple spell was cast, a potion that gave Jim over-sized elephant ears, but the fantasy turned sinister. Inspired by the cleaning promotions at work Jim was to suffer a fatal poisoning, first by consuming a pint of chlorine scented bleach, imaginary Jim not batting an eyelid at the peculiar taste. He wasn't to escape with just the one demise, Louise's mind ran through other possibilities; there was the rat poison in his curry, arsenic in his coffee, hemlock in his salad, cyanide in his sandwiches, wolfsbane in his underpants, dimethylmercury in his toothpaste and belladonna in his eyedrops.

Louise was woken from her daydream, and miserable mood, by the phone call they'd been waiting for. The baby had arrived.

Louise, a technophobe known for taking days to reply to text messages hadn't noticed the incoming text to say that Trinity was in labour and that they were on the way to hospital.

On being informed of the joyous arrival Louise booted up the laptop and jumped straight on social media, sure that her precious grandchild would probably be an internet star at just minutes old. There were several photos of a rather scrunched up, red faced babe and an exhausted looking Trinity. Itching to get her hands on her grandson, the Wilsons were in the car and up the motorway in record time, collecting an emotional aunt Ellen on the way.

Entering the hospital armed with balloons, teddies and cards the excited Wilsons descended on the maternity ward. Louise worried that there might be a clash of the grannies, staking a claim over the new arrival, but Trinity's parents were nowhere to be seen.

Holding baby Jared transported Louise back to the birth of her own offspring. It seemed like only yesterday that she was cradling Frank as a new born, soaking in his soft skin and inhaling his baby smell. Louise's smile told the world she was in love, reluctantly passing him to the next pair of outstretched arms.

Louise relished her new role as granny, her zeal for life returning with newfound abundance. Even Jim seemed excited, probably as he knew he could hand the little one back and wouldn't be asked to change a nappy or get up in the middle of the night with a bottle. Louise was determined to be a hip granny not a cranky granny. Louise thought back to the conversation she'd had with her son and secretly wandered if marriage may be back on the table soon, Frank was besotted with his son. Louise wasn't religious, but she prayed that it would be the start of a beautiful family for Frank.

23

Louise woke up in a bad mood, she'd had a good night's sleep, nothing was troubling her, she'd simply 'woke up on the wrong side of the bed', although Jim was snoring soundly on his side. The usually gracious bird chorus was loud and irritating, her breakfast was tasteless, she just wasn't feeling the love that morning. On her drive to work Louise encountered every grandad out for their Sunday drive, a few days early, the number of tractors would suggest some farming emergency, but their speed assured her there was not. It was going to be one of those days.

Within seconds of walking into the brightly light supermarket a small demonic child could be heard wailing like a banshee from a far-off aisle, wet floor signs were dotted around like forensic flags for spillages and customer services had a queue that almost snaked out through the automatic front doors.

Several of the leadership team had already started to congregate in the staff room, waiting for the bio-monthly meeting, the main focus of the agenda being post-Christmas sales.

Skyla, for who a calorie would do no damage to her slight frame, had taken it upon herself to calorie count the entire workforce providing laborious lectures rather than considerate counselling. Louise had never been one to watch what she ate, and she had the bottom to prove it. She wasn't over weight, but she was by no means slim and the middle age spread was threating to take over Louise's fat cells, leaving no prisoners.

The staff room at work was hardly big enough to accommodate the row of lockers that formed the west wall. The round table, designed so that nobody was at the head, was as crammed into the room much like a pair of ample boobs into a corset. There was barley room to swing a cat, you probably couldn't even swing a mouse. The restricted communal area afforded no room for the suitcase sized handbags that fashion dictated her colleagues own making them trip hazards which constantly teased Louise's clumsiness, any claim made void due to her colleague's ignorance. It seemed that no matter where Louise hung her coat somebody would have to impose on it. The rack could be near empty but no, the coats would always be side by side, a fabric love affair. It was just one of lives annoyances that bugged Louise. Normally she would rise above it but today she let it get under her skin and fester.

If the world was a considerate as her, then it would run smoothly. She loved that diversity and difference made the world the dynamic place that it was but sometimes, just sometimes, Louise imagined what it would be like if she ruled it, like an inter-planetary Goddess. If only she had the power, she'd beat the manner-less and teach the rude. In Louise's eyes the world owed no one a thing and no great birth right gave you the entitlement above others, but money and social standing proved that it did, and Louise dealt daily with those who expected the earth.

As usual, the meeting went as predicted, nobody's ideas complementing each other's but nobody relenting on their new year's vision. Louise made a few suggestions, but they fell on deaf ears and she had no fight in her to commence with a battle. She would act as a dutiful losing side and put into action whatever notion was deemed the most profitable. The meeting ended with the invitation to a health and safety course including a presentation on the new uniform which Louise volunteered for, the argumentative team surprisingly quite in the face of this 'exciting' opportunity. It would be a day away from the branch if nothing else.

It was a quite night in the Wilson household, Louise still in a miserable mood, Jim not faring much happier. Louise's night was about to improve as, unbeknown to Louise, Jim had absent-mindedly walked past the downstairs toilet without realising it was occupied. Louise innocently exited and, in the process, caused Jim to jump a mile. He even let out a girly scream which made Louise jump in response as she'd been as unaware of Jim's presence as he had been of hers.

"You scared the life out of me." reprimanded Jim.

"I'm sorry." replied Louise genuinely, before allowing a very real smile to fill her face. Although she was glad that she had managed to frighten Jim she was dissatisfied that the feeling was not as great as it would have been had it been a planned scaring.

Louise had to travel a little way to the venue, but she made good time and was one of the first to descend on the plate of shortbread provided for the attendees. Taking her seat at an empty table she arranged her notebook and pen in an organised row and waited as the empty seats filled with staff from around the county. Louise nodded to the few faces she recognised and smiled a greeting at those she didn't. Her mood was much improved, she just hoped they'd be no role play activities.

The health and safety training was agonisingly boring. The duo delivering the presentation had had a personality lobotomy, their tone more punishing than Jim's, any hint of fun firmly off the agenda. It was strictly business, but at least the catering was good, and the room was warm.

The uniform was marginally different, most probably won't register the change in design and Louise had already forgot the majority of the drones' speech. She drifted off into a daydream as the presentation took a turn into appropriate, and inappropriate, foot wear, Skyla will be pleased.

The daydream looked much the same as the room she was in now, a projector stood ready, but she was the only participant on the course. The lights dimmed, and the projector came to life. A serious looking full-size image of Jim appeared on the screen. The fantasy played out as a series of slides in a PowerPoint presentation showing all the ways in which the new lanyard, to be introduced to the uniform, can potentially kill you.

Jim was innocently walking to work when a gust of wind blew the lanyard and it got caught in a passing tree, hanging Jim from the branch like a 19th century murderer.

The next slide showed Jim bending over a shredder, his lanyard dangling dangerously over the machine before getting caught and sucked into the mechanism, strangling Jim before an error message stopped the shredding of Jim's ID and life. Jim shouldn't have tried to use the lift with his lanyard on as it got caught in the doors and strangled him as he changed floors. Louise's safety video advised staff not to wear their lanyards outside work in the event that a criminal could use it as leverage. The health and safety Jim was taken hostage, with the lanyard fashioned into a lead-come-torture collar, one sharp pull decapitating the unfortunate worker. It was a sheepish looking Louise that cooked tea that night. Jim none the wiser to the days imaginary events.

24

Louise had just returned from a weekend of granny duties whilst Frank took Trinity away for a long-deserved sleep. Jim couldn't get the time off work. Louise was as in love with her grandson as the day he was born and savoured anytime she could spend with him. All the better to have no Jim, she didn't like to share Jared anyway.

Before long there would be great grandchildren on the scene, her own children's upbringing gone in the blink of an eye, the traumas and tantrums a long distant memory. Baby Jared changed a little every time Louise saw him, he was sitting unaided now and would be saying his first words before long.

Louise had been more eager than normal to escape to Basingstoke as there was an agonising decision to be made, one that she didn't want to be part of.

Jim's mother had been showing the early stages of dementia and Jim could no longer dismiss the signs as old age. Jim had been struggling to accept that the fiercely independent woman that raised him would begin to lose what made her 'her' and would need assisted living. There had been calm discussions, heated discussions, emotional discussions but no discussion that come up with a definitive care plan or solution that worked for everyone. Louise favoured a residential home with 24-hour specialist care, when the time came, whereas Jim's inclination was to bring Mary Wilson home. Louise knew that she was being selfish, for not wanting to dedicate her free time to being a carer but she knew that she would end up with the lion's share of the burden.

Jim and Louise's arguments were legendary, feuds could last for weeks and arguments simmer until the situation was blow out of all proportion and an insignificant spat could result in world war three. They were short lived when the kids were little so that peace could be restored quickly. But as the kids grew and could take sides, the disagreements escalated, Louise no longer suppressing her fiery nature which, ironically, first attracted Jim to her. Some days it was like being in the Alamo, both sides taking fire but neither ready to surrender.

Louise's favoured tactic was to stop talking to Jim, a punishment most husbands would be happy with, but to Jim it was torture. He would coax answers from his wife by acting like everything was normal and Louise would fall for it, temporarily, until she remembered that she wasn't speaking to her husband and would slink off, angry at herself for being tricked, equally as angry at Jim for tricking her into conversation. Louise could only last a few days before allowing the indignity of whatever had caused the disagreement in the first place to dissipate, she liked the view from her high horse.

A much as Louise hoped that Jim had looked at the brochures she had left behind on the table she feared that her attempt at gentle persuasion would backfire and Mary would be in residence when she returned. She was not. Nor had the brochures moved a millimetre.

The chat went much the same as the previous times, Jim refusing to acknowledge that his mum was getting worse with Louise sympathetically pitching the care home, her main justification being that they didn't own the dog Jim longed for owing to their work commitments, retirement a long way off. Briefly consider and quickly rejected was the option for Jim to become a full-time carer leaving facilitated living on the cards. Pensions were still over a decade out of reach and with her new-found nan responsibilities Louise had to be firm with her husband.

To avoid making a final decision Jim slunk off to his mums to run a few errands she had asked him to do last week. Mary must have had a long list of jobs as Jim didn't return to early evening and when he did he was accompanied by the disgusting smell of singed hair and his eyebrows were partially missing. It transpired that one of the many D.I.Y jobs that Mary had lined up for Jim consisted of removing the colony of ants that had taken up residence in her composting bin. In his infinite wisdom he had concluded that the most efficient way to destroy the ants was to disintegrate them with fire.

Having dowsed the compost heap in a flammable substance it failed to ignite promptly, Jim reported. He then proceeded to investigate by prodding the damp heap of rotting plants and food when it ignited, an explosion of flames leaping at Jim's face. Though he was quick to react, saving most of his face, Jim's hair was executed in the line of being a dutiful inventive son. Jim had little choice but to take his wife's reprimand on the chin, admitting himself that it wasn't his finest hour.

A flaming Jim ran into Louise thoughts forcing Louise to stifle a giggle and retain her school teacher demeanour. "The ants. Get the ants" screamed an inferno Jim as he ran around his mum's make-believe garden, any recollection of the 'stop, drop and roll' taught by the kids forgotten. There seemed no end to the human torch as Jim continued to leap and hop around, more concerned that the extermination of the ants was a success than extinguishing himself before the flames extinguished his life.

In the meantime, Ellen was in a much better frame of mind owing to a round of speed dating that had resulted in a very busy month of first and second dates, a few even making it to the third date. Louise was just waiting for that phone call to say that Frank had proposed, she was sure it was coming soon.

Giving Jim a few days to recover from his heated debate with the ant colony Louise approached the subject of the additional sockets that she wanted installed. Louise had been moaning for months, years, that there weren't enough plug sockets to take all the electrical devices without meters of extension cables and Jim's most recent dice with death had highlighted the urgency to fire proof the home. She had already baby proofed it in preparation for Jared. Louise had been threatening to get in a tradesman, but Jim had steadfastly refused, assuring her that he was perfectly capable of installing extra sockets, he'd done it in the past. It took Louise to start searching for an electrician before Jim got his box of equipment out and start hacking at the walls. Jim was notorious for neglecting to do the jobs he had at home but would help out others. He was happy to pop over to their neighbours, the Henderson's, especially after him next door shuffled off his mortal coil, leaving behind a perfectly abled and spritely wife.

Louise was on standby with the hoover to clean up after Jim had finished, he never tidied up after himself. With the exception of a few grunts and several swear words the do-it-yourself electrical work was complete. Louise would have attempted it herself but after changing a light switch long, long ago she accidently crossed the live wires resulting in a 'fuzzy hand' for several days and a black streak up the wall which always found its way through whatever paint Louise used to disguise it. Jim was not impressed.

The memory of her own foray into electrics opened up a daydream where Jim's skills were less polished than in reality. With childlike movements imaginary Jim used a screwdriver to levy off the socket resulting in his electrocution. In classic *Scooby Doo* style Jim's skeleton was outlined with a jagged ring of electrical currents, his teeth braced together in a grimace, his limited hair standing to attention. For several cartoon minutes Jim's body shook at a diagonal angle to the socket before falling to the floor. Wisps of smoke filling the air setting of a fictional sprinkler, the water reacting with a charged Jim causing him to convulse as the water mixed with the electricity coursing through him.

25

Going through the days mail Louise suspected that the postman had been hording her post, she was sure he hated walking down the bumpy lane to her house and there was more mail than usual with no birthdays or Christmas in sight to take into account. She'd have to have a word at some point, not that she'd missed anything important, he always seemed to deliver the bills on time.

One piece in particular narrowly escaped being filled with the rest of the junk mail - utility companies addressing the householder and offers of credit cards from banks she'd never been a customer of. The envelope was non-descript, looked like a mass mailing but something about it caught Louise's eye and made her look at the return address. She recognised the sender as one of the many weekly magazines that she read.

Intrigued as too how they had obtained her address and what they could be offering Louise opened the envelope with uncharacteristic anxiety. A feeling of exhilaration filled Louise as she pulled the letter from its brown encasement.

The correspondence informed Louise that she had won competition.

Louise had been entering competitions for as long as she could remember, fancy dress competitions as a toddler, art and poetry competitions as a teenager and magazine puzzle competitions as an adult. She had never won anything of substance or value, a raffle prize here and there but nothing of this magnitude. Jim was dumbfounded at his wife's optimism and despaired at the wasted time she put in though she would remind him that somebody had to win and 'you've got to be in it to win it', her justification for blindly entering competitions regardless of the prize.

Louise was resigned that it would be fake, made to look real to trick the recipient into opening it and losing a small fortune. She left it on the side whilst she heated up a frozen tea and contemplated what to do with it. The prize was tremendous, an all expenses safari. There had to be a catch, Louise was just too excited to see it.

Nervously Louise presented Jim with a plate of toad-in-the-hole and a side of winnings.

Jim was convinced of its authenticity, but Louise still doubted her good fortune and phoned the company who were happy to confirm it. She even contacted the fraud action line to ensure that she wasn't about to becoming embroiled in a fraudster ring, not that the letter had asked for any money, they said that it sounded genuine.

It took further booking confirmations for Louise to believe that the trip was real and not part of a fantasy she had made up in her own head. All that was left was to arrange the time off work, let family know they'd be away and arrange a cat sitter.

The only expense to the Wilsons was the transport to the airport, regretfully over two hundred miles away but they were getting a free holiday so a trip up the motorway and a night in a hotel made it the cheapest getaway they'd ever had. They even got spending money. Louise was still waiting for the catch.

Louise was ready to murder Jim before they had even departed the UK, before they had even checked into the hotel. Jim had taken offense to the parking charges, paid for by Louise, which were notoriously over-inflated for the captive audience at an airport. His moaning could be heard as Louise checked them in on the automated system, she wasn't great with technology but enjoyed playing with touch-screen systems.

Louise had a restless night, she couldn't decide if she was nervous or excited. She half-expected the airport to laugh at her when she presented the tickets, and if she got on the flight then she was expecting some calamity at the other end, the hotel not having their booking, the itinerary of trips not the fairy-tale adventure she hoped for. She was just waiting for it to rain on her parade.

Getting Jim up and moving when the moon was still ruling the sky proved to be Louise's biggest challenge of the day. Louise wasn't enamoured with waking at such an ungodly hour but the airport check in dictated what time they had to be there, and she wasn't going to be late and risk missing their flight.

It was Jim's thing to be late, it was one of his traits that Louise loathed with a passion, she'd never understood why everything had to be at the last minute, why couldn't they be early and wait, was her company that bad? It was the same with everything, arriving by the skin of their teeth and it drove Louise bonkers. She couldn't remember the last time they had arrived at the cinema when the lights were still on. She was the first to admit that the safety notices and trailers were not the highlight of the show, but it annoyed her to find a seat in the dark, or have to accommodate a late comer, a Mexican wave of movie goers clutching oversized drinks and tubs of popcorn as they allowed them to squeeze their way through the narrow rows of seats. As she always said, Jim would be late for his own funeral, which would be happening sooner rather than later if he didn't get a move on through the dimmed sleepy corridors of the hotel.

The Wilsons arrived at the check-in desk with ample time to spare, Louise regretting the coffee she had fed to Jim to get him moving. It had backfired as he was merrily making unfunny jokes about smuggling a grandchild in the bag it was so heavy, causing a panicked clerk to call a supervisor over to verify the luggage did not contain a small child. Humiliation number one nearly got them arrested, but Jim wasn't finished yet.

Next came the torturous security checks. This time, instead of the usual ping as Jim walked through the metal detectors, he always failed to remove something, a belt, a key, a pen-knife, it was Louise who received a ping. Embarrassment crept up her face as two burly security guards pulled her from the line to perform a frisk search. Louise had complied fully with the security checks; the offending item was an opened bottle of water. A bottle of water that had last been in Jim's possession, a bottle which he said he had left in the toilet when quizzed over its disappearance. Humiliation number two nearly got them arrested and Louise had to endure a lecture from the terminal staff about the dangers of unsealed bottles like a teenager caught smoking. Airport staff are not the joking kind.

There was a catch to the trip after all – Jim.

There was a connecting train to take them to the other side of the airport, where their departure longue awaited. Jim and Louise stood in stony silence on the platform waiting for the connecting train to whisk them to paradise. As Louise stood on the platform she contemplated pushing Jim under the train as it arrived to carry passengers off on holidays of a lifetime, vacations to see family or international business trips. Jim's death would be quick, a high velocity impact that would splatter him all over the terminal. It was lucky for both the Wilsons that the track was cordoned off by an automatic glass door, saving Jim from heaven and Louise from prison.

Louise could scarcely believe that the trip was really happening. The flight had departed as scheduled, leaving Louise with only the concern of touching down at the Jomo Kenyatta International Airport and what to expect when they headed to their destination. She hoped that it would not turn into their final destination, well, maybe it might for Jim, that depended on his behaviour. Jim wasn't going to turn his nose up at a free holiday, but he wasn't looking forward to the African heat. He'd happily sit around a hotel pool in the Costa-del-somewhere resembling a lobster in shorts but wasn't a fan of moving in the heat.

Jim was practically snoring by the time the plane levelled off following take off with Louise briefly fantasising what it would be like if Jim accidently fell out of the plane and disappeared into the distance. She had brought enough to keep her entertained on the eight and half hour flight, settling into the uncomfortable claustrophobic aisle seat she turned to page one of the mammoth book she hoped would take her mind of the journey and on a trip to the past.

26

Stepping out of the terminal into the African heat transported Louise back to Florida and the magical yet exhausting few weeks the Wilsons spent there when the children were young. There was nothing quite like a foreign climate. Just for a moment Louise wished the kids were at her side instead of her husband whose face was already contorting into a picture of discomfort as they stood in the queue waiting to be loaded onto transportation to the hotel.

Thirty minutes in the heat and humidity of the sun left Jim gasping and his very British skin was starting to tinge a pretty shade of pink, the bottled water downed in one. Louise embraced the suffocating temperature, breathing in lungs full of warm air and coughing up minute dust particles.

The forty-five-minute bus journey to the hotel was more traumatic than the plane journey. The experienced native tackled the populated roads like a formula one driver, his passenger's mere spectators on the death defying drive. The commercialised landscape speed past in a blur, Louise unable to focus on the sights.

It was with much relief to all onboard when a sign for the hotel was spotted by a fellow traveller located near the front of the bus.   The mood changed from surprise and terror to excitement.

The hotel was hidden from the main road by an assortment of tropical plants but opened into an attractive complex of beautiful lodges topped with triangular roofs. Palm trees sprouted from manicured lawns and swimming pools with crystal waters encircled the main building.

Louise and Jim were escorted to their lodge by a gentleman with a delectable accent and a good grasp on the English language. The polished floors gave a distorted mirror image of the polished dark wood furniture and cream drapes that hung from the windows and four-poster bed. Louise felt like a princess in a palace and dived, head first onto the mattress like a child - when the porter had gone.

The communal breakfast was a delightful assault on Louise's senses, the smell was deliciously tempting, despite the number of guests jostling for space the sounds of nature breathed into the room from the open doors and the multilingual conversation was a complementing serenade to the variety of food available. Louise opted for a staple breakfast of fruit, unsure if the native cuisine would wreak havoc on her digestive system. She had no intention of spending the free vacation in the bathroom. Her eyes were working overtime, committing to memory the layout and decoration of the breakfast hall and taking a peep at each of the other people dining.

Louise often people watched, making up stories to suit their appearance or behaviour, it made it more interesting as dining with Jim was a mundane experience. There was the loved-up elderly couple on their second or third marriage, this time for love, the touchy-feely 20something newly-weds on honeymoon, or in the throes of an illicit affair and the international jet-setter eating alone before a lucrative business deal.

The excursion that formed part of the prize was scheduled for the following day, so Louise and Jim had the freedom to explore the complex and surrounding towns at their leisure. To keep the peace Louise had resigned herself to an idle morning while Jim lazed on a lounger by the pool and roasted alongside the other tourists. Louise retrieved her book in the knowledge that any conversation with Jim would be as sluggish as his body.   By lunchtime Louise had lapped the resort several times and was itching to see the surrounding sights. Jim knew that trying to cage his wife on holiday was like trying to find the end of a rainbow, and if he didn't go with her she'd happily head off on her own.

Before being permitted to leave the site, Jim took a refreshing shower in the lodge. Within minutes he had come running from the bathroom, towel wrapped precariously around his waist murmuring hysterically about a humungous spider. Humouring her husband's arachnophobia Louise went to investigate the size of the spider before deciding on its means of disposal, Jim had been known to overestimate before. The offending insect's body was around an inch long, though it wasn't huge or hairy Louise wasn't taking any chances.   She captured it under a wine glass, leaving it in a clear tomb for the house keeping staff to remove, unsure if it was deadly. It wasn't.

Louise forced Jim to report the intruder to the hotel staff whilst she indulged in a quick fantasy where the spider found Jim first. A girly scream alerted Louise to the pretend danger. She ambled in the direction of the commotion to find Jim trapped in a corner by a spider who was stood on two legs, waving the remaining six menacingly at Jim. Giving the arachnid assassin a high five Louise left Jim to a tortuous death of paralysis and suffocation as the spider sank its poisonous fangs into Jim's big toe.

The spider had put Jim on edge and every step he took around the district was with care for fear of attracting the attention of the local wildlife. The sights and smells outside the resort were vibrant and overpowering with the locals plying their trade in the tourist orientated market. A misplaced hose caused Jim to jump out of his skin and practically fly across the narrow street, fearing it was a snake come to finish him off. Jim had clearly not overcome his near-death dalliance with his bathroom stalker.

"You OK there Jim?" giggled an unsympathetic Louise. His response consisted of a venomous look and what resembled a snort.

It was time for the ultimate part of the holiday and Louise could barely contain herself, she felt like a child on Christmas morning, bouncing around the lodge, eager to get going. She'd always wanted to go on safari, see the animals in their natural habitat and not the tiny inferior homes that zoos offer.

A group had already assembled at the collection point by the time Jim and Louise arrived, minutes before the briefing. A frosty exchange passed between them as Louise berated Jim for his tardiness with her facial expressions.

Louise was expecting a luscious backdrop of trees and serenity but was meet with a terrain that was predominantly beige, a sandy floor and camouflaged vehicles in an open landscape dotted with a sporadic handful of plants broken with splatters of green. Even most of the tourists where masked to the backdrop.

They'd been shown a safety video before they left, the basic stuff like don't pet the lions and stay in the vehicle at all times, the usual staying alive notices. The tour guide reminded us all again of the dangers, in broken English, before we set off into the pride lands.

Every passenger was glued to their side of the truck, possessively hoarding their vantage point in the vain attempt to be the first to spot our prey. It was the experienced eyes of the guide that primarily spotted the tell-tail movements in the long grass.

To Louise It was like star gazing on a cloudy night, the more you looked the more could be seen, a disguised hide here, a branch like tail there. She was in her element, seeing nature first hand without the confines of fences to divide the endangered species of the world. Her camera clicked and zoomed its way through the memory card but how many would be in focus was anybody's guess. Jim let out half-hearted 'ooos' and pointed in random directions. Louise secretly chastised herself for expecting anything less, she knew he behaved depressingly in zoos and had shown little interest in the main feature of the holiday. Africa wouldn't have been Jim's first choice of destination, it wasn't in his top five, but it was gratis, sort of. He had to admit that his idea of a holiday was a break from everything, including walking.

Louise was internally furious at the driver owing to her perfect shot of a mother lion licking her cub being lost when the safari shuttle hit a rough patch of dirt. Not that she'd say anything, she'd have to be content with the invisible daggers that were now sticking out his back. Louise was beginning to wonder if the driver worked for the lions as his sole purpose seemed to be to shake the passengers out of the truck as food or to preserve the lion's modesty and prevent the spectators from capturing an award winning or compromising photograph.

One particularly large bump or pot hole had the passengers rising from their seats by almost half a foot and Louise was sure she saw the experienced driver grin in satisfaction. It did, however, give rise to a daydream fuelled by Jim's nonchalant expression at the whole safari experience. Not that Louise was surprised as he'd shown zero enthusiasm to come along and trips to zoos when the children were little had been mainly solo affairs. Jim did enjoy the safari, but he had noticed a worrying glint in his wife's eyes. Hidden by the glare of the sun Louise was oblivious to her husband who was eyeing his wife with suspicion.   She looked on another planet.

The safari transportation had morphed into an overgrown child's toy with passengers balanced precariously around the edges. it was Jim who was unceremoniously flung from the vehicle. As he made his slow-motion departure a pride of lions stood in wait, licking their lips and rubbing their front paws together in anticipation of the meal. Jim wasn't about to make it easy and gave chase, the mini truck keeping just ahead of the doomed man. The lions weren't prepared for their lunch to make an escape so took up the challenge to reach Jim before he reached the safety of his travelling companions, half of whom were routing for his survival, the other half, including his loving wife, on team lion.

The Kings of the beasts took down their prey like a frightened gazelle, a beautiful maned male sinking his gleaming canine teeth into Jim bottom. Jim's screams silenced by a magnificent lioness, her powerful jaws ending the game of cat and mouse in a feline victory. Jim made a delicious meal for the pride and having one less made the cramped journey back to the resort more comfortable.

Louise was brought back to reality by the shrill yell of "giraffe" coming from the red haired woman next to her and the image of Jim's bloody corpse being devoured was evaporated.

Jim looked as bored on Louise's return from her fantasy as he did when she left and was oblivious to the alternative Jim's fate. Louise snapped a few pictures of the giraffes as they were driven back to the resort.

A feast of local and international dishes was served up to commemorate their stay and the Wilsons retried to their room full and content. There hadn't been enough sex to constitute it officially as a second honeymoon but that night they made sure that they would leave Africa, united as a couple.

In her dreams Louise swapped the African continent for the golden shores of Australia and the plains of the safari for the bushes of the outback. Jim was safe from marauding lions but fell victim to a kangaroo which boxed him to oblivion and a team of brightly ringed venomous snakes who coiled themselves around his limbs and took off with their prey, a slithering sea of reptiles supporting their human vessel. Louise woke refreshed, if not a tad disappointed that Jim had not been mauled to death or spirited away by some voodoo priest.

The outward flight home left as the sun set bringing their holiday to a romantic conclusion. Louise arrived back into England tired and cold, eager to get home and upload her photographs, so she could have a proper look at them.

The record of their first, and last safari, was a series of snapshots showing blurred animals and surprised looking natives. Louise selected those that were identifiable for viewing by her family and friends.

27

A week after arriving home the trip was fading into a long distant memory and the dark clouds that had hung in the sky since touching down were starting to wear on Louise's positive exterior. Work had them both busy as they caught up on the jobs left idle while they lounged under a perfect sun. Louise liked to be kept active. She found her mind was too dynamic if it did not have the stimulation of tasks to contend with and a quite mind for Louise meant new ways for Jim to die or interior design projects to be born.

It was part of Louise's personality to move through life at one hundred miles an hour, it was a flaw that she readily admitted too but didn't see as a fault herself. It was a point that both husband and wife agreed on through Louise saw no need to slow down as Jim was slow enough for the both of them.

Jim had hoped, in vain, that the pace of life in Africa would have made Louise take a step back, as he'd surmised, it had not. The only thing to slow Louise down was illness, and even then, she battled through it with the determination of a heat seeking missile. It was a trait in his wife that he both admired and loathed in equal measure.

Louise tried her upmost to remain in a happy frame of mind, but she could not abide the unfairness of the world, or other road users. It pained her deeply to even acknowledge, let alone admit, that she suffered from road rage, but she did. She'd tried calming music, holistic crystals, leaving early but once she experienced the slightest annoyance on the highway it was quickly amplified and blown out of proportion.

Every Tom, Dick and Harry was on the road that morning and everyone seemed to be going Louise's way. "It's a 30 not 25 you moron for crying out loud," Louise shouted at the car in front, not that the car ahead of that was going any faster. She was not late for work but was in a questionable mood when she got there, and the day passed in uncomfortable annoyance. The journey home fared no better as an accident had caused a tailback of cars. Louise considered abandoning her vehicle on the hard shoulder and walking home, almost.

Jim had done nothing wrong, he'd done nothing at all. He'd not put his shoes away or done any housework, but this was commonplace. He just looked at her 'that way' but it was enough. Still riled up from the grandpa driving Louise stormed to the kitchen to prepare tea. On autopilot, she dug in the freezer for that night's ready meal when her mind began to contemplate a new way to dispose of her faithful husband.

The daydream ran in reverse. Jim's dead body the opening scene. The fantasy played out like an investigation documentary, exploring the different ways that could lead to death at the hands of an automobile. In the first scenario Jim skidded on a patch of frozen ground and spun out of control, a metal barrier and steep ravine stopping the car and Jim's heart. A similar loss of control resulted in Jim hitting a tree, his unrestrained body exiting via the windscreen. There was the tire that punctured on the motorway causing the imaginary Jim and his car to veer across the lanes and end up beneath the cab of an articulated lorry. The brake line had been cut so when Jim turned downhill he was unable to stop and continued straight onto a pier and was launched into the sea, a metallic fishing rod with Jim as the bait. The final death was caused by the carelessness of another driver and not a vehicle malfunction or work of sabotage. Jim was shunted from behind which caused a domino effect of cars, each one squashing the other until only cubes of metal remained.

As Louise scrapped the lasagne from it plastic container onto the plate she couldn't help feeling upset over Jim's demise. He'd done nothing to warrant it and did not deserve to die in such a fashion. Besides Frank was banking on inheriting his dads beloved car as soon as Jim became to infirm to handle it, so it wouldn't do to have it wrapped around a lamp post.

Louise's sullen mood lasted for days, weeks. She was beginning to wonder if it might be the onset of the menopause but put it down to post-holiday blues.

The kids were about to rouse her from her depressing state with news of love, laughter and happiness.

Ellen was the first to lift her mum's spirits, after months of being heart-breakingly single Ellen had popped over with the revelation that she had meet the man of her dreams. His name was Norman and he was a forty-five-year-old divorced GP. Though she was pleased that her daughter was happy Louise couldn't help but feel slightly reserved of the choice of candidate, and the closeness in age to her own father. It irked Louise that she felt any inclination of prejudice owing to the age gap. She reminded herself that Ellen's happiness was at the forefront of the dilemma and invited the newly formed duo to Sunday lunch. A phone call invitation to Frank was rewarded with the promise an exciting exposé. Louise hoped that at last they'd be hearing wedding bells.

The veg was simmering and the meat cooling as the Wilson kids and their partners, along with little Jared, piled into the kitchen. Louise immediately clocked the sparking bauble on Trinity's ring finger but waited patiently for the official announcement, a swift kick under the table indicating that Jim was to do the same. Ellen was so wrapped up in Norman that a U.F.O could have landed in the middle of the table and a troupe of aliens perform a dance and she wouldn't have noticed. No proclamation of marriage was declared over the dinner table, so Louise had to sit politely as rays of light agonisingly refracted around the room from the ring, not yet able to admire its existence.

Coffee and desert came and went with not a peep from either of them. At the rate they were going the babbling Jared would learn to talk and reveal all before they did. A well timed and perfectly executed raised eyebrows and eye gaze to the ring instructed Frank that

Louise was not ignorant to his relationship status and that she was going to explode if he didn't make it public knowledge, soon.

Frank briefly considered winding Louise up and drawing it out, but she'd always been his advocate as a child, snuck him food or slipped money into his coat pocket when Jim had said no so he felt guilty. Any previous plans such as "Jared did a whooper in his nappy today" or "you wouldn't believe what came out his nose when he sneezed" were shelved. The threat of the holiday snaps slide-show also spurred on his announcement.

Frank stood in front of the assembled audience and beckoned Triny to his side. Louise felt her hands tense in excitement and a smile, barely contained, start as she waited, expectant with joy. There was no speech, Frank just came straight to the point "Triny and me are getting married".

Louise was up and hugging her son and future daughter-in-law before the words "married" had left Franks lips. Ellen's squeal of delight startled Norman who spilt his drink while Jim sat in his chair looking a little dumbfounded but none-the-less pleased.

The ring was scrutinised, an over-sized diamond balanced delicately on a band of silver. With hugs, kisses and congratulations exchanged the party were in a jubilant mood. Triny recounted Franks proposal, Louise and Ellen delighted in the romantic tale, tears of happiness caressing their cheeks. Even Jim's eyes had a glossy appearance. Louise glanced towards Norman, conscious that this was quite a first 'meet the family' but he seemed content, if a little wet from the split drink over which he had had no fuss at all.

Louise was beaming with pride that her son had followed her years of proposal advice and had done so in a memorable and idealistic way, and not the "shall we do it then?" that was Louise's one and only proposal of marriage.

Frank had taken Triny for a candle lit meal at her favourite restaurant. Unbeknown to her a pose of their friends were hidden in adjoining booths, along with little Jared. Halfway through the meal Frank excused himself to return shortly with their son, both dressed in matching suits. As Frank dropped to one knee, Jared held his hand out to Triny. Inside it was the engagement ring. As Triny took the ring Frank boldly asked, 'Will you marry me Trinity Hollyworth?'. Right on cue their friends revealed themselves as a shocked and tearful future Mrs Wilson sobbed "yes, yes, I'd love to marry you".

28

Within the week every colleague had heard the rendition of Franks proposal as Louise told anyone that stood still long enough. Even the customers noticed that she was more animated than usual, and those kind enough to enquire were treated to the romantic tale alongside their weekly shop.

Louise had visited every bridal outlet in the vicinity looking for the perfect outfit. The mother of the groom was just as important in her eyes, more so even as Jim & Louise had made a substantial donation to the wedding fund and Triny already regarded Louise as a surrogate mother. Her own was unsuccessfully fighting the demons that had plagued Triny's childhood.

Louise had three outfits that she was deciding between, the assistants in each shop swearing that she looked magnificent, their fake smiles an attempt to flatter her into a purchase. Louise was wise to their antics, so Ellen accompanied her mum to cast the deciding vote. As bridesmaid her outfit had been picked for her, a peach accompaniment to the brides' white gown.

Louise throw herself into the wedding preparations and Jim's mortality was hardly given a second thought. It felt an age since Louise had devised a way to dispose of her spouse. This was all about to change as family descended for the combined pre-wedding outing.

Frank and Triny had organised a modern celebration where the Wilsons and Hollyworths, along with an assortment of close friends, would spend the day together before separating into the traditional stag and hen parties.

Jim was indifferent, but Louise had worked herself up into quite a state about meeting Trinity's parents and she was in danger of being overwhelmed by an ibs attack.

As was customary where Jim was involved they were among the last to arrive at the venue, coming a close first to Triny's dishevelled parents, leaving Louise ready to throttle Jim and struggling to control the cramps that were starting to bite at her intestines, the medication not yet effective.

Louise hoped that her smile was welcoming but feared it was a grimace and prayed that Mr & Mrs Hollyworth were themselves too nervous to notice. As it happened they were too drunk to care.

To enable all those that the engaged couple held nearest and dearest to get to know each other the venue had arranged a series of team building activities with the only rule being that you cannot work with a partner you have known for more than twenty-four hours. Louise internally groaned at the thought but graciously greeted her primary partner. The day was surprisingly fun, and, with controlled visits to the bathroom Louise enjoyed herself. The only moment of tension was when mother went against mother in an all-out game of table tennis. Fortunately for Louise alcohol was not conducive to keeping track of an unpredictable bouncy white ball and Louise won the match.

To end the joint day, they descended upon the mini golf course - men verses ladies. Louise hated golf of any kind, normal, mini or televised. Even as a child, family outings and get togethers seemed to end up on a miniature course stalked by strangers with identical objectives. Even from the hole behind them Louise could see the concentration on Jim's face as he tried for a hole in one. He always took it so seriously it drove Louise mad, he couldn't even let a four-year-old Frank win his first game, the memory caused Louise to momentarily see red.

During more than one game Louise considered what she could do with the golf club, primarily using Jim as a caddy, his exaggerated stance making the notion even more tempting.

Louise's back niggled as she swung the tiny club and sent the fluorescent ball hurtling towards its goal. It didn't reach its mark, but a gentle tap saw if fall down the hole and Louise's turn was over until the next hole. Cheering on her team mates Louise twirled her club like a majorette baton, her mind drifting off into a sporting fantasy.

With just the two of them on the course, Jim positioned himself to take the winning shot. Jim wiggled his bottom and waved his shoulders as he took up his golfing stance, unbeknown that his wife was also limbering up for the winning shot. Before Jim had the opportunity to strike the hard little ball with his iron Louise struck his soft large skull with her own driver club. Jim fell to the floor, unconscious, his nose nudged the ball toward the hole in a valiant effort to finish the course. To ensure that Jim wouldn't resume his position as number one Louise clubbed him to death where he lay, at hole nine. Whistling merrily to herself Louise used her bloody club to complete the course taking victory over her husband.

Back in reality Louise's score was trailing behind, letting down the female team but she wasn't the only source of embarrassment. A combination of the uneven terrain, impractical heeled shoes and a skin-full of larger was an accident waiting to happen, and it happened in spectacular fashion. Louise almost missed it, in her daydreaming state, but looked up just in time to capture Trinity's mum, Lauren, trip over her own feet and barrel down the course, an oversized ball of black lace and screams. The men gallantly came to the rescue, Frank helping his future mother-in-law to her feet whilst her own husband, Edward, looked on grateful for the intervention. Lauren had a bruised pride as well as a bruised knee but was otherwise unscathed, her drunkenness dulling her pain and humiliation but causing her daughter to flee in a flood of embarrassed tears.

The two groups separated for the remainder of the night, each donning the required fancy dress and heading off to an undisclosed location for an evening of drinking and entertainment.

The girl's destination was a cocktail bar with luxurious cuisine followed by a show. By the time they had consumed their banquet and taken their seats Louise was herself quite drunk. She'd had *sex on the beach*, visited *Manhattan*, became friends with *Margarita* and *Daiquiri* and was rather in love with *Bloody Mary*. Rapturous cheers went up from the hen party as three chiselled hunks took to the stage. It took a few songs for Louise to realise that she was at a real-life showing of *Magic Mike* and before long the only thing to cover their modesty was the microphone they were holding. Louise hated to think of herself as a prude, but she didn't know where to look as the men dangled their livelihoods at their audience.

Louise copped an eyeful as they made their way into the crowd wiggling their bits at their guests as hands came from the crowd to stroke their sculptured chests and gasps of admiration escaped the lips of Louise's new-found acquaintances. It was all Louise could do not to burst out laughing as they bunny-hopped in unison, their little guys slapping their flat stomachs with each thrust. To avoid making direct eye contact with the dancing manhood's Louise turned her attention to what the stags were up to and allowed herself to dream.

She knew that the boy's itinerary consisted mostly of burgers and beers followed by a reduced grand prix. The carts they were using were not dirt track cars but fully motorised carts that could reach alarming speeds for an indoor track, separated by bales of hay.

In Louise's mind Jim was going down in a blaze of glory regardless of the security measures in place. In pole position Jim shot round the track like a pro but his advantage was soon lost when he collided with the hay barrier and his arm was ripped from its socket. A race attendant waved Jim's severed limb in place of the safety flag to warn the other drivers to the danger ahead but Frank couldn't stop in time and smashed into his father's go-cart. The impact happened just as Jim was exiting his crashed vehicle and his leg followed the same path as his arm, his own son inadvertently dismembering Jim's limb, dragging it behind the cart like a bloody talisman. The course reset, with all Jim's limbs present and correct, and the boys were off again, vying to get around one another. Jim's confidence had been knocked after severing body parts in the previous race but undeterred he performed a risky manoeuvre to move out of third but misjudged the skill of his opponent and again became victim of the hay. This time the cart overturned and squashed Jim like a mouldy satsuma. The third and final race left Jim an inferno of flesh and metal, his damaged cart igniting a bale of hay with a rogue spark.

Louise didn't remember getting into bed, but her dreams were plagued with willies driving clown cars around a weaving track.

Breakfast was a subdued affair, the majority of the party sporting mammoth hangovers and faces devoid of the war paint from the previous evening, except that to stubborn to be removed by blurry eyes. It felt like a heard of elephants had taken up residence in Louise's head and all she could stomach was water and dry toast, the smell of the cooked offerings washing waves of nausea inside her belly. Lauren, as fresh as a daisy, bustled around the room before plonking herself and her fully stocked plate beside Louise.

Pleasantries and kind wishes were exchanged along with hugs and air kisses as everyone departed back to their own lives, to be forgotten until reunited at the wedding.

Jim, Frank and Edward had beaten the girls back home and were enjoying a celebratory whisky in the garden when Louise pulled onto the drive. Louise was half-heartedly a little disappointed to see Jim intact but hugged him nonetheless, their embrace making Louise realise that she had actually missed him, a tiny bit.

29

With all the talk of weddings, love and family Louise was feeling sentimental. When Jim arrived home from work Louise was in the living room surrounded by a library of photo albums, a crime scene of their life together.   A half empty wine glass and discarded tissues indicated that Louise had been on a tearful, but happy, journey. They both found it hard to believe how quick time had gone, it only seemed a blink of the eye that Frank was in nappies, and now he had a child of his own.

Unbeknown to Louise, Jim's reason for avoiding reminiscing over old photos was it forced him to address his own mortality and face the fact that he had eclipsed his prime and was firmly in middle age. Jim spent some time with his wife, laughing at once fashionable clothes and hair styles before retiring to his study.

Louise cracked open another bottle as the past holiday snaps came out. Clear blue skies shone behind palm trees on the streets of Orlando and Louise was transported back to the humidity and contentment of first hand experiences. Foreign wildlife always intrigued Louise, much of her album a record of the native flora and fauna, and she had been chiefly taken with the prehistoric gators, fascinated by their stillness and close proximity. Louise vividly recalled accidently knocking a piece of wood into the enclosure, mesmerised by the anger and velocity of the attacking gator. Her memories twisted in her mind to form an alternative scenario.

Standing on the bridge observing the pre-historic reptiles, alligators or crocodiles Louise never could remember the difference, Jim leant over for a better view presenting the perfect accident. Louise feigned bending over to tie her shoelace and, with moves worthy of an olympic athlete, she grabbed Jim around the ankles and propelled him over the side of the bridge into the croc invested water below. As soon as he hit the surface his scaly assassins were upon him. A limb each they disappeared into the murky depths, a fading ripple and handful of bubbles the only evidence of anything untoward. Checking that her deed was witnessed only by the beady eyes of her co-conspirators, Louise left her husband to a watery grave. The practicalities that Jim would have had possession of the vehicle keys lost in the improbability of the daydream.

Glossy prints of the seaside reminded Louise of cold and sandy trips with the children, too afraid to let them venture past their knees in the sea and too disheartened when they readily flattened the architectural masterpiece she had constructed with the grainy particles. As she fought the irrational tears that the memories caused she fashioned a death for Jim to distract herself. Bobbing on the waves on-board a striped surfboard Jim looked like an oversized seal to the shark stalking the sea, hidden beneath the swelling tides. Louise spotted the dorsal fin from the shore but did nothing to warn her husband. He dumbly waved back to the other beach goers who were attempting to warn him of the predator, wondering why his own wife had not returned his gesture, assuming that she was waiting expectantly for him to get to his feet. She was waiting expectantly but not for Jim to perform the bottom turn manoeuvre but for the marine mammal to gobble him up. In classic *Jaws* style the silver king of the ocean leapt from the waves, it's razor lined mouth open and ready to swallow Jim. The slippery beast and Jim disappeared from view to a melody of screams, the only evidence of the attack was an unoccupied surf board minus a bite shaped piece floating lonely back to shore.

Triny invited Louise and Ellen to lunch at the wedding venue, Willow Lodge Hotel, to finalise the wedding menu. Louise felt a pang of guilt that Triny didn't invite her own mum but understood that the drink made the relationship volatile and was grateful that Triny was comfortable around her. Louise felt   honoured to be involved in the nuptials, in a way normally reserved for the mother of the bride.

Willow Lodge was secluded behind a wall of trees, only visible as you turned the corner of the long winding driveway. The property was breath-taking, a collective 'wow' went up from the backseat duo as Triny parked haphazardly on the gravel drive in front of the two-storey brick construction.

The women were ushered to a private room by the resident wedding planner, Tamsin. A slender young woman with pinched features and sleek black hair pulled tight into a plate that swished like a horse's tail as she walked. Tamsin proceeded to coordinate the upcoming day with Triny while Louise and Ellen were left to marvel at the décor. When their input was required they were called over like waitresses to cast a deciding vote or to be given instructions for the day and dismissed.

Louise's tummy was rumbling by the time the wedding taster buffet was served. There were delicate portions of every dish available, all laid out in a long line, the chef describing each morsel to the ladies as if they were edible works of art. Louise chuckled to herself at the thought that they should have been handing out rosettes, judging each dish on its tastiness. Ellen, who had appeared slightly distracted all morning, was munching through the buffet paying little attention until she heard the chef mention a collection of shellfish in one of the hors d'oeuvres and was gripped with a sense of alarm. She'd heard that you shouldn't eat shellfish when pregnant and began to panic that she had unwittingly harmed her growing foetus.

Louise instantly felt the shift in her daughters demeaner and asked, "what's wrong Ellen?"

"I've eaten shellfish." replied a worried Ellen.

"So," came Louise's confused reply.

"But…. But." stammered a neurotic Ms Wilson

"But what." said Louise and Triny in unison.

"It's … it's…. er…" Ellen responded, realising that she was about to give away her secret.

"Well, it's not as if you're preggers is it, and anyway, the docs say that it don't matter anymore anyway." responded Triny through a mouthful of food.

"I .... er ...... thought .... er... that I ... might be allergic to shellfish." lied Ellen.

Knowing full well that her offspring had never been allergic to anything Louise silently put two and two together. Although she may have come with five, she was pretty sure her second grandchild was on the way.

Dismissing the outburst as a consequence to the alcohol the party finished the buffet and sat down. Over another glass of bubbly, they deliberated over the choices and came up with a wedding menu.

A tour of the venue and grounds brought the meeting to a close and Tamsin left. It was perfect, all except for the pond, that was a little too close to the decking for Louise's liking, and accidents happen.

Louise burst through the door, a tipsy whirlwind filled with delicious food and pricey champagne, talkative with excitement for the big day. Jim was despondent, absorbed in some app on his phone, and after seven minutes of grunted acknowledgements and well-timed 'a-ha's' with fleeting eye contact Louise sulked off, mid-sentence, to seek solace in a steaming soapy bath.

Louise lost herself in a daydream as she relaxed in the hot fragrant water. Her mind brought forth a magical wedding, complete with fairies, unicorns and maidens in flowing dresses and floral crowns. Amongst the merriment Jim was sullen and withdrawn, his phone a bigger draw than the fanciful creatures at the Mid-summer marriage. It was easy to push Jim over the rickety wooden barrier that protected guests from the pond. By the time Jim's body floated into the distance the bath water had cooled and Louise had goose bumps on her exposed skin. Shivering, Louise dried herself, and as she did her thoughts returned to the wedding.

There was no longer gleeful dancing under a bright summer sun, the familiar landscape now glimmering with crystal snowflakes that illuminated the winter wedding. The scene of Jim's prior demise was frozen over, a stage where confused birds would land with a soft thud. In a valiant effort to save a 'distressed' bird, that promptly flew off at Jim's balanced arrival, he found himself abandoned precariously. All that separated Jim from the frosty depths of the pond below was a layer of ice. As horrified onlookers shouted words of advice zigzags began to form at Jim's feet and spread in a web across the glistening surface. The echo from the crack lasted longer than Jim's descent into the icy waters, ejected from the cold stage via the trapdoor. Thankful for the hot towel rail and the warm PJ's Louise felt a miniscule sense of guilt as she saw Jim's frozen face disappearing from view in a floating frozen tomb.

It was a sheepish looking Ellen that arrived on her old doorstep the following day. Louise shouted up to her dozing husband that she was heading out and that she expected the broken fence panels to be gone on her return.

Louise patiently waited for Ellen's confession, which came over a cream tea. At only six weeks Ellen had been in two-minds about making the revelation but knew that her Mum already suspected and could be assured of her discretion.

When Louise returned her excitement over the latest news was forgotten in a wash of frustration when she saw the damaged panels had not moved an inch. Louise marched into the house, on a war path, her husband the enemy.

Jim was in the kitchen nursing a steamy cup of coffee and looked like he'd just woken.

"You're back quickly love." he said, attempting to placate his seething spouse with a warm smile.

"No Jim, you went back to sleep, didn't you?" snapped Louise.

"No." he faltered at Louise's back as she stormed upstairs.

Louise found the marital bed in its usual state of distress, one side a crumpled duvet and misshapen pillows, its twin neatly made with plumped cushions. She cursed her husband as she straightened his side. Noticing that the sheets were still warm Louise's face contorted into a snarl. Most men would get busted with another woman, but Jim was found with himself in bed. Vilified that she had caught her husband out she returned downstairs, a storm brewing in Louise's mind. Jim, aware that his deceit had been detected had retreated to outside and was loading wood into his rickety trailer, desperate to avoid an argument or a dressing down from his wife.

Louise shoot imaginary daggers at him through the window, her mouth pinched like a cat's bottom, but she rose above her anger and let it go. Despite liking the view from her high horse, she wanted to present a united front at their son's wedding.

30

With the wedding just a week away there had to be a last-minute change of bridesmaid dress as there was no way that Ellen and her baby bump were squeezing into the pre-ordered dress and no amount of letting it out would suffice. Trinity was furious, having spent the last month meticulously watching every morsel she ate and her future sister-in-law seemingly eating every morsel in sight. Trinity herself was in danger of having to have her dress taken in. It was a fraught hour spent with the seamstress, the party leaving with gowns in hand, and a flea in the ear. Louise couldn't have been more thrilled with the change of attire as the previous choice made Ellen look like a giant peach blancmange.

Louise, never one to be concerned about her appearance, had bought a selection of fascinators for the big day, to accompany one of her own hardly worn outfits hanging forgotten at the back of the wardrobe. Jim was wearing one of the hired grey matching suits.

Though they had started a family out of wedlock the engaged couple followed tradition by spending the eve of their wedding apart, Frank not catching a glimpse of his bride until she walked down the aisle. The lads were given a gourmet full English breakfast to start the day and soak up any remaining alcohol from the night before. Louise was to nervous and excited to eat.

The bedroom looked like a jumble sale gone wrong by the time that she made her final decision. Louise pondered on her reflection, she'd never be one hundred percent happy with what she saw no matter how hard she tried in the fashion world, but her understated makeup complimented her turquoise dress. To add the finishing touch Louise wore the same jewellery she wore on her own wedding day. Louise wondered if Jim would recognise the sparkling additions. He did not.

"Is that necklace new?" enquired Jim, nervous that the gems were real, and his wife was sporting a small fortune around her neck.

"Just a little treasure I picked up darling, it didn't cost too much." teased Louise knowing that the jewels were as fake as her response.

"Beautiful." gulped Jim, his face noticeably dropping a shade or two.

The time had come to get Frank to the altar and start the next chapter of his life. For Louise it was an emotional car journey, her son had flown the nest years ago, had forged a career and life for himself but in her heart, he was still her little boy and now she had to pass him into the care of another woman.

Apart from the collection of family huddled together, faces from the last weekend of freedom and a handful of Frank's childhood friends who had remained local Louise didn't recognise anybody lingering at the venue. Louise made a beeline for her sister Fran whilst she left Frank to great his guests. Trinity's parents were already there, and already swaying having consumed a liquid breakfast. Franks grandmother, Joan, arrived in spectacular fashion, just minutes before the bride. Fran having forgotten to collect her on the way.

Although the front row provided the best view of the service they were last to see the bride and missed most of her infamous last walk as a single lady. Jared squealed with delight when he saw his mum, having spent the night with Louise, and was promptly sick on his miniature matching three-piece suit. Granny Louise had him cleaned up by the time everyone had finished gawping at the bride and the registrar had completed the welcome speech.

The service was perfect and went without a hitch, no dropped rings or mumbled vows. Louise couldn't help crying, her children looked beautiful and she had just gained a daughter. Louise would never admit it, but she thought that Triny kind of looked like a layered white meringue in her puffy princess number and was unwittingly upstaged by the elegant 1920s style halter neck dress that hung gracefully over Ellen's inflated bosom and pregnant belly. An undignified cheer went around the room as the newly formed Mr & Mrs Wilson made their way, hand in hand, into married life.

There was a forty minute window as the staff frantically ran around preparing the wedding breakfast and the newly-weds were whisked away to endure the enforced nuptials paparazzi. Some guests used the time to launch an unofficial photo shoot in the beautiful surroundings whilst Trinity's parents lead a possession to the bar.

The day was organised to perfection and nothing was left to chance, Tamsin had rightly earned her exorbitant fee. In one of her final duties of the day she called the increasing tipsy party to order and presented the married couple, as one, to their assembled family and friends.

The chef was good to his word and every bite was as tasty and succulent as what they had eaten on the taster day. Louise over indulged and was left feeling a little bloated, her stomach straining against the fabric of her dress.

Louise used the lull between the afternoons proceeding and the arrival of the evening guests to settle Jared for a nap and catch forty winks herself.

Feeling refreshed and ready for round two Louise and Jared returned to the party, disjointed by the interim period of change. At some point the wedding gift table had an addition of a collection tin for one Aaron Tyler to do a parachute jump. Cheeky chap thought Louise but a good idea, money tended to flow where love and alcohol were concerned.

Jared had gone back to the care of his parents, temporarily as he was spending the night with granny and grandad. It gave Louise a little freedom to soak up the atmosphere without being on J-watch. Louise was signing the guest book and filling out tokens of love when her eye was drawn to the boldly placed donation tub and she was momentarily lost in losing Jim.

Louise imagined herself standing in the middle of a deserted field looking skyward at a plane hovering around fourteen thousand feet above the ground. One by one small dots fell from the plane and hurtled towards earth. Louise had to squint to see the aerial acrobatics, preferring to watch the Gopro images projected onto a screen for those only brave enough to watch. Although it seemed longer for those on the ground the skydiver's parachutes began to open after only thirty six seconds of freefall. All except one who was still going down when the others had been jerked upwards by the lifesaving material. Screams began to emit from the onlookers and the sky as Louise observed, with morbid fascination, her husband hurtling to his doom like a human meteor.

Jim came into focus as he swam through the air, arms and legs desperately trying to form wings and save him from his impending departure from the world. Poor Jim was terrified, his face changing from panic to fear to resignation and back to panic again as he swooped towards the ground like an eagle after their prey. Nobody could save Jim from his demise, all they could do was watch in horror as he crashed into the earth. A mushroom cloud of dirt projected into air as his body formed a crater in the ground with the force of his fall. His airborne buddies landed gracefully around the fallen skydiver, his body covered with the colourful fabric of the parachutes.

Louise was brought back to reality when she heard "OMG, Mrs Wilson you haven't aged a day" screeched at her by an excitable young lady.

"How are you dear?" replied a slightly shocked and confused Louise as she struggled to reconcile the grown woman with the child she had once been. It took a moment to twig but Louise recognised her as little Jenny

Thompson, one of Franks friends from primary school. Louise knew she had moved away but had no idea her and Frank were still in contact.

The day moved almost as fast as her own wedding and before long the DJ was playing a slow waltz to the remaining guests as they clung drunkenly from each other, rotating in wobbly circles. With a kiss for the newlyweds Louise and Jim wrestled an over-tired Jared from his parents' arms and retired for the evening, leaving their first born to consummate his marriage, but hopefully not yet add to the family.

31

Louise's head was pounding the following morning. There was no lie-in as Jared rose with the sun and his gurgles in protest that his breakfast was not yet served where increasing in volume forcing Louise to attend to her very awake grandson before he woke the rest of the guests.

A Farley's rusk, bottle of milk and a black coffee later and the two were off for a walk around the slumbering grounds. Crystallised droplets of dew clung to the grass and balanced precariously from the leaves of the trees as birds swooped and danced overhead in a melody of the dawn chorus. The delicious smell from the hotels kitchens began to waft in their direction. The two generations of Wilsons were first into the dining room and had finished their leisurely breakfast before any of the other wedding guests made an appearance. Despite the fact that Louise was hung over she consumed a hearty feast but avoided the hair of the dog. Louise was not a drinker, hadn't been since vodka and graveyards as a teen, but every couple of years she would revisit the temptation of alcohol. She had tested her tolerance in recent months in preparation for the toasts, the last thing she wanted was to embarrass herself or her children in a drunken moment of madness.

Everybody dispersed in trickles, returning to their own lives. Louise and Jim took Jared back with them leaving the new couple to ponder their gifts and have a few days without the trappings of a young family.

Aside from ibs attacks Louise was generally a healthy person, the occasional cough and cold but nothing to write home about. There had been a sickness bug doing the rounds at work, an infectious parent co-worker had kindly reduced the work force to half by contaminating the staff room. Louise thought she had been spared the dreaded lurgy but, as her colleagues were returning to work in dribs and drabs, the illness had saved the best for last and she came down with a particularly bad bout of sickness. Louise hoped that she was just rundown after all the excitement and build-up for the wedding but on her second day in bed she began to suspect otherwise. Her nose was blocked, her throat was dry and sore and every bone in her body ached. "Oh my god, is this what it feels like to get old?" Louise moaned at the empty room. Jim had left early for work leaving Louise to wallow in her own self-pity. He wasn't good around sick people, he wasn't great with people in general, but he couldn't abide ill folk.

When she was conscious the painkillers she was on rendered her senseless, she couldn't taste or smell anything and was a miserable mess of snot and sweat. Louise's waking hours brought waves of pain and nausea, her time asleep provided her with night terrors, visions of darkness and the unpleasant sensation of falling. Jim had been living off of takeaways as Louise was either asleep or incapacitated, and she wasn't about to let Jim catch it by cooking him food. Jim had been banned from coming within ten feet of Louise. He'd just have to fend for himself, he could afford to lose a few pounds. Alternatively, Jim could have made his own meals, but he'd always had an aversion to cooking, his idea of providing a meal was collecting it from the takeaway. It was a pity McDonalds didn't offer loyalty cards, Jim would have been in for some rewards this week. As a peace offering for avoiding his wife Jim had brought home Louise's favourite, a chicken meal with a gassy coke and salted fries. Though it was only junk food Louise felt better for having had a hot meal.

It was the best part of a fortnight before Louise felt well enough the return to work, she knew she was feeling better as she had daydreamed about losing Jim.

In her fantasy the couple had traded roles, Jim was the maverick and Louise the timid picture of innocence. Dream Louise had slaved away over a hot stove to make Jim a homemade chicken Rossini using the cute little arrow tipped mushrooms she'd found growing in the garden that morning. Unbeknown to the naive Louise the mushrooms she had so lovingly picked contained hallucinogenic properties and Jim was about to be taken on an involuntarily trip. Jim's behaviour deteriorated throughout the course of the meal, by the time he had swallowed the last mouthful he was singing like a drunken sailor, spraying bits of chicken and mushroom over Louise and the table.

"Vroom, vroom." shouted Jim as he ran around the living room, arms extended, pretending to be a plane. "All aboard for flight seven-sixty," laughed Jim as he stopped momentarily beside Louise before flying off upstairs. Jim had been gone for a little while when Louise felt a draft and went to investigate. On inspection she found the window of their bedroom wide open, the curtains billowing in the breeze but no Jim to be found anywhere. Louise carried on the search for her missing husband outside. She found him. Jim was below the open window, his legs sticking out of a rose bush with broken branches and petals strewn upon the floor. Louise assumed that Jim had taken his desire to be an aeroplane to the next level and had launched himself out of the top floor window in an attempt to fly. Jim flew as well as a lead balloon and fell to his demise.

It would be easy for Louise to manufacture a scenario when Jim fell out a window, but the more she thought about it the more unlikely it would be that Jim was cleaning them and he wouldn't be closing them. In hindsight, it would probably be Louise that would fall to her death shutting a window Jim had opened. Jim had never been one to fling open his doors to waifs and strays but was delighted to open their windows for any unwelcome flying insect. The neighbours had become accustomed to the terrified screams of Ellen as a child at bedtime as she was attacked by the 'moths trying to kill her'. Harmless and beautiful night-time butterflies attracted to the night-light she refused to part with until her teenage years. Louise hated Jim's uninvited guests as much as the open windows that beckoned them in. Not only did the windows allow in unwanted bugs they were also responsible for the drafts that whistled through the house or damaged her ornaments, knocked over by unpredictable gusts of wind.

Where Jim would open windows Louise would come along in his wake and reduce the gap, so it allowed for a slim passage of air but nothing that had more than two legs. Both irritating the other with their preferences, both believing themselves to be correct, and neither accepting the others rational opinions. If Louise wanted the weather inside the house, she'd make a hole in the roof. To Louise the definition of inside meant you were away from the elements outside and if she wanted any fresh air she would go outside, where it should be. Not only were the window openers a bone of contention, so were the coverings. Jim was content with the blinds that came with the property, but Louise detested them, it made the room look like an office. The fact that Jim liked them was not Louise's only motivating factor for loathing them, she liked them fully open to maximise the natural light, Jim did not. She disliked the gloomy ambience that half opened blinds cast across a room, and the striking rays of light that filtered through the gaps in the slats. Louise refused to clean them, and Jim rarely did.

Jim came home from work to find them tied up like criminals caught by a vigilante Louise who was exceptionally pleased with her handy work. She had amateurly strung up nets and hoped it would hold. Louise knew that Jim wouldn't put the effort into removing them, so she just had to ride the storm. Patterned curtains now danced along the top of the radiators or fell in a cascade of thick lined material, the curtain poles clinging to the walls in a mixture of nails, grip-fill and crossed-fingers.

"Louise, it's Norman, Ell's gone into labour." came the panicked voice on the end of the phone. The remaining vestiges of sleep were abolished with the startling news. "I'll call you when I know more." said Noman and hung up before waiting for a reply.

Louise couldn't get back to sleep, the baby wasn't due for another month and waiting for news was tortuous. Louise had to stop herself from jumping in the car and heading to the hospital. Jim found Louise pacing the living room but disappeared to work, leaving his wife to agonisingly wait for news.

She had entertained every childbirth scenario and had convinced herself that something dreadful had happened. Despite the fact that she had been willing the phone to ring it still made her jump when it vibrated in her hand. Expecting to hear Norman's voice Louise was shocked by the feeble voice on the end of the phone.

"Mum, it's Ellen.   You've got a granddaughter".

"Congratulations sweetheart, I'm so proud of you, do you have a name yet? Ellen… Ellen are you there?" Louise replied, panic starting to fill her bones.

"It's me again Louise," interrupted Norman. "Ellen wanted to tell you herself, you know what's she's like. Anyway, the nurse said you can come in around six, they've had to take the baby down to the specialist unit. Louise, I think Ellen needs her mum".

With surprising resolve Louise ushered instructions for Norman to return to her daughter and headed off to Mothercare on a prenatal shopping spree. At six o'clock sharp she was stood in the maternity ward, again under the weight of balloons, teddys, nappies and Babygro's, a bewildered Jim at her side.

A harassed midwife waved the Wilsons in the direction of one of the rooms. Tentatively Louise knocked on the door. Ellen was sat up in bed, exhausted but satisfied, cradling a ball of cloth. On closer inspection her new granddaughter was huddled inside the layers of fabric, just a delicate nose, scrunched shut eyes and tiny fingers protruded from the hospital linen. Norman looked as beat as Ellen, his first marriage having not produced any offspring, but all the years of GP training didn't prepare him for the emotional arrival of his first born.

Jim tried to suggest that the men disappear to wet the baby's head, but the notion was met with death stares from both women. Although baby had arrived a month early she weighed an impressive four pound twelve ounces, which explained why Ellen looked like she was carrying twins. She had a good set of lungs on her, much to Jim's displeasure as she chose his time for cuddles to make her feelings known to the room. Jim thrust the new-born back at Louise who was more than happy to have the angelic bundle in her arms, screaming or otherwise. It was a reluctant Louise that handed back the yet-to-be-named bundle of joy.

Louise's elation was short lived as the Wilsons had an unexpected shock when they returned to the car park. Louise's beloved, yet scrappy, car had been in an altercation with another vehicle, and lost. There was a deep dent that ran from the back to the front. The bumper lay severed on the tarmac. Louise's car was a mangled muddle of metal and rubber. Louise called the AA whilst Jim reported the incident to hospital admin. The report from the garage the next day was not good news for Louise's trusted car. The repairs would outweigh the value making it economically unviable. Jim assured her that the insurance would pay for a new car, but to Louise that wasn't the point, she wanted her car. Louise out right lied to her husband and told him it had gone to the scrape yard. The scrape yard had been visited, but to salvage parts to repair her car. The mechanic thought she was insane, but it was custom. It was mostly cosmetic damage and this way Louise kept her car. Jim was beyond furious when he arrived home from work to find the car he thought was rusting was in fact sat smugly on the driveway. Louise was decked out in a superior smile and sexy undies, Jim's frustration forgotten with a wiggle and jiggle from his misleading wife.

32

Every time the phone went Louise thought it was the call that would reveal her granddaughters name. By day four she was getting increasingly irritated by the cold callers offering PPI claims or making inquiries about the accident she'd never had.

It was during a bloody operation on *Casualty* that Ellen chose to call with her final selection. With her face twisted into a picture of disgust and hands hovering by her head so she could cover her eyes Louise glared at Jim until he answered the phone. Jim ambled off muttering something about the "bloody TV". He was at a loss why Louise watched her medical dramas when most of it was spent behind a cushion. He was repulsed by the characters that popped up on reality programmes, was to sensible for the supernatural and hated soaps. Louise had asked him once what he considered the most effective weapon to kill an immortal and Jim had replied, "I don't like vampire or zombie movies". "I wasn't asking if you liked them, I asked how you would kill them". It was Louise's generic response, adapted to the current topic. Jim often replied with indirect answers to questions, it was like trying to get blood out of a stone sometimes. It was another area of their lives that they couldn't agree upon. She briefly considered how she would kill Jim if he were one of the undead. She disliked zombies so decided she'd hide and hope he went to eat Mrs Henderson instead.

"Hello Darling…... yep……… right ………… ok …… that's pretty ……… yes………I will…......bye." Jim hung up the phone and returned to his chair.

The fictional life or death operation was a success and the patient was recovering on the ward when Louise enquired after the caller. "Who was on the phone? Was it Ellen with a name at last?"

"Yea." grumbled Jim

"Well, what's she called?" snapped Louise.

"Oh, Sophia." answered her disinterested husband.

"Sophia," confirmed Louise "that's so beautiful."

"Um." replied Jim ruffling his paper indicating that the conversation was at an end.

Louise returned to her show, too exasperated with Jim to bother pursuing further communication. She should have known better, he wasn't a paternal person, she often wondered why she thought he would change with grandchildren.

The arrival of another generation had made Louise consider her own mortality. She devised a plan to get Jim to partake in more exercise, but not in the way that would have got him excited enough to be a willing participant. Her plan was to maximise the regions beauty and get Jim out into nature, after all he was a keen scout as a boy.

The novelty had worn off their rambling adventures and getting Jim motivated was as hard as raising a teenager from their bed before noon, in fact it was as hard as raising Jim before noon. Unperturbed Louise forged on with her health regime, offering Jim cues for involvement like deciding if they were heading to the woods or the cliffs, but not the beach, Louise didn't care for sand getting everywhere.

Today's hike took the Wilsons along a familiar path surrounded on one side by fields full of local flora and fauna and a sheer drop to the crashing waves on the other. Jim stood staring out to sea, the outline of an island peeking over the horizon, as the tides crashed against the jagged rocks below. Louise watched a large bumble bee move from plant to plant collecting pollen from the adjacent field. The winged assassin made a beeline for the Jim, providing Louise with a murderous situation.

Whilst stood admiring the coastal landscape his wife was concocting his death and fashioning a watery grave for her innocent husband. In Louise's mind the bee provided the motive. She innocently defended herself against the onslaught of the winged beast, waving her arms around in a valiant attempt to remain sting free. In the commotion her husband was knocked off the cliff and plummeted to his untimely end. Mission complete the stripy accomplish flew away and Louise retraced her steps back down the trail and to a life of freedom.

Jim penetrated Louise's daydream as he called "Earth to Louise".

"Can we go now?" he asked once he had his wives' attention.

"Sure love" she replied, and they made their way back home, Jim catching his wife's hand to steady her on the uneven surface. Louise's cheeks burnt momentarily with shame.

Louise prided herself on her birthday celebration organisational skills. She had a reputation in the family for pulling off spectacular shindigs and was more than happy to don the crown of party queen. She had her work cut out for her this year as Jim's fiftieth birthday was fast approaching and he was notoriously hard to please.

Jim had no hobbies that didn't involve either the latest technology or the two metallic pride and joys nestled in the garage. Louise wasn't in the remotest bit technologically minded and steered clear of the vehicles, so she didn't dent them. She hadn't heard him mention needing anything and Jim was less than subtle with his hint dropping.

She's been considering getting him an experience, after all they had everything they needed, and Jim could go out and buy anything he wanted. Despite owning two racing machines Jim showed only a passing interest in motor sports on TV and had declined any previous suggestions of a day at Silverstone. Jim had never been into football so that was a fight that never happened in the Wilson houschold, and it was a strike for any present ideas.

On principal Louise refused to entertain the idea of seasons tickets to next year's Wimbledon. Though it was very British with the rain, cream teas, strawberry's and all, it was torture to Louise. Jim loved the sport, but Louise loathed it, watching a ball being hit back and forth, blah blah blah. Jim had never been into gambling, a few pennies in arcade machines, hence a day at the races would be wasted.

Louise was starting to lose her mind trying to find the perfect gift. She had multiple search tabs open, trip advisor verifying credentials, google maps calculating distances and a glass of wine to keep her focused.

The wine did not help her focus and she found she was thinking of ways that a healthy lifestyle could have a killer effect on Jim. The first death was at the hands of his preferred sport. After a brutal defeat in a doubles match Louise sliced and diced her losing spouse with the tennis racket. By the time she had finished her husband had been reduced to a pile of cube shaped bits of Jim. His next athletic death came on an olympic track. A rogue javelin targeted Jim as he completed laps of the indoor course. He was speared like an Amazonian fish. A stray dart took the same trajectory as the javelin and found its mark through the centre of Jim's eye.

To lighten the fantasy the Wilsons were playing a friendly game of snooker. Louise was lining up the winning shot. She hit the shiny black ball with the force of an elephant and it shot off the table like a bullet from a gun. The ball connected with Jim's forehead, right between the eyes, and he fell to the floor. To add insult to injury Louise performed a world class trick shot, each ball falling in timed succession onto Jim's already dented head. His body convulsed with every individual impact until the final ball fell into Jim's open mouth, and he expired.

Neither Wilson had ever been a gym rat, Louise had joined the odd class over the years, but nothing had ever lasted. Louise would have loved for Jim's body to be more appealing and sculpted, as she was sure he would prefer she didn't wobble so much but had never forced him to exercise. She tried once, bought him a membership as a present. It went down as well as a man buying his wife a vacuum cleaner for her birthday. She hadn't approached the subject since. Imaginary Jim had decided to hit the weights with vigour. He metamorphosed from a beer bellied couch potato into a six-pack adrenalin junkie. However, pretend Jim was not content with his transformation and pushed his bulging biceps to breaking point. Jim did one strenuous repetition to many and his muscles burst spraying Jim all over the equipment.

Satisfied, Louise recommenced her search for the ideal gift. She settled on a flight, now all she had to decide was plane, glider or helicopter.

33

The kids wanted to organise a surprise birthday party. They were great with ideas, but the actual planning and payment was left to Louise. Following a family meeting, minus Jim, the theme, venue, and date were decided. Gangsters, the function room of the local, the weekend after Jim turns half a century.

The flight was booked, and Louise was very proud of herself. She was highly regarded for her unique taste in gifts and ability to organise a memorable get-together but had outdone herself this year.

Although the topic of birthdays had been suspiciously sparse of late Jim was sure that his wife had not forgotten. She'd tried to forget her own on a few occasions but never anybody else's.

As the big day approached Louise informed Jim that she had booked a table and that the kids would join them for a meal. Disappointingly he had to wait until the weekend to accommodate the grandchildren's care. Jim, a little perturbed at the understated turn his celebrations had taken had assumed that fifty years would have elicited a more excited response from his nearest and dearest.

Louise presented Jim with her gift on the commemoration of his birth, over a home cooked, non-frozen tea. Well the chips were frozen but the steak and veg were fresh, and costly, from a newly established farm shop. Beautiful produce at a price reserved for special occasions.

Louise had left an envelope beside his plate, Jim's name inscribed in calligraphy on the front. He tore open the hand-crafted paper like an expectant teenager. Bemused, he turned over the card, a spoilt child looking for the rest of his gift. Louise had to compose herself, take a deep breath, before sweetly explaining the exact nature of his present.

"We thought you'd like it," explained Louise, realising that she was crediting the children with her own idea "you get to fly the plane yourself."

"Ahh." was not the response that Louise had expected.

"I thought it would be different. You always say you like flying." replied Louise defensively. She hadn't envisioned having to inject excitement into the recipient.

"Yea, yea, it's a good idea, thank you." came Jim's compulsory reply.

Louise did the dishes, as usual, too frustrated at Jim's lack of enthusiasm that she couldn't even muster a fantasy. Putting on a brave face and plastering on a forced smile she spent the evening at her husband's bidding. A family tradition that the birthday person gets treated like a god, for the day. No longer oblivious to the offence he had caused with the response to his carefully selected gift Jim was attentive the following day, guilt niggling him into submission.

The children had been tasked with getting the decorations to the venue. Not that Louise couldn't but because they should. She was sure that Ellen would do her proud, no matter how hard it was to relinquish the responsibility to another. Louise knew that the small gathering of family, friends and neighbours would be assembled before they arrived and sent a discreet arrival text as Jim parked the car. They waited in the bar whilst the staff 'got their table ready'. Jim led the way, ignorant to the hidden group ready to celebrate the Wilson patriarch.

A riotous reception greeted Jim as everyone shouted either "Surprise or Happy Birthday" in unison. Jim nearly broke Louise's foot as he jumped back, momentarily scared and disoriented by the welcoming. Jim calmed down and assured the guests that he was not suffering from a heart attack. Ellen had done a good job, if not a little overboard, with the decoration. '50' glittered at Jim from every corner of the room on banners and balloons. The gangster theme had fallen by the wayside in favour of table props for the selfie loving generation.

The meal was lovely and the company entertaining. The evening went swimmingly with laughter and anecdotes filling the room.

Louise, full and content, soaked up the atmosphere. She couldn't help falling into a daydream as the light reflected mesmerizingly off one of the many helium balloons that bobbed around the room. Fantasy Jim was celebrating his birthday too but was in more of a drunken state than the original version. Fantasy Louise tied masses of helium balloons to Jim and watched him float away. She visualised herself waving to Jim as he left the atmosphere, his thrashing body silhouetted against a full moon.

Back to reality Louise looked longingly at one of the balloons. Louise was a logical person at times and her own mind would pose problems with the fantasy. She couldn't help questioning herself on how she could manage to tie enough balloons to Jim, to make him air bound, before he stopped her. She decided that Jim would have to be paralytic, or unconscious, for her to even get close to achieving this mammoth feat. And, if she managed it, how many balloons would be needed to lift a grown man? Thousands she imagined.

Jim booked his flight.

The forecast had been clear, but the day was cloudy. The airfield was hoping for better visibility, but it was safe to fly so they would be going ahead, the views just wouldn't be as spectacular. Jim had mandatory training and safety checks before he would be allowed inside the cockpit.

Louise sat in the purpose-built profitable café whilst Jim prepared for his co-piloted ride. She'd started a new book about space pirates and dragons. The kids turned up, families in tow, disturbing the peaceful realms of Linaria in which Louise was engrossed, spellbound by the adventures of Moroda.

The Wilsons congregated on the air strip to observe Jim ascend to the clouds. He waved nervously at the spectators as the small plane trundled down the runway and lifted into the air. They disappeared into the distance until they were a spec on the horizon.

Jim hadn't had any private lessons, he'd been on plenty of flights but only ever as a passenger. Louise imagined possible aerial disasters. There was a mid-air collision. Jim's plane entered a cloud, unbeknown that fellow air travellers were playing a dangerous game of hide'n'seek. His plane struck an aircraft which was hiding inside the cloud and 'boom", one player down.

In another comic scenario Jim was on a sight-seeing tour when he gets excited at the sprawling landscape below and accidently hits the emergency button and ejects the pilot from the plane. As the puzzled pilot glides back down to earth Jim and his winged coffin nose dive from the sky and crash land in a debris of dirt, metal and trees.

Louise was woken from her imagination as the tannoy buzzed with the announcement that Jim's plane was heading back and would soon be visible, and that Jim was at the controls. Louise looked on in fascinated horror as the plane wings wobbled whilst Jim made his decent. With closed eyes and fingers crossed Louise waited for a gasp of fear or cheer of excitement. He landed it with precision and walked away, intact.

Jim left armed with leaflets and positive intentions. All the way home he talked about the scenery, the freedom, the adrenalin and of getting his pilot's licence. Louise hadn't seen Jim so passionate for years. He got riled up over politics and annoyed at parking charges, but he seemed genuinely excited at the prospect of learning to fly. Louise was ecstatic that her birthday treat had inspired her husband however by the time they got home she was beginning to regret it.

34

A week in and everything was aviation oriented. It was like Jim had been possessed by the spirit of Amelia Earhart. A small wooden replica of the plane Jim had flown appeared on the mantlepiece and a pile of books had materialised on the coffee table. The most surprising thing was Louise didn't even know Jim owned a library card, wasn't sure he even knew where the library was. If it was possible Jim was doing even less around the house. After tea he would scuttle into his study and pour over the pages of his borrowed books. Even the grandkids were being treated to tales of the sky.

Louise had heard of a football widow and had friends whose husbands would disappear for the weekend with just their fishing rods for company, but Jim had always been consistent in his lack of inspiration. Louise envied her friends but now she was in the same predicament she felt a bit lonely at times, and disgruntled that Jim's minimal household duties had decreased further.

Louise left Jim sleeping, as she usually did and got on with the day. The sun was shining, the birds were singing, and Louise had a list as long as her arm to get through. She tidied up from the night before, removing sweet packets and an empty beer can discarded by the sofa. As she toiled away she was taunted by the polished wood of the model plane gleaming at her. Nothing else shone with the care and attention that Jim lavished on his treasured possession, including the ornaments that stood dusty beside it.

Unknown to Louise, the day was going to spiral into an uncontrollable mess. The first incident in a series of unfortunate but comical events to befall Louise was the sporadic set of traffic lights that were tormenting the drivers trapped at its mercy. The three-way setup had been programmed by an imbecile for it followed no logical pattern. Instead of allowing a stream of cars from each angle the lights allowed a possession through, then a handful from the next queue before reverting back, ignoring the line that Louise was in. The expectant driver in pole position almost ran a red light and Louise was hovering over the accelerator in anticipation. When the light decided they could go only three cars managed to escape before the red light halted progress. Frustrated Louise swore at the lights and waited, almost patiently. Eight minutes after joining the stagnant line of traffic Louise was admitted passage to continue her journey.

When she reached the supermarket, it appeared that the inhabitants of the town were all experiencing a case of Mother Hubbard and needed to fill their bare cupboards. The car park was full, every space filled with some cars abandoned precariously by their hungry owners. Louise lapped the car park three times before finding a departing couple and swopping into the space before another driver did. She began to wish she'd abandoned the trip when she saw the chaos on the shop floor. Had she missed a weather bulletin forecasting snow? Through gritted teeth Louise weaved through packed trollies, screaming children and geriatric shoppers to purchase the weeks groceries. Her main mission was to track down an ironing board as the faithful servant that had lasted twenty years, and numerous repairs, had finally supported its last pair of trousers. Mission complete Louise gave her sympathies to the harassed till staff before loading her purchases and joining yet another queue to exit. As the car idled in traffic her remaining fuel dwindled forcing Louise to make a pitstop before returning home.

The garage was deserted, seemingly nobody needed fuel for their cars, just themselves.

"Number twenty-two" announced Louise confidently to the cashier.

"Don't you mean twenty-two pounds of fuel Ma'am?" replied the amused cashier, looking at the empty forecourt, with its six pumps.

Why could she never remember the number of the pump, it always happened. Did the automatic doors of the kiosk contain a memory altering devise that removed the knowledge when you entered? "Sorry yes," said an embarrassed Louise as she held her card against the machine. "Not a problem Ma'am, happens all the time" smiled the experienced worker.

Louise was hungry and ready for lunch. She almost stopped off at McDonalds but her boot full of frozen food dissuaded her from taking the lazy option.

Louise noticed instantly that the curtains in their bedroom were still drawn which meant one of two things. Jim was either still in bed or was being too lazy to let sunlight drown the room. Either were possible but Louise knew which one to bet on.

With her mouth pinched tightly, and nostrils flaring Louise stormed into the house all guns blazing and took the stairs two at a time. She unceremoniously threw the curtains back causing a stream of sunlight to flood the room and blind Jim's sleeping form. A groan emitted from the slothful mate as sleep left him and he registered his wife's annoyed form retreating from the scene of idleness. The words "noon" and several swear words were all that she left in her wake.

On waking Jim resembled a disgruntled rodent with molelike eyes, squinting at the bright light of day. His hair looked like he'd been pulled through a hedge backward, especially against Louise's styled mane. Jim attempted to fix the greying mop on his head, incoherent grunts filtered to an irritated Louise. It wasn't that Jim was a night owl, it was his lack of energy and tardiness on a morning that kept him awake at night, he just wasn't tired. His job was not physically demanding, and he avoided the gym like the plague. Also, he only gained control of the TV when Louise had retired to bed or fallen asleep on the sofa, so she was partly to blame. His body clock wasn't geared for early mornings he'd argue to counter Louise's accusations of laziness. Louise had spent some twenty plus years of his last fifty trying to prise him from between the lush cotton sheets of the martial bed.

The block of cheese bore the brunt of Louise frustration. The chokingly thick doorstop wedges nestled with pungent onion on a bed of salad cream between slices of bakery bread.

Louise happily allowed her mind to wander and serve Jim up with a side of suffering and a main course of death. Already incapacitated with slumber the execution should have been the easiest yet. Using her pillow, she held it over Jim's face in an attempt to smother him. As he struggled for breath his flight or fight response kicked in and he fought against his murderous wife. Fearing she would lose the battle Louise sat on the pillow. She pinned Jim's flailing arms under her legs and used her weight to gain the advantage. She continued to pin Jim down as his strength diminished. Tiny feathers tickled his throat as he inhaled the pillows stuffing, pulled through the fabric by his desperate gasps to cling to life. Jim was still for several minutes before Louise released her hold on the soft weapon. Dream Jim was dead. Louise retuned the pillow and made the bed as best she could with the form of her forever asleep husband in residence. With a wiping of her hands and a smile on her face Louise nodded at her handiwork and left the room, satisfied.

Jim gratefully received his breakfast/lunch combo, keeping his eyes downcast to avoid the contemptuous gaze of his other half.

The fantasy had dampened her irritation with the day, but her mood had not settled, and she still felt agitated. Louise was no preacher, she hated negativity and she tried to live a happy life but sometimes she felt that obstacles were put in the way just to try her. If she was religious, she'd say God was testing her but as it was she knew it was just the trials and tribulations of life. She tried to stay positive, but she had an evil side, could hold a grudge to eternity and back. She loathed to speak ill of others but if you crossed her there was no going back. People say that they wouldn't wish it on their worst enemy, Louise would, or that you wouldn't piss on them if they were on fire, Louise wouldn't, she'd throw alcohol to fuel the flames. Today was turning into 'one of those days'. Louise hurried with the cleaning before completing the days tasks; a trip to the charity shop to make a deposit and a trip to the tip to dump her rickety old ironing board.

Avoiding the traffic lights Louise went the long way into town, which was still quicker with the crazy lights dictating journeys. Delivering the bags to the charity shop was a moments work. Louise thought her fortunes were looking up as space right outside the shop presented itself as she drove up the steep street.

Arriving at the recycling centre there was a parking space right beside the dumpster she required. Her fortunes were looking up. Leaving the keys in the ignition she closed the drivers' door and pulled on the handle of the rear door. Nothing happened. She pulled again but the door wouldn't open. Not thinking anything of it she went to open the drivers' door, but it wouldn't budge. Pulling violently at the handle Louise's heart skipped a beat as the cold realisation set in that she was locked out of her car. She frantically, and fruitlessly, ran around the car desperately yanking on all the handles in the desperate hope that one would miraculously open. She was sure she'd pressed the unlock button but must not have. Realising that she was stranded, she couldn't call Jim for help because her phone was sitting torturously in her handbag on the passenger seat, she pleaded with staff for the use of a phone, but Jim was not answering any device. With the centre closing in less than an hour Louise was in a quandary. She could call the AA, but her phone and membership details were in the car, and they'd likely be longer than an hour, she could keep calling Jim, she could smash a window to gain entry, or she could run home and grab the spare set of keys. Louise was confident she'd just make it, so she set off on foot.

By the time she got home she was a hot puffing mess, her chest was heaving, and she was wheezing from the exercise. To her surprise the front door was locked. Jim hadn't said he was going anywhere, not that she was really speaking to him and his van was still on the drive. Frantic, Louise was temporarily unsure on her next course of action. The key box which housed a spare key had rusted shut from lack of use. At a loss and with time rapidly running out Louise grabbed a stone from the garden and started trying to smash the box off the wall. The din that she was causing as rock struck metal had caused Jim to emerge from his hiding place. What on earth was he doing next door questioned Louise.

It was an understatement to say Jim was shocked to find his partner in such a state, angry tears gushing down her face as she attacked the key box, her knuckles bloody from scraping against the wall. She told him what had happened between sobs. Jim gave her a cuddle and together they took Jim's van to retrieve the stranded vehicle.

Louise's cheeks were still red, and she could feel the heat radiating from her face as she stood in the kitchen preparing tea, over an hour after the humiliating episode.

35

Jim had an amused look all night. Though he was sympathetic to Louise's plight she felt that he was just a nudge away from bursting into laughter over his wife's calamitous day.

What was Jim doing next door Louise wondered. They had a good relationship with their neighbours, but Jim wasn't inclined to be the most social creature Louise in the world. He would moan if they were invited for a summer BBQ or a winter tipple. Since Mr Henderson had departed this world his dedicated wife had taken to asking the Wilsons for help. Louise had never seen any family and there were no photos of young or grown children on the walls. Not one to pry, Louise never investigated further. Usually Heather Henderson would conveniently happen upon Louise as she got home from work or put out the rubbish. A plea for help would normally follow and Jim would be dispatched to change the lightbulb, cut the grass or fix a cupboard. Louise knew Heather to be roughly ten years her senior, but she looked weathered for her age. Heathers hair was white, and she was tentative in her step, appearing fragile beyond her years. All home cooked meals and sewing Heather put Louise's domesticated knowhow to shame.

Unable to stem her curiosity Louise asked Jim "What did Heather want you for yesterday?

"My body!" replied Jim, his face showing no hint of mockery.

Unsure if Jim was serious Louise's official reply was "Huh, say that again." and under her breath she muttered "and a trip to Specsavers."

"She just wanted some company and you were out." answered Jim innocently.

"Ok, that was kind of you." came Louise's suspicious response.

"Yea. I'm off to see mum now." Jim said, ending the conversation with a depressed tone. Louise was perplexed over not getting a straight answer. Although not really suspecting that Jim had been up to no good with Mrs Henderson she couldn't help the tiny niggle of doubt that took up residence in her gut.

Mary's dementia had worsened, and she no longer recognised him. It was heart-breaking for Jim to visit her and see his beloved mother a shell of the loving care giver that she once was. Louise didn't go anymore. The home they had chosen for her was a lovely building set in landscaped gardens with professional staff and high fences. Neither Jim nor Louise had the time needed to provide adequate care, and this way Jim didn't have to witness his mother's decline on a daily basis.

Jim was distraught when he got home. Mary's weight had plummeted. The staff were in a constant battle as Mary would forget to eat and refuse food as she "wasn't hungry". Louise feared that Mary would not be long for this world. At least she would be reunited with Jim's dad and her only son could properly grieve the loss of his mother. He had painfully accepted that the person Mary was had been lost but he couldn't move on whilst her body remained, an empty image of a wonderful woman.

Louise phoned her own mum, guilty that she was sometimes a bit sparse in communication. Joan was feisty and had more sense than most and the only cause for concern she gave her daughters was what was she going to do next.

Jim was compliant in odd job requests from family, friends and neighbours but when it came to doing jobs at home Jim's attitude was out of sight out of mind. What bothered Louise didn't register with Jim, yet Louise could easily live with faults that Jim deemed repair worthy. Louise was no good at D.I.Y, she'd always give it a go but just didn't have the mindset. Louise would point out a job and wait for Jim to put it right. When she got fed up of waiting for Jim to do a job she'd do it herself. Or bodge it as Jim would say but she fairly gave him every change to man up and do it before ploughing in herself. Louise was reasonably competent with a screwdriver, dangerous with a hammer, downright lethal with a drill and stuck many things together she shouldn't with superglue. But she tried. Every time she went into the spare room the lopsided door on the wardrobe taunted her. Technically the kid's rooms were spare now, but Louise still regarded them as Frank and Ellen's rooms, every ready in case one needed to come back home. To Jim there was always an excuse not to repair it, besides it wasn't as if anyone stayed in it expect

Louise's sister Fran. Sometimes a note written to 'herself' to fix something, left in plain view, had the desired effect and Jim would jump into action but not this time. Armed with a tool box and plenty of determination Louise did it herself.

Every D.I.Y job left its mark on Louise. Usually in a physical way, a cut hand, a bashed finger or a dented toe, they rarely produced satisfaction alone. Today was no exception. Louise got her finger trapped, the blood welling to the surface but finding no broken skin to escape. It smarted as Louise sat down for a well-deserved rest, and hot chocolate.

Louise looked at her injured digit and couldn't help but find Jim responsible. After all, if he'd fixed the wardrobe like he'd been asked she wouldn't have had to risk life and limb to do it. Her trivial annoyance gave way to a kill Jim fantasy, the open tool box her inspiration. She had ample choice of murder weapon, duct tape to tie up the victim and a saw to chop up the body.

Louise could stab him with a screw driver. The handles have good grips, so she should be able to plunge one through the delicate layers of flesh. The bradawl was super pointy and poked nice holes in wood, so it should poke some holes in Jim. The Stanley knife was strong, but the blade wasn't long so would only suffice to slash a throat or wrist. The handful of salvaged screws and nails would make for a nasty pie or mini projectiles but probably wouldn't cause death. She could use the saw as a weapon, but the blade was bendy and unpredictable and would serve better to slap him than murder him. The hammer presented the opportunity to bash his head in, not a unique use for this tool. The bunch of allen-keys were useless, too blunt and small to render operational as an offense weapon. She came to a similar conclusion of the pliers. Great for torture to extract a tooth or twist off a dangling appendage but Louise would have needed some muscle to brain Jim with it. The final tool in her arsenal was a chisel. It could possibly be used to stab or beat Jim. As she stayed clear of power tools she had none to hand to fuel the fantasy but couldn't help thinking of the havoc she could cause with one. It would be over quicker, but the blood splatter would have been further reaching and harder to clean up.

Jim was methodical in his repair work, which explained why he remained injury free. Louise on the other hand just wanted it done and her fingers were usually the casualty of her eagerness.

When he got home from work Louise was waiting for Jim and indicated for him to follow her upstairs. Jim nearly had a heart attack, he thought his luck was in. The disappointment was evident on his face when he realised that he wasn't getting his end away and that Louise had brought up him to show off her handiwork.

"You're proud of yourself, aren't you?" stated Jim rather than asking.

"Yes I am thank you." replied Louise smiling triumphantly as she walked out the room, leaving a dumbfounded Jim to ponder on whether to repair Louise's efforts or to leave it. To her credit the door was no longer lopsided, and it opened and closed with only a slight stiffness.

36

Though they'd been man and wife for decades they had varying tastes in film, tv and music. 'Opposites attract' is what Jim used in reply to any comment or argument from Louise on the subject. Every year Jim moaned he'd never been to see a live tennis match at Wimbledon. Louise had never stopped him, just refused to go. Whereas Louise had always wanted to go to a film convention and Jim had always found an excuse not to take her. She'd threatened to go on her own countless times, but her pleas had always fallen on deaf ears, Jim calling her bluff.

Frank had been making an annual pilgrimage to see his comic heroes for years but had failed to invite Louise, despite her hint dropping. Her time had finally come, and she'd been invited. It was for her babysitting ability as much anything, but she relished any time with Jared so jumped at the chance. Frank was never one for forward planning, so Louise was only given two days' notice and reduced to rummage around the house to muster up an adequate costume.

Jim wasn't interested in coming. He'd been complaining of a headache for a few days, so Louise was happy to leave him at home.

Meeting in the packed car park Louise was in awe. Three different sized Spiderman walked past to join an array of Marvel characters before a call of "Avengers unite" rumbled across the crowd and the group descended on the venue. Louise was glad she had made some form of effort and not turned up in her civvies, she would have stood out as a non-costumed attendee. She had used her posh Halloween frock, a medieval style dress that she loved but had little occasion to wear. If anybody asked she'd say she was from Game of Thrones or Merlin, or something like that.

Louise let the convention veteran take the lead. It was sensory overload, there were people everywhere, swarming amongst the stalls, security guards and celebrities. Louise's headed wiped from left to right trying to take it all in all whilst retaining a gentle yet unescapable grip on Jared, so he didn't get lost.

"Oh that's, umm, oh, it's thingy from, um, oh that show your dad likes." Stammered Louise in admiration, her voice diminished in the din of traders and excited cos players.

Jared was in his element, surrounded by real life versions of his heroes his eyes were in a permeant state of excitement, his grin as big as the Jokers. Louise soon learnt that dressing-up wasn't just reserved for school children, there was a whole fandom out there of adults imitating their favourite tv, film, cartoon or comic book characters, indulging in harmless cos-play. By mid-day Louise's memory card was full of pictures of Jared beaming with superhero's, the cast of Star Wars as well as character's that Louise had not seen or heard of but were clearing part of Jared's universe.

Lunch-time brought a lull in the proceedings with the noise level dropping to a soft murmur. Jared, and Louise, were exhausted from a star-struck morning. The cos-players had retired to fuel up for an afternoon of crazy antics and role play and the celebs had taken a break from signing, smiling, posing and chatting.

Frank and Triny took back their parental responsibilities allowing Louise to have a wander around the stalls and decide if she wanted to meet any stars. She didn't recognise the majority, she'd heard of the shows but hadn't watched them.

Sitting and relaxing with her son and his family Louise watched the cos-players as they began to filter back through and commence their role play scenarios.

Louise allowed herself her own fantasy where Jim had accompanied her but fallen prey to overzealous amateur actors. Despite his aversion to the cold-blooded ones Louise's mind had dressed Jim in a Dracula outfit. Unfortunately for Jim, with the popularity of steampunk, a group had dressed as Van Helsing and his band of monster slayers. Spotting their prey, the reality challenged group began their hunt, chasing a confused and screaming Jim around the room. Thinking it an over-active dramatization the crowd stood by and watched, cheering on the hunters, booing vampire Jim. Out-numbered, Jim was captured, and a stake driven through his heart to stop his supposed immortal body from resurrecting. The event organisers quickly removed Jim's body, the blood trail evidence washed away as elaborate Hollywood makeup and Jim declared an exceptional actor. In another Jim had taken on the persona of a mutated creature, which was vanquished in a battle of blades by fellow commy-conners. A Potter inspired fantasy saw a Death Eater Jim conquered by a particularly vindictive wizard wielding a wand and uttering the killing curse "Avada Kedavra" to a chorus of "I destroy as I speak".

Amused and refreshed Louise was back on granny duty for the afternoon and she had her own battle to contend with. The temptation of all the toys combined with the fun and excitement of the Marvel universe under one roof was just too much for Jared. He'd turned from a bundle of excitement into an agitated ball of energy. Louise chose not to meet any stars of stage or screen, mostly for fear of how they would react to the demon child she had in tow. There were a few faces she vaguely recognised but none she was keen to get up close and personal with, so she took Jared outside in the hopes that the fresh air would freshen his attitude. It didn't but a cuddle and lullaby from Granny induced his afternoon nap and peace was restored. Louise's arms felt like she'd done a thousand press-ups by the time Frank and Triny noted their absence and had come to find them.

"It's just as well you're a natural grandma." Triny said to Louise as she gazed upon her sleeping son. "You'll be super busy in six months' time."

It took a few seconds for the comment to register but when the realisation sunk in that Triny was pregnant Louise could have jumped with joy. However, she was restricted from embracing them in cuddles as she was still cradling Jared. Her ear-to-ear smile showed her genuine pleasure.

"You'll have to retire Mum, be a full time Nanny." suggested Frank, raising his eyebrows in jest.

"If only son, I'll be eighty before I get to retire." replied Louise, loving the notion but hating the reality.

Louise couldn't wait to tell Jim that grandchild number three was on its way. She was ecstatic that Jared was to get a new brother or sister. When she got home she found Jim on the sofa, with his head in his hands. She initially thought he'd fallen asleep but as she muttered under her breath about laziness Jim responded that he wasn't feeling well.

It transpired that Jim had been sent home from work. His persistent headache was still gnawing at his skull and he felt rough, uncoordinated. Jim was rarely ill, so Louise was sympathetic, helping Jim to his feet and up the stairs. Her bedside manner was second to none when the illness was sincere. His usual bouts of sickness coincided with self-induced activities such as a night out with the boys, or a dodgy takeaway so he received no sympathy from his wife on these occasions. It was still early, but Jim looked exhausted and let Louise mother him. It was rare she was this attentive anymore, so he was making the most of it, appreciative between the waves of pain that shimmered across his body and mind.

37

A trip to the doctors provided little in the way of relief. Usually it would take days of nagging to get him to see the GP. Not this time, which instilled a slither of nerves in Louise that she was not yet ready to succumb to. "It's probably a virus." they were told, "Rest, drink plenty of water and come back in a few days if you haven't improved." was the medical advice they were given.

Trusting the professionals Jim took up residence on the sofa with the remote, a tradition of the sick off work or school, a blanket covering him from chin to toes.

Louise had a shift so left Jim with a stock of water and snacks, and the phone.

When she returned Jim was in the same position, but his supply of food had dwindled to empty wrappers strewn haphazardly in his general vicinity. There was a faint scent lingering in the air that Louise couldn't place. An aroma of flowers that was vaguely familiar to Louise, it reminded her of someone.

"Can you make me a cuppa love?" asked Jim, his voice pleadingly innocent.

"Sure." countered Louise as she rounded up the stained evidence suggesting that he had been consuming a steady supply all day. As Louise picked up the last cup she detected a whiff of Jasmine, only slight and for an instance but the scent was unmistakable.

The smell played on Louise's mind as she brewed a fresh batch of coffee. Louise struggled to remember where she knew the scent from. She didn't wear perfume, and there were no air fresheners in the house that smelt like that. Louise rolled her eyes at the state she found her kitchen in. There were water drops on the worktop, the sugar bowl was empty, the milk on its last few drops, and teaspoons abandoned on the draining board. Jim's excuse was he didn't know where Louise kept spare sugar and he was too poorly to tidy up after himself. Couldn't be bothered and too lazy was more accurate Louise thought to herself. Substituting cream for milk and filling up the sugar bowl Louise allowed her frustrations to boil into a quick fantasy as steam from the kettle filtered around the kitchen.

Instead of a steamy mug of aromatic coffee fantasy Louise served up a helping of frying pan. Walking serenely into the living room imaginary Jim looked up, expecting to be handed a caffeinated drink but instead saw the hefty metal pan seconds before it impacted with his face. Louise chose the largest pan she could find, it was an inch off being a wok, and it had a large handle allowing Louise to get a firm grip, with both hands. It only took four heavy blows to resolve Jim's headache forever.

On returning with the freshly brewed mug of coffee Louise caught another whiff of perfumed scent. She almost yelled out loud when the eureka moment hit. The smell was Lily of the valley. She knew it well as it was her nan's perfume of choice. She'd loved it that much that, when Louise was little, she thought she used to bathe in the stuff. The fragrance always arrived before her nan did and lingered for days after she left. The memory brought Louise to tears, her nan had been gone for donkey's years. When Louise had calmed down she rationalised that there was a reasonable explanation for the smell. She briefly entertained the idea that her nan had made a ghostly visit to check on her granddaughter but dismissed it as nonsense. Louise spent the evening pondering her puzzle. She racked her brains for the source, but it remained elusive until bed time. As she was drifting off to sleep she had the sudden realisation that their next-door neighbour, Mrs Henderson, also wore Lily of the Valley. Louise knew she did as she'd bought her a bottle years ago as a Christmas present. That meant that Heather had been over whilst she was at work, yet Jim hadn't said a word.

Louise had a fretful night's sleep and the first thing on her mind when she woke was her neighbour. Louise lay awake, waiting for her alarm to go off, thinking about the unfaithful reasons for Heathers visit. Jim had barely the strength to walk up the stairs, so she didn't think he'd done the dirty, but it did leave the question of their sudden exaggerated friendship.

Even at work Louise was distracted. Would Heather be at there's? What would her other neighbours be thinking?

She absentmindedly waved in response to the greeting from warehouse Joe and Skinny Skyla's remarks fell on deaf ears. The only person getting under Louise's skin today was her neighbour. The latest anti-social antics at Bull Heights didn't break Louise's preoccupied façade, even the customers noted that Louise's mind was not on the job.

The journey back home was to test Louise's patience further as an accident had caused a tail back. A car had collided with a bike. Twisted shards of metal and sprinklings of glittering glass were strewn across the road. The sirens of the ambulance faded into the distance as the cyclist was rushed to hospital. Police scurried around gathering evidence and preparing to reopen the road. The traumatised driver was sat in the back of a squad car while they waited for a second ambulance to arrive. Owing to the width of the section of road involved most travellers were stranded in the queue. Louise didn't even attempt to turn her battered saloon around as she was sure she'd get it stuck and have to have the fireman come and rescue her. Tempting as the option was Louise decided to stay put. She texted Jim to say she'd be late. It took ten minutes to get the reply 'K', the 'O' being too much for Jim to text as well.

A handsome young police officer in a fluorescent high-vis jacket informed the patient queue that they should be on their way in about fifteen minutes, thanking them for their patience. Louise reclined the driver's seat backwards, so she could relax whilst the scene was cleared of debris and the mangled metal removed. Louise allowed herself to daydream, the crash her muse.

There were so many ways that Jim could die at the hands of a motor vehicle. He could drive head on into a tree or a lamppost, he could drive of a cliff and plummet to his doom. He could be driving too fast, lose control, and smash the car into a wall or swerve to avoid an obstruction and roll the car, shaken like a maraca. Jim was momentarily the victim of a hit-and-run driver, bounced around the road like a ball. In another fantasy he chose to ignore the train signal and became stranded on the track, a high-speed city train dragging Jim and his car to the next station. Not all deaths were the fault of Jim, some were down to vengeful acts. Cutting the breaks lead Jim to a fatal crash. His foot pumped helplessly on the pedal, but the car didn't slow down. The car gained traction as it sped down hill, it's destination either a coach full of elderly tourists or the low wall of the docks. Hero Jim saved the passengers and doomed himself, the wall failing as a crash barrier allowing Jim to plummet into the sub-zero depths of the river below.

Louise ended this round of Jim's deaths with an unfortunate accident. She pictured Jim, at home, maintaining his beloved Lotus. Propped up on blocks he was working underneath the car, a range of tools within easy reach. Unexpectedly the blocks holding up the car exploded causing the one hundred and seventy-three stone vehicle to crush Jim. Louise was brought back to reality with the sound of engines firing back up, forcing her to leave Jim laying flattened beneath his worshipped machine, the wicked husband of the south.

Jim was still suffering. He was complaining that his head was even worse, his face deathly pale. He was nauseous too. Louise rang the doctors for an appointment. The duty doctor phoned her back, begrudgingly agreeing to see Jim after Louise threatened to jump the queue and head straight to hospital.

She wished she had. The usual waiting time applied, forty-five minutes after your scheduled appointment. The GP was with Jim for less than five minutes before declaring that he needed to be admitted to hospital. If Louise couldn't leave with him immediately they'd get an ambulance to take him. Having seen enough of the emergency services that day Louise opted to drive Jim. He'd be in the hands of the professionals within thirty minutes, the main hospital was only in the next town.

The journey took a hair raising seventeen minutes. Louise shaved vital seconds off by ignoring the speed limits, challenging amber lights and taking a few short cuts, known only to explorative locals.

Jim was whisked away by a matronly woman, sympathetic yet stern. Louise was lead to the family room to wait for news. The cosy area was filled with out-of-date magazines and children's toys that had seen better days.

Louise found herself blindly staring at the small TV mounted on the wall. It was tuned to a news channel, the volume low and the remote M.I.A. The accident had made the evening news. It transpired that the car had clipped the wheel of the bike. Inevitable really, the road narrowed in many places, to the point were two vehicles would end up in a metallic love affair should they happen to meet. The driver had rounded a bend and the bike was there. Oncoming traffic prevented him from swerving to the right and the built-up hedge verges stopped him hankering left. Despite breaking, the slow-moving bike was nudged sending the inexperienced rider careening off his bike and into the path of on-coming traffic. The rider sustained broken bones. Nobody was charged in relation to the accident.

38

Louise was on her fourth cup of watery tea by the time somebody came to see her. An exhausted consultant in dark blue scrubs made brief introductions before launching into a medically laced explanation of the diagnosis and treatment of her husband.

Since his arrival Jim had been poked, prodded and examined, trapped in an MRI scanner and tortured with a lumber puncture. Tests revealed that Jim had been suffering from a brain aneurysm. The headaches he had been getting was his body's way of altering him to the life-threatening danger that was forming in his head. The consultant was concerned that the weakened blood vessels could rupture at any time so had transferred him to a specialist unit. The hospital, however, was in the next county. Time was of the essence, so the conversation was finished as she was led to say a tearful goodbye to her husband. Possibly their last. Unfortunately for Louise Jim was whisked away moments later and all she could do was look on as her husband was wheeled out of sight.

Jim was as a scared as Louise, but he didn't show it. They both projected bravado they didn't feel. Jim wondered if this is what it left like to be arrested, unsure when, or if, they would see their loved ones again, left to battle the unknown, alone. He refused to contemplate that his life was hanging in the balance. If he didn't think about it then it wasn't happening. Jim lay still, with his eyes closed and tried to imagine riding his bike. He tried hard to ignore the sense of panic that was clawing at his insides.

Louise had no choice but to return home, alone.

It surprised her how much she worried about Jim. On the rare occasions he went away, she relished the time without her idle husband lounging around the house. She was free to do as she pleased without fear of oppression, but his absence had tainted her freedom with concern. A knot of worry had formed in her gut and it refused to be placated with tales of survival and hope.

Like most people, Louise hated hospitals. They are sterile places of great sorrow and immense joy, of endings and beginnings, of loss and hope. Apart from the odd x-ray as a child Louise had avoided hospitals like the plague, until the birth of her first child, and then she'd escaped as soon as possible, and against the wishes of the midwife. Her pregnancy with Frank had started off smoothly, except for the sickness, which was not limited to just the morning, it lasted all-day, every day. Frank had been conceived within weeks of trying and hadn't waited to arrive either, making a dramatic entrance a month before he should have. Louise was suffering from a rare yet fatal form of pre-eclampsia, her organs on the verge of shutting down before her condition was diagnosed. Frank was delivered by emergency caesarean section, the only option to save both mother and baby. Since her reluctant release she had only been back for the birth of Ellen, an explorative appointment and as a visitor. Louise pondered if Jim felt so isolated when he she was fighting for her life, he never talked about it.

She couldn't rest until she had received the call. The wait was agonising.

As much as Louise wanted life to be sweetness and light it simply wasn't, life was a bitch that would bite you in the arse every opportunity it could, and it often did. Louise always smiled though, no matter the internal struggle, she strived to give the appearance of tranquillity and managed chaos. Even her midwife commented how smiley she was, even when she was squeezing Ellen into the world. She was quick to advise her children, friends and colleagues to dream big and go for it but rarely took or applied her own advice. Her smile had vanished, replaced with an anxious frown, her mind already being to imagine life as a widow.

How would she tell the kids, when should she tell them? On the verge of calling Frank Louise rationalised that there was no point in unnecessarily worrying them, they couldn't visit or do anything. Also, Louise wanted to keep the line free for when the hospital called.

Louise had fallen asleep. She hadn't realised until the phone woke her. The veil of sleep shrouded the news and Louise had to ask the caller to repeat themselves.

Jim had survived the surgery and was recovering on the ward. Louise took in no other information other than her husband was alive. She called the children. Naturally they were concerned and relived. She went to bed, happy in the knowledge she would see Jim again and had a fitful dreamless sleep.

She woke the next morning feeling like she had a hangover. She didn't, but her head was pounding, and she felt a little 'off'.

Louise picked Ellen up on route and Frank met them there. Louise was glad of the sat nav, her mind was still distracted, she was having trouble concentrating. Thankfully Ellen was vigilant for the both of them and intercepted a few potential collisions.

The Wilson women followed the signs to intensive care through a maze of identical corridors. Louise had to produce identify to be admitted onto the secure ward. They were ushered into a waiting room; a muted TV and a row of chairs was all that occupied the space, Louise had previously been spoilt with old celebrity news.

A caring nurse in baby blue scrubs came to talk to Louise. She explained that Jim had been taken to surgery as soon as he arrived. The surgeon had worked for almost four hours to clip the aneurysm and safely remove it. It was an invasive procedure and required a craniotomy. The extent of any damage would not be known for a couple of days, but they were expecting Jim to make a full recovery.

Louise was composed in most situations, but she was unprepared to see her husband helpless and reliant upon tubes and wires. It was a blow to her and she reeled from the shock. A bandage covered Jim's skull and machines beeped with his vitals. Louise sat gazing at her husband, his hand held in hers. He was weak, found talking tiring so they sat in silence. Jim was exhausted from recovering from major surgery, so visiting was to be kept to a minimum. Louise tried to prepare the grown children as best she could, but she heard the cry of exclamation from her daughter. Taking ten to compose herself Louise went outside for a dose of fresh air. She didn't feel any better.

Returning to the ward Louise thought the unhandled doors were automatic. When she realised they weren't she absentmindedly reached out to push the door open but saw what she thought was somebody heading out, so she stood aside.   She's been brought up to respect others and prided herself on her polite manners. After nobody had exited the door, Louise beckoned them through, her mind was distracted with thoughts of Jim. She squinted at the person on the other side mimicking her actions before realising that the person she had seen was her own reflection, she had been waiting for herself. Frank and a tearful Ellen were. She kissed her sleeping husband and returned to the family home, alone.

It was another six days before Jim was allowed home. He'd been transferred back to the local hospital for good behaviour. His recovery was excellent, he hadn't lost any cognitive or coordinated ability, but his temper was shorter than it was, quicker to lay blame. Louise put it down to being frustrated at being stuck on the ward, though she imagined he was relishing being sat in bed, waited on hand and foot.

Jim was thinner than before, his face gaunt from lack of nourishment and his receding hair had been partially shaved. An angry red line ran from his hair line and curled around his ear.

Louise had to admit that looking after her husband was hard work, it was like having a teenager in the house. Clothes and food everywhere and responses grunted rather than formed into articulated words. Louise was grateful that her husband was alive, but his constant demands were wearing thin. She'd be thankful when he was well enough to return to work.

As much as she wouldn't admit it Louise was becoming over-whelmed. Being a carer, a wife, a mother, a grandmother and holding down a job, in addition to being a domestic queen, was turning Louise into a stressed-out wrench.

She hadn't allowed herself to daydream since Jim was admitted but needed the escape. A hot soapy bath was the conduit she needed to spend a little time in the realms of dream-death. She felt like her life was being sucked into oblivion and that's what happened to Jim. In her imagination Jim's gravitational stability was reversed and he found himself floating. Gripping desperately to anything he could find, Jim was losing the fight. His grip couldn't hold his own weight and he was pulled upwards. A human helium balloon, Jim was sucked into the voids of a black hole and disappeared.

The struggle with her own apathy towards her sick spouse manifested in the demise of Jim. He had become stuck in quick sand, the reason he was there not addressed in Louise's mind, probably down to another's mistake. The more Jim struggled the quicker the sand took over his body. Before long he was only a head and a hand sticking out from the grainy surface. Louise waved goodbye as the sand consumed Jim, devouring his mind, body and soul. Louise had never felt too bad about her fantasies before, sometimes a little guilty, occasionally regretful but this time she felt ashamed of herself for even considering entertaining the notion.

It wouldn't last.

39

The area had been living under the threat of severe storms for several days. Normally they missed the worst of the weather, avoiding the snow and mini tournedos but if there was any hint of rain then it would be a certainty that they would get it. It even rained when it wasn't forecast. The nearest the world-famous storms and hurricanes came were the news and a tail wind that would wreak havoc on lose garden furniture and roof tiles. The air had been hot and humid, a taste of California in the grey skies of England. Those complaining last week of being fed up of the cold where lobster red and pleading for the return of the gloom by day three of the blistering heat wave. Louise was loving it, Jim was hating it. The shelves had been raided for ice cream, water and BBQ supplies. Louise had been reluctant to leave Jim, but she had no more holiday left to take, and had pulled a payless sick day already. Besides Mrs Henderson seemed more than happy to fill the role while Louise was at work.

Louise joined the staff on the supermarket floor. There was no point sitting at a desk when her colleagues where fronting the battle lines. Last minute shoppers held the harassed workers responsible for the lack of stock, and for not pre-empting the demand owing to the uncharacteristic change in the weather.

Louise lost count of the amount of people that had said something along the lines of "we need a good storm to clear the air". In this neck of the woods they were always in disagreement with the weather, rarely happy with what was on offer.

The weather had soured Jim's temper further. He had never coped well in excessive warmth, the heat seemed to intensify his own natural body heat, unlike Louise who was always cold - the opposites so abundant in their relationship.

A drop in the natural light indicated that the promised storm was on its way. The clear blue skies were now concealed behind dark clouds. Louise did not possess the type of personality that allowed her to be idle. She was constantly doing something, her mind or hands always active. Even when she had the time to be still, to appreciate life, her mind conjured daydreams or conundrums to keep her busy. She didn't even rest in sleep, her subconscious playing out the day's events or creating a dream death for Jim.

Louise beat the thunder and lightning home. The wind screen wipers had worked double-time just to give a slight level of visibility against the giant rain drops that heralded the arrival of the storm.

Mrs Henderson had already made Jim's tea, and cleaned up. They had better be the only wifely duties the woman is performing complained Louise. Louise would like to blame the heat for inflaming Jim's nerves but since the surgery he wasn't the same man. The subtle differences, hard for the outside world to detect as his appearance was unaltered, were obvious to those that knew Jim. His face was the same but underneath a darkness had taken hold. Jim had always been grumpy, borderline miserable and emotionally stunted but never rude or aggressive. That was changing. Louise loved him, would stand by him, try to be patient and understand him but little remained of the outgoing, loving man that she had married.

Louise was upset to wave goodbye to the sun, but her plants were in need of a shower and she loved nothing better than a good lightning display. She'd slept through the last storm to sweep across the region. she had seen some sheet flashes, turning night into day, but had lost the battle to wait up for the fork lightning. Not this time. She was determined to witness, first hand, what they'd all be talking about at work tomorrow.

A low gentle rumble from the heavens started Louise's sky watch. Like a child on Christmas eve, trying to catch a glimpse of Santa, she stood by the window eagerly awaiting the claps of thunder to see what style of lightning would follow. Disappointment was written all over her face when the first wave consisted of boring sheet flashes, even the birds weren't impressed. Determined she kept her vigil, retiring to an upstairs room when Jim's complaining became too much. Apparently, it had been irritably hot all day and now it was too noisy for him to sleep. Admittedly the rain was creating a crescendo of tapping against the windows and roof of the conservatory.

Louise's spirit, and legs, were tiring as the storm raged overhead. Just as she was abandoning all hope of the forked rays she loved so much her patience was rewarded. The night came alive as bright ragged zigzags crackled against their black background. Lasting just seconds the forks darted vertically, horizontally or diagonally in a powerful and beautiful display. Louise   marvelled at the storms magnificence, in awe of the theatrical performance by mother nature.

Even though she held her breath the window still steamed up, so Louise decided, in her infinite wisdom, to get an unimpaired view. Without her customary concern for safety she went outside. Watching the storm from the garden was magical. The forks disappeared behind the tree line, the silver lined clouds lit up with each flash and the ground shock as the disembodied drums of thunder vibrated the land.

One particularly loud boom followed prematurely by a flash caused Louise to rethink her idea and dart back inside. Jim laughed. Louise smiled weakly, heart beating as loud as the sky. A little unnerved from her close encounter Louise let go her husband's mockery, after all she must have looked a picture having scared herself half to death with her own bravery.

Watching the remainder of the storm from the safety of the sofa Louise allowed herself to daydream as Jim lounged next to her. His attention was half on the documentary he insisted he was following and half on his phone.

The sensational storm provided the perfect backdrop for Jim's dalliance with death. Louise imagined Jim as a fearless storm-chaser. Running into the eye of the storm, to capture a striking memory. The beastly weather turned on its pursuer. With jets of lightning shooting at his feet he was forced to retreat, running, screaming for his life. Louise could barely contain herself as she imagined Jim charging around, trying to out run, and outwit, the piercing flashes. Louise couldn't decide his fate, should he get struck by lightning and disappear in a puff of smoke or crushed by a falling tree – that was itself hit with lightning? Before she could conclude Jim's fate her victim saved himself by making a melodramatic exit to the toilet, shattering Louise's illusion.

The storm had run its course. The thunder was now a gentle echo and the flashes a dim light on the horizon. Louise tried to settle on the sofa for the evening but was a slave to Jim's refreshments requests and dictation of the remote control.

Pondering the theme of natural disasters Louise wondered how else the earth and her forces could eliminate one of the population. She chastised herself for even contemplating how. She was allowed the lightning fantasy as Jim had laughed at her, but he had been ill, she'd nearly lost him, for real, forever. She really should stop fantasying about ways he can die.

Before bedtime Jim had drowned in a tsunami, fallen to the Earth's core in an earthquake and been pelted to death with giant hailstones. He'd also been consumed in the lava from a volcano, frozen in a blizzard, engulfed in a wild fire and buried by an avalanche.

40

The aneurysm had terrified Jim. He hadn't been dependent on another since he was a boy. The only other time he felt helpless as an adult was when Frank had been born. He'd had to place the life of his wife and unborn child in the hands of a stranger, not knowing if either would come out of the operating theatre alive. In recent years his mother had given him cause for concern. The onset of her dementia had upset Jim, but he had accepted her fate without a fight, resigned to losing her little by little. In his working life he had accomplished what he had intended. He hadn't thrived to be the best of the best, just to live a comfortable uninterrupted existence.

Jim regarded himself the master of his own destiny, able to navigate his future as he pleased. Not one to see fault in himself Jim didn't consider his tardiness a problem, took no issue with his 1950's attitude towards household duties and thought himself a reasonable lover. However, the invasion of his brain by an enlarged bubble in the blood vessel had challenged his mortality and questioned his existence. He knew the tampering under his skull had irreversibly altered him. On a good day he resembled the old Jim but on a bad day he was unrecognisable, even to himself. His mind was swamped in dark judgements, his tolerance was non-existent, and he seemed at odds in his own skin. Jim wasn't vindictive towards others, didn't care enough to be, most people were neither this nor that to Jim but since his operation he had been tetchy, permanently irritable. He found he couldn't control himself, couldn't stop himself. It was like being a teenager all over again, not knowing what mood you'll wake up in or what the day would bring.

He was still on sick leave, looking at a phased return back to work, becoming increasingly bored by the day. He'd taken to having an early afternoon nap. Just as Jared was outgrowing day time sleeping Jim had taken up the pastime.

Jim rarely remembered his dreams, could recall a handful over his lifetime, but this one would return to haunt him. The vivid detail alarmed Jim. He wasn't a creative person so worried about the depth of his dream deception.

The dream started off innocently enough. Just another day in the Wilson household, Jim watching TV, Louise cleaning the house. Dream Jim was taking an unprecedented weekend away leaving Louise the run of the house. However, before he left Jim set up an elaborate booby-trap. Knowing that a long soak in the bath, with candles, wine and music would be high on the list of his wife's weekend plans the bathroom would be the setting. The engineering involved to rig up the device was worthy of Isaac Newton.

Jim had rigged up an intricate system of pulleys, springs and wires that ultimately connected to his tablet. He had attached a cable which would deliver an electrical charge to the water pipes, in turn causing a spike of electricity to shoot from the tap into the water. Electrifying the victim.

At the same time the tablet would send a command to the high-tech box that Jim had fitted to the door of the conveniently situated airing cupboard, which would then open. In so doing it should trigger another spring-loaded box set up to dislodge the mop. The mop then falls over and hits the three-foot-high sculpture of a seahorse. The innocent seahorse would titter on its base before falling towards the bath. The unwitting accomplish would then collide with the precariously placed radio which when slips into the bath. Tada, accidental electrocution.

All of this would be activated by the word 'Hallelujah'. Jim's tablet was hidden and on standby, ready and waiting, just like Googles *Alexa*, idle and forgotten until called into action. Jim was pleased with the plan he had devised to cover his tracks to make it look like an unfortunate accident.

Thinking about the dream, Jim had no idea if any of the setup was even a possibility, if the technology existed, but, as was the way of fantasies, anything was possible in his imagination.

Dream Louise got into the bath, relaxing in the perfect setting. As the heavenly rendition of *Hallelujah* started so too did Jim's invention. Louise, lost in her karaoke performance didn't notice the impending doom, until it was too late.

It worked like a charm.

Returning from his weekend away dream Jim was 'surprised' to find the house seemingly unoccupied. Had his experiment worked? Would he get away with murder? In this twisted tale the roles had been reversed with the universe seeing Jim murder Louise.

He crept upstairs and into the bathroom. Louise was floating in the tub, her lifeless eyes open, a pool of water beneath her outstretched arm. Her skin was mottled from the stone-cold water, her limp hair clung to her face which was contorted into a grotesque mask. The 'murder weapon' had sunk to the bottom of the porcelain tub. All Jim had to do was disconnect the wires and remove any evidence of tampering. Once that was done he could call the police and report the devasting accident he'd come home to. The coroner recorded a verdict of accidental death.

With guilt as the motivating factor Jim had made tea, himself. No Mrs Henderson or Ronald McDonald were involved. He tried to rationalise his dream, to explain it away as his subconscious rebelling against the confines of his altered personality yet didn't want to acknowledge that is neural pathways had changed him. His guilt not yet subsided he also attempted to instigate an adult role-play session with his very alive wife. Louise knew instantly what he wanted, it was the only time Jim was attentive and his eyes transformed in a weird smouldering kind of way. So predictable. Louise wasn't an adventurous lover, a lay back and think of England kind of girl but that didn't stop Jim trying. She'd always been embarrassed about sex, she wasn't a prude, just body conscious and an over thinker.

Even after all these years together both expected the other to bend to their will, to change, but neither would.

Jim really should learn to think before he speaks. Even as he dropped the hints of a superheroic stint in the bedroom a plan was formulating in Louise's mind. Jim was surprised that his seductive suggestion was received with such vigour, already excited at the prospect of his wife in a skimpy little number. *SuperWoman* onesie to the rescue. It was what Jim had asked for, it just wasn't delivered in the way that he had hoped. Amused, Louise slept dreamlessly till morning.

41

Somehow Jim and Louise had ended up with both the grandkids for the weekend. Jim had hoped to inject some oomph into the stagnating relationship, his attempt at seductive role-play having fallen short of the mark thanks to his creative wife.

The weekend was dirty for all the wrong reasons. Instead of a weekend from the pages of *Fifty Shades of Grey* Jim got a weekend out of a *Peppa Pig* book, mud pies, nursery rhymes and the alphabet.

Louise loved having the little ones over, loved a house full of craziness but Jim struggled. The effects of the aneurysm had stunted his patience further, obliterating his ability to be tolerant to smithereens. Jim could manage a few hours before he'd become overwhelmed and retire to his study or go out for a drive. It made little difference to Louise. Jared refereed to Jim as "Umpy Anda", the best he could manage on the 'grumpy grandad' name that Louise had been teaching him and little Sophia was too young to be bothered by his absence.

A day of playing and nappy changing had exhausted Louise. Even if she'd been inclined to accommodate Jim's intimate intentions she was too exhausted, snoring through Jim's advances. Louise could succumb to being a modern age granny, with electronic devices to keep the children appeased but she was old school and believed in fostering their imagination. Also, she loved seeing the toys that had occupied Frank and Ellen for hours being loved again, it was like she had slipped back in time. The one thing she didn't miss was the mess. More than once Louise had stood on Lego, which was very unforgiving to the delicate sole of an un-shoed foot. The classic construction toy was as popular with son as it was with his father and again graced the floor of the Wilson house, bringing back happy, yet painful, memories.

Many a time Louise had falsely declared "I could kill him" when Frank had left Lego all over the floor for the umpteenth time, a trait inherited from his father. Death threats weren't uncommon to hear in the Wilson household, Louise had lost count of the amount of times she had directed a fake threat at her husband or children. "Oh-my-lord (substitute name) I'll swing for you one of these days" was one of her favourites. The threats however were now just used against idiot car drivers or Jim. Her daydreams allowed her to carry out the deed, repeatedly, without fear of prosecution or estrangement from family and society.

Louise took the grandkids out for the day. Giving Jim a break from the noise of their pre-schooler wards. She wasn't being as kind as she seemed as she had left him a short list of chores to accomplish in her absence. They had a fun packed day on the beach, building sand castles, paddling in the sea and searching rock pools.

To her disappointment, but not surprise, Jim had managed to cross a grand total of zero off the list. It would appear that he had been in the process of taking out the rubbish but must suffered a fit of lazyitus forcing him to abandon the chore, half finished, and take a seat on the sofa, the recommended cure for such a condition. It must have been a bad bout as he was still on the sofa when they returned. Louise dispatched the toddling alarm clocks, they could be Jim's problem whilst she made everyone tea.

Another of Jim's irritating flaws was his inability to admit when he was wrong and getting an apology was like pulling teeth. He rarely took the blame and since his real-life near-death experience he was even worse. Louise didn't like to think of herself as selfish but sometimes she could be self-centred, put herself first. She supposed that she was asking too much of Jim, that she shouldn't be burdening him with housework. Going the extra mile, striving to impress is what had landed her in this situation in the first place, yet she never learnt her lesson. Louise always saw the best in people and believed they could shine, she was rarely right.

The departure of Sophia brought the arrival of an invite. Ellen had asked her mum to accompany her to watch a show, a pop-up theatre production of *Magic Mike*. What was it with the younger generation and willies thought Louise. Needless to say, Norman wasn't prepared to take his wife to ogle at another man's dangly bits. Louise was excited at the prospect of a girly outing but was reluctant to leave Jim overnight. Franks moods were driving Louise crazy, so she accepted the invite on the proviso that Ellen's hubby kept an eye on Jim.

Louise hadn't realised how tired she was, being a grandma was exhausting. She must have fallen asleep on the sofa as she woke with a crick in her neck, a half-drunk glass of wine sat on the end table and Jim snored, open mouthed, next to her. The sci-fi show they were watching must have finished as she woke to the conclusion of a murder case. The killer had dissolved his victims in hydrofluoric acid to dispose of the remains.

In a semi-conscious state, in the realms between sleep and wake, Louise's mind turned to murder. Louise was often yanked out of her daydream before the details of the burial had been revealed so she let her mind run with the fantasy and contemplate how she would secure evasion from the law.

According to the prosecution in the case on the small screen, the murderer was caught due to his blatant excessive purchase of the corrosive liquid. All twenty-one gallons bought from the same supplier over an unrealistic period of a couple of months. Louise thought that she'd have the sense to plan ahead. She'd use different suppliers and pseudonyms to amass the amount of liquid required to consume a human carcass and use a fool proof sealed container that would withstand any leaks or be breached by the acid. She prided herself on her organisational skills and would be aghast at being busted due to carelessness. It would take several days for the bones and connective tissue to be reduced to pulp leaving behind a congealed mush of flesh and organic matter. All that remained of Jim could be hidden - a bit buried here, dropped down a drain there, with some deposited in the food waste receptacle or fed to the waste disposal.

Louise really hoped that she would be more forensically aware than the redneck on TV and evade capture. She was sure she'd cover her tracks so that, even if she was a suspect, there would be no evidence to charge her. She knew as well as anyone that a case could scarcely be built on circumstantial evidence alone, the Crown Prosecution Service wouldn't let it get to court if it was.

Ellen had done a sterling job of organising the day, had booked first class tickets on the train and even drove them to the station. Louise had never travelled in style before, always had to opt for the cheap seats.

Enjoying a cup of tea from the waitress service in the spacious and clean seats, the train pulled into a station. Louise payed little attention to the hubbub of the travellers coming and going but one passenger caught her eye. She recognised him but couldn't put her finger on where she knew him from. He sat facing her, seven rows away. Every eight minutes or so Louise poked her head around the seat for another glimpse, hoping to jog her memory, and to check he was still there. Ellen was so engrossed in her book that she'd paid little attention to her mums stalking behaviour. Louise couldn't focus on her own novel, she was too distracted franticly recalling faces - was he a customer, someone she'd seen on TV?

"That's it. I know who he is." declared Louise, a little loudly, roughly nudging Ellen. "He's the dad off the show I used to watch".

Ellen looked blankly at Louise, her finger holding her place in the novel.

"Yes, you know, the funny one about the family. Three kids." Ellen's expression was still puzzled, having not been aware of the focus of her mum's attention. "Not the one with *Citizen Smith*, the other one, with the boy with crazy hair." Louise ploughed on, gesturing wildly with her eyes in the direction of her celebrity find. "Look, over there." Ellen took a stealthy look behind her "See".

"Oh yea, the bloke of Outnumbered. Cool" acknowledged Ellen before returning to her book. She'd never been as star struck as her mum, who would get tongued tied over a D-lister.

Louise had her mobile out and was attempting navigate the phones controls and establish an internet connection. Ellen could only take a few minutes of Louise jabbing at the screen, muttering that it wasn't doing what she wanted it too.

"It just keeps taking me to a site about glasses, stupid phone." complained Louise in response to her daughters offer of help.

Passing over the "blasted contraption" Ellen secretly despaired at Louise's lack of ability to grasp digital technology. Jim liked his gadgets, was probably more tech-savvy than Norman but Louise seemed to fear the advancements of modern mankind.

"If you'd been on Google instead of goggle.co.uk you might have had a bit more luck Mum." sighed Ellen, her fingers flying across the screen as she spoke. "There you go. One Mr Hugh Dennis."

"Yea, that's the chap. God I'm awful with names, it's ridiculous." confessed Louise, "and you're not much better with technology" thought Ellen to herself.

"Should I go over? No, I shouldn't, should I?" deliberated Louise, leaning over to check her prey was still there. He was. Ellen warned her she'd regret it if she didn't but had no intention of going with her, she was old enough to introduce herself.

Two stations came and went while Louise mustered the courage. Each time Louise hoped she hadn't missed her chance. She hadn't.

Louise rose from her seat ready to make her move but bottled it at the last moment. The second attempt failed, so did the third. By the time she had found the nerve for a fourth attempt her heart was beating at an alarming rate and her palms were unflatteringly moist. She launched herself forward before she had time to think. Walking unsteadily towards her unwitting target she willed him to make eye contact. As she approached he did. With her body working as a separate entity from her brain her arm extended, and she found herself smiling like a mad woman, a rushed greeting tumbling from her shaking lips. To Louise's relief Mr Dennis was very accommodating and graciously answered Louise's barrage of questions. He even posed for a selfie. Triumphant, Louise faked a trip to the loo, a guise to accidently met the sitcom star. She couldn't resist waving at her new friend as she passed by him returning to her seat. The harassed comedian was quick to disappear on the platform, eager for anonymity.

The Pop-up theatre was half the cast and a condensed story line but was none-the-less a great performance. The chiselled chests rippled in front of the excited audience, but they ensured that everyone got their money's worth of nakedness, with some copping more of an eyeful than others. Louise struggled to keep attention on the torso. She'd never found a penis a particularly attractive organ, but it was hard not to focus on these as were creating a musical extravaganza slapping around and dancing in time to the music. Louise had to stop herself from laughing as she pictured them with tiny hats. Her mind fashioned a sombrero for one, a French beret for another, one donned a top hat and another in a bowler. A baseball cap topped a fifth and a beanie hat capped the final performer's little performer.

The return journey was uneventful.

42

Jim knew he had changed since the aneurysm, not that he'd admit it. He'd never been one to acknowledge his flaws, didn't like to confess he wasn't perfect. His father and grandfather were the same, laws unto themselves with the moral compass of a wombat. The neuropathways had suffered such horrific trauma that it was inevitable elements of Jim would be lost or altered but it didn't make it any easier for Jim to deal with. Louise had been magnificent at the beginning and Jim couldn't fault her, but his transformed personality had put a strain on the relationship like nothing before.

A trip to see his mum put into perspective what he still had to live for, but he was powerless against the waves of paranoia, anxiety and desperation. Despite his deep feelings towards Louise he could not help himself and it was his spouse who bore the brunt of his depression, not that Louise didn't use his as a sounding post when she was frustrated. Jim's mum Mary had been getting progressively worse with every visit, she still failed to recognise her own son. No amount of promoting provoked any form of memory and Jim left feeling dejected and petrified over his mums future.

Louise had had a long day at work. She was bashing around the kitchen when Jim got in. The smell of cottage pie wafted out of the kitchen, but his favourite dish wasn't enough to lift his spirits. Louise found her husband slumped on the sofa, his head in his hands. Jim explained the devasting news that his beloved mother had reached the point of no return with her illness, yet he was too angry to allow the tears that threatened his eyes to fall.

Louise was tentative that night, sympathetic to her husband and upset as she loved Mary too. Jim's dad had died before they had married so she hadn't really known him. Mary was a vibrant artist woman with a zest for life.

To envision the vitality that made her the woman they adored had dwindled to nothing stung Louise, but she couldn't imagine how Jim felt, she'd never lost anyone she was close to before, only distant relatives that she knew only from photographs. Her own grandparents were in their nineties and living together happily in a care home. Louise visited every few months. Her grandfather was the fourth, two of the others meeting their ends through heart attacks and the original losing his life to a tragic fishing accident when Louise's mother Joan was just a little girl herself. It was a wonder that her gran hadn't been arrested for murder.

The next morning Jim was up and out of the house without a word and back in the evening moaning about the traffic, his colleagues and the unfairness of life in general. Jim could never ever have been classified as an overly happy person, he was even a serious child and he was generally negative, seldom positive, but Louise was struggling to cope with Jim's new attitude. He's memory and cognitive skills   had returned almost to normal, but Louise wrestled with his unpredictable moodiness. This is what men must feel like everyone month, as their wives and daughters explode in P.M.T filled emotional outbursts of hormones, thought Louise. She was glad he was still with her and not six feet under but at times she was more than tempted to turn one of her fantasies into a reality. She had always been a martyr over housework, running around like a blue-arsed fly, juggling tea, homework and diplomacy when the kids were at home with Jim arriving after work like royalty taking up his throne in front of the TV. Things had not improved and were unlikely to. Jim was quick to learn that Louise couldn't abide a mess and would clear it up regardless of the culprit. Even when she abstained from being a domestic goddess she could only last a few days before the need to tidy got the best of her and she'd set to work. Jim would moan Louise was doing too much, Louise would moan that Jim was doing too little, it was a vicious circle.

The Wilson household had returned to its new normal when they got the fateful call from Mary's nursing home. They needed to come in to discuss Mary's deteriorating condition. Jim held it together whilst the doctors spoke to them about palliative care and what to expect but Louise could tell that he was retaining little of the information. He'd turned into a nodding dog, making the right noises at the right times but he refused to acknowledge that his mum's time on earth was drawing to a close.

Jim withdrew into himself. He had no siblings or cousins to rely upon, his father had long since passed and he was desperate for his mum not to join his dad, even though what remained of her mind had already made the journey to be with her late husband. The rest of her followed a few weeks later.

Jim was hit harder than Louise had anticipated. He knew the woman he called mum had checked out a while ago, leaving just a familiar looking vessel behind but he was struggling with the finality of her death.

The crematorium had undergone a remodel and looked more like a wedding venue than a place of endings, the chairs had new coverings and the mood lighting was more at home in a disco than a funeral parlour. Even though the bulbs were set on low they were flickering and producing the effect of strobe lighting causing Jim to become irritated. He was the same at home, if a programme didn't pre-warn viewers, or more accurately he had ignored the announcement, he would get angry, cursing at the TV channel, vowing to send a strongly worded email. As he bid a final farewell to Mary Jim's annoyance mixed with grief, tears and frustration resulting in a meltdown and he left. The funeral was a sparse affair as most of Mary's friends had already departed this world or had lost their faculties. Jim's uncle Eddie was present, but he had as many marbles left as Mary and didn't really remember who it was he was commemorating. Louise, Frank and Ellen allowed the service to finish before going on the hunt for Jim. He hadn't got far, was wandering around the car park.

They held a personal quake at home. Bottles of prosecco were drunk whilst watching *Rebel without a Cause*, Mary's favourite film. Louise could picture her now, up at the pearly gates trying to get a glimpse of the brooding actor, she wondered if you could get banned from heaven for stalking someone.

Louise helped Jim to sort through his mother's belongings. There was not much to show for a life lived. The majority of his inheritance had been swallowed by the nursing home fees with her furniture and possessions sold when she was admitted. Her clothes were donated to charity and what few assets she had left were boxed up. Apart from the treasured yellowing family photo from Jim's childhood the boxes were put in the garage to gather dust. Louise let Jim grieve, but she would not allow him to disappear into the depths of self-pity.

As part of her plan to pull Jim from his despair she had arranged for the grandkids to come and stay for the weekend. Triny was ready to drop with grandchild number three so could do with a break. Secretly Jim loved spending time with the mini Frank and Ellen, had the time he never had as a father. He wouldn't admit to it though, not that he had to, Louise knew him well enough to know when his smile was one of joy or trickery. There was a new farm park that had just opened, making a perfect venue for a day out, with play areas, animals and mud, what more could two small children and one big one wish for?

Louise made the fatal error of telling Jared the night before of the following days plans resulting in the household being up at the crack of dawn, except Jim who could sleep through an earthquake. By the time they arrived at the park both kids were fast asleep having torn around the house until it was time to leave.

The pot-holed dirt track that led to the attraction failed to raise the children from their slumber, but a freshly opened bag of crisps did the trick. The over-enthusiastic young worker issued stickers and a map as Jim held onto the two excited guests.

The kids were having a great time, running from pen to pen feeding and stroking the lambs and goats. Jim was standing guard to prevent any two or four legged escapees whilst Louise was rather taken with the sow and her little pink piglets, neglecting grandma duties to capture the day on film. Lunch was run off inside the play area. Sitting back and letting the little ones run riot was great in principle with the multiple levels of attractively coloured soft play equipment entertaining numerous children until Louise realised that the child is thought was her grandson was in fact wearing near identical clothing but was a complete stranger. Once her heart had stopped racing and she had safely located her kin she decided it was time for another trip to see the animals.

The afternoon saw Jim suffer a series of unfortunate mishaps that left him feeling embarrassed and he struggled to control his temper. Louise did feel compassion for her husband, he couldn't help how his brain made him react, and she couldn't help but to see the humour in his calamity. The boys were running around a field playing chase while the girls sat in the sandpit, Sophia happily squashing every sand sculpture Louise made. Despite the difference in size Jared was giving his grandad a run for his money but, just at the moment that Louise looked up, Jim lost his footing. The momentum made him lose his balance and he plunged towards the ground, arms instinctively outstretched. It all happened in slow motion as Louise watched in amused horror, unable to save her husband from his humiliating fall. Luckily for Jim the grass provided a relatively soft landing and the only thing really hurt was his pride. It was the first time he'd had grass strains on his clothes for a very long time. Louise fussed over Sophia to detract from the grin she was desperately trying to conceal, her giggles passed off as playing. Before leaving Jared begged his grandparents for one last go the slides. Uncharacteristically, Jim accompanied the children into the play area leaving Louise to order coffee for the journey home. Louise was carrying the polystyrene cups back the table when Jared came running up shouting "Nanana Umpy Anda stuck".

Jared dragged Louise to the bottom of a long curved red tube. Sophia was in the ball pool at the foot of the slide, but Jim was nowhere to be seen. A disturbing mumbling noise and series of bangs came from the tube and Jim's feet materialised from the opening. Another loud bang followed by some grunting produced Jim to the knees. Louise and Jared took a leg each and helped to pull Jim free of his entrapment. Looking red-faced and traumatised Jim declared they were going home. After one last trip to the animals to appease the upset children, who had to witness a slide regurgitate their grandad, the Wilson clan headed home.

As Old MacDonald played through the car speakers Louise drifted into a daydream, the blurred landscape zoomed past as she stared blankly out the window, Jim scowled at the road ahead. Pigs. Louise had always loved pigs. She would have got one of those micro-pigs, but she'd heard so many tales of people being duped and ending up with a full-size hog that she hadn't dared take the chance. But, if she had a pig she could feed Jim to it.

Louise pictured the back garden, a sty in one corner whilst Rufus, that's what she'd name her pig, lived a life of luxury. He'd have mud baths, succulent grasses and a diet of Jim mixed in with dinner scraps and pellets. Rufus' Jim rich deposits would fertilize the garden and make the roses grow the most magnificent shade of scarlet that couldn't fail to impress even the Queen of Hearts.

Louise was as exhausted as the kids, who had both fallen asleep again on the way home. "No matter" thought Louise, they'd be collected shortly and be their parents little nightmares, she loved being a grandparent, the ultimate revenge on your own children.

When they got back the answerphone was flashing indicating a missed call. Expecting an automated telesales message Louise pressed replay as she unloaded the bags.

"Daddy." shouted Jared at the telephone.

Not having heard a car pull up Louise ran out of the kitchen just as she heard her sons voice say "…I'll call when I can, gotta go mum, look after Jared".

Puzzled and a little alarmed Louise rewound the message as Jim retreated into his study, grandpa duties over for the day. The answer phone message informed them that Triny had gone into labour, so they wouldn't be round to pick up Jared. Following this was a drunken message from Trinity's mum Lauren about the impending arrival of the new baby.

Within thirty six hours Louise was cradling her third grandchild, Lucas.

43

The arrival of baby Lucas was celebrated with a lavish Sunday roast. The entire family was descending on the Wilson residence. Louise was in her element preparing the mountains of meat and veg to feed the hordes. Even at Christmas the Wilsons were not host to this many people, not all at once. Jim was in a mood that he hadn't been consulted about the gathering. Jim felt a little out of place, being an only child, he never had the sibling bonds that Louise and their own children had and struggled to understand the close relationships of the women in his life. Louise felt for Jim, sympathised that his own mother was too far along the dementia path to recognise her own son, but she wouldn't allow it to prevent her from enjoying her own family, celebrating every success and commiserating failure.

With the arrival of grandchildren came the rediscovery of toys he thought Louise had long since given away but had instead craftily hidden. It was nice to see them being used again though, and it triggered memories of when Frank and Ellen were small. Jim saw it as an ill omen of his advancing years, of a youth that has long since disappeared into the past. Much to Jim's displeasure there seemed to be a new edition creep into the house every day. The former playroom downstairs had slowly been overtaken with baskets full of blocks, cars and dolls, even the kitchen cupboards were filled with plastic cutlery. He didn't however complain about the copulas amounts of sweet treats that had also found their way into the house. His Tom Clancy books gave way to Roald Dahl, his herbaceous boarder was lost to a mud kitchen and peaceful days were filled with tantrums and enthusiastic brightly animated children's shows.

The grandchildren used the newly purchased high-chairs but even with the scrubbed down garden chairs they were short on seating. Jim was dispatched to borrow chairs from Mrs Henderson, next door. Jim returned with three dining chairs and an extra diner. Jim knew that Louise would make too much, she always did. Louise took his kind invitation as a slight against not being consulted but she smiled graciously whilst rearranging the dining table to accommodate their unexpected guest.

"It's only polite, we are borrowing her chairs after all." reasoned Jim.

"Not a problem, dear." smiled Louise through gritted teeth.

Fran and John had made the trip from the Yorkshire Dales and arrived with suitcases in tow, and Joan who they'd remembered to collect along the way. The siblings always made a bit of a holiday of seeing each other, with over half the country separating them, and Frans affair with the bottle, contact was sporadic, with Louise, as the older sibling, initiating visits and phone calls. When Fran was present and sober she was a caring sister and aunt. At least there were enough children to go around, when the baby wasn't being cuddled there was a puzzle to complete, a tower to build or a picture to colour. Frank, Triny, Jared and Lucas were staying over too, making the most of the extended bank holiday weekend.

Snakes & ladders and skittles gave way to monopoly and poker as the children slept and the wine flowed, and Ellen abandoned all pretence of going home. The blow-up bed would be coming out.

Louise went to bed with her head spinning, welcoming the tranquillity of sleep to quieten her drunken mind.

Louise heard the grandkids stirring and the respective moans of their parents, the free-flowing booze now regretted in the light of a six am start. Saint Granny to the rescue.

Louise crept into each room, the early rays of daylight just starting to peak between the gaps in the curtains and took the offending bundles downstairs to feed them.

Lucas feel asleep in Louise's arms, milk drunk from the luke-warm bottled he'd just drained. Sophia and Jared were plonked in front of the TV while Louise tidied from the night before and made herself some breakfast, and a strong coffee, heavy on the sugar and light on the milk.

Louise left the house in an orderly state and took her band of multi-coloured mini hippies out for some fresh air. Louise loved dressing the children from her stash of mix-and-match hand-me-downs, her eccentric mix of stripes and dots in a multitude of colours were at odds with their parents' choice of coordinated matching outfits. Grannies house, grannies rules. Jared, especially, enjoyed the freedom to plaster his clothes in mud and food with no reprimand for his actions. His cousin Sophia may act like a little princess, but she wasn't above getting messy. They returned to a house full of noise and the smell of bacon - the Wilsons tried and tested hangover cure.

The only member of the family absent was Jim. Louise went to locate her missing spouse to find him opened mouthed and snoring. She knew that slamming the bedroom door would wake him. She stomped back downstairs, her blood simmering

"Dad still asleep then." commented Ellen, smirking.

"He's not about to break the habit of a lifetime, Darling." replied Louise snidely as she took up position on the only empty chair. She grabbed a bacon butty before it disappeared inside Frank, if Jim stayed in bed much longer the piggy feast would be all consumed.

Jim's laziness was the topic of conversation over the table, Frank and John regretting their decision to get up and Norman was already dressed and heading out the door, he was the locum on call for the hospital that day.

Jim finally came down, as the clock struck noon. The plates had been cleared but a whiff of bacon still clung to the air, informing Jim of the treat that he had missed. Not a scrap remained, cooked or uncooked. Jim consoled himself with toast dripping in honey, he must have spread half a beehive over his burnt bread remarked Louise.

Jim was acting like a bear with a sore head. He'd been really moody recently. That was one of the reasons for the inflated family get-together, Louise needed some love and joy injected into the tense atmosphere. It was like living with a teenager again, walking on egg shells and being irrationally snapped at. An innocent comment taken to heart would be the source of anguish for days. Louise tried to remain calm, tried to continue as if nothing was wrong but it put a stain on her positive personality. It had been almost a year, but   it was hard. Louise tried not to nag Jim, in fact she rarely nagged, never had, her style was to drop hints and loudly comment, hoping desperately that Jim 'got the message'. He never did. If he wasn't picking his clothes up off the floor at age forty then he wouldn't be doing it age fifty, but Louise was ever the optimist and lived in hope that one day Jim would miraculously turn into a domesticated God.

Changing the grandkids nappies required a nose-peg. Louise didn't know what they'd eaten but preyed that they'd never have it again in her presence as the contents were toxic, throw that at your enemies and they'd run a mile. The scent of the revolting excrement lingered in the air, the floral air freshener did nothing to disguise the smell, yet the perpetrators had left an hour ago. Jim had been dispatched to return the borrowed furniture.

"Huuuhhh," sighed Jim with relief as he passed Louise, a grin appearing on his smug face. "That's unusual" thought Louise to herself, Jim usually basked in the flirtatious behaviour of their widowed neighbour. Having mistaken the source of relief it was a moment before the offensive smell assaulted Louise's nose, the culprit already disappearing into the safety of his study pretending he was oblivious to the nasal carnage he'd left in his wake. "revolting man" muttered Louise. Jim was no gassier than most blokes on the planet, or the women for that matter, not that they'd admit to it. Even in yoga class nobody ever laid claim to their bottom burb, and not being at school meant the class could continue without disintegrating into fits of childish laughter. Regrettably for all but Jim, his motto in this matter had always been 'better out than in', maybe for Jim but certainly not for Louise.

She imagined him being the picture of male courteousness at a social occasion with the queen, not even Jim would pass wind in the presence of her majesty. It was the perfect setting for fantasy Louise to test her theory – would Jim explode if he was forced to hold in one of his own farts? Would the noxious gas build up and combust, causing Jim to pop like an over-inflated balloon? The rational part of her brain her reasoned that it was impossible, but the murderous side concluded that it would be a hilarious experiment and Jim could indeed explode like popcorn, that would be his just desserts for years of expelling his wind.

44

Louise hadn't realised how much science actually went into killing someone, if you were trying not to get caught. She knew that some poisons were undetectable once they had entered the victim's body and the lethal concoction would present as an innocent heart attack or other medical catastrophe for which they would not be in time to administer a cure. A verdict of misadventure would be recorded, a severe allergic reaction to a foreign agent. There were the classic ones freely available in the British countryside like foxglove and hemlock that mothers warned their children not to touch, to exotic species of plants such as the Nerium Oleander that was harvested for its deadly properties. It would be a moments work to mix a teaspoon of the poison into a spicy curry, the overpowering taste of turmeric disguising any hint of foul play. Louise would be guaranteed to survive as she'd avoid the poisoned dish, Jim knowing that she didn't eat eastern cuisine. She was happy to experiment with ingredients, as long as she wasn't required to taste them, luckily for her Jim had an iron-clad stomach and would eat her trial meals with good grace. Jim would far rather she was experimental in the bedroom rather than the kitchen, but he'd take what he could get. He may not be susceptible to the eye-watering spices, but he wasn't immune to germs that had clearly been left as a gift for nanny and grandad. Jim had caught a cough, and Jared was the likely gift giver.

Louise was in the shower when the pilot-light blew out and the hot massaging pressure tuned into cold droplets of agony. Jumping out of the shower Louise grabbed a towel and stomped to the boiler. Her soapy hair dripped down her back and she left a trail of wet footprints in her wake. After a few minutes of his wife cursing and threatening the boiler with dismantlement Jim conceded and agreed to call out an engineer. Jim's temporary solutions held for a week or two, but Louise had come to the point of no return, if Jim didn't do something about it, she would. She could boil kettles, but she had earned the right to demanded instant hot water, it wasn't the stone ages and Jim would afford her the luxury, willingly or otherwise.

Technology was not on Louise's side. After calming down from her traumatic shower Louise decided she'd do a bit of on-line surfing, perhaps start looking for Christmas presents for the kids. Jim had left for work and the house was peaceful and quiet. The festive season was a little way off yet, but Louise prided herself on her gift giving ability. She always found the perfect gift, and that didn't happen by spending an afternoon on eBay. Following a mammoth update from Windows, which saw Louise watch a film in the time it took the laptop to assimilate itself with the new software, Louise was to find that her account had been hacked. Her profile had been used to front a scam. Half the stock from PC World had been listed for sale; computers, phones, TVs, if it was electronic then Louise's account was selling it but from the tone of the messages, the buyers weren't receiving it. It took the best part of the afternoon, screeching hold music and being passed between departments to convince the online retailer that she was not responsible. After all, it was highly unusual activity for Louise, to suddenly become an internet tycoon. She was renowned for her ability to buy, not to sell.

By the time that Jim arrived home from work Louise was in a less-than-happy mood and the house was being vacuumed to within an inch of its life, the skirting boards and chair legs taking the brunt of her frustration. The engineer that was scheduled for the boiler had not turned up.

"For God's sake women, what the hell is wrong with you?" snapped Jim, compounding the situation, but not waiting for an answer. His cough echoed around the hall.

"Go boil your head." muttered Louise under her breath. Jim retreated into the safety of his study wittering something about the menopause. Louise had considered the fact that she could be menopausal but had refused to accept that her body was changing, again. The frequency of her monthly periods was sporadic – check. Hot flushes – check. Low Libido – Jim would report it's always been low, but Louise was less inclined these days - check. Louise was experiencing trouble sleeping but that was more down to Jim coughing. She didn't tick off any of the other symptoms from the NHS website so declared herself not in the grips of the menopause. She'd only bug the GP for a formal diagnosis when she could tolerate the symptoms no longer. Jim would continue to avoid the war path when P.M.T was raging, he'd managed the last quarter of a century, he could cope a bit longer. Or, as Louise had said before, "there's a door right there".

"An engineer will be here in the hour." called Jim from the sanctuary of his office, adding "Love" as a last-minute platitude, followed by a cough, for which he received no sympathy.

"Um." replied Louise doubtfully, the kettle rocking on its base in the background as it reached boiling point.

True to the second phone call an engineer did make it within the hour, fifty-seven minutes after the call but within the hour, Domino's Pizza would be after them as a delivery driver. The young engineer must have barely passed his qualifications, but Louise showed him the offending equipment and prayed that he would have a solution that wouldn't cost the earth. After thirty minutes of banging and scarping and two trips back to the van for parts the young engineer declared the boiler fixed and ready to go. Louise had to endure a patronising lecture about servicing and maintaining gas apparatus and the dangers of carbon dioxide. Louise relayed the information to her husband. Jim had always hated the school teacher tone she'd take sometimes, and she'd employed it to remind him of the dangers of faulty gas appliances. Accordingly, Jim responded like an insolent teenager being told off by trying to correct the engineers opinion and down play the hazardous nature of a defective gas supply. Tea passed in mutual silence, a heated prepared frozen chicken served on a bed of chilli infused rice.

Louise unwound in a hot soapy bath. She'd deliberately filled it to the max because she knew Jim hated it. She positioned her book on the corner of the sink, so she could reach it without getting out of the bath. Louise lowered herself in carefully, to quick and she would have caused a wave of aromatic soapy water to spread across the bathroom floor. She washed as quickly as possible, she'd run the bath to read, getting clean was a forced by-product. This was her sanctuary, since the children had left home anyway. Jim wouldn't walk upstairs when they had a toilet located on the ground level and opted for the en-suite when upstairs, so Louise was guaranteed peace, unless the phone went, Jim wasn't an effective answer phone. Louise relaxed in the scorching water and drifted off into a daydream before she'd had the chance to open her book, Detective Deans would have to wait. She had her own murder to commit.

With all the talk of gas leaks and Jim's deadly D.I.Y it seemed a natural progression for Jim to succumb to toxic fumes. Professor Louise, complete with a white lab coat and black rimmed spectacles, used a wand-like stick and A-board to highlight the scientific elements of causing death using the periodic table. Prof Louise informed her imaginary class that the substance of carbon, in its purest form was lethal. If you could get the victim to ingest the substance or expose them to a concentrated jet of gas you may get away with murder. Louise instructed her students to ensure the scene was set, remove any form of coal or other carbonated substances before reporting the death. The coroner would record a verdict of natural causes as it would present like a heart attack. There'd be no scaring or medical evidence, so they would have to hope that the autopsy was not completed as it would detect foul play and they would test for poisoning, the real cause of death. Louise instructed her students that the best course of action would be for the victim to have an existing respiratory condition, that way carbon dioxide or nitrogen could be used. The doctor would confirm the existence of a life-threatening medical condition and sign off the certificate as death by hypoxia. Louise heard the dull reverberations of Jim coughing from somewhere downstairs.

"Here's an example class," said imaginary Louise "take this individual, a middle-aged unfit male with a history of smoking and working within an industry that uses chemicals. He would be a prime candidate for execution. Keeping a dry environment will help to trigger a coughing fit. Hands up who can suggest the perfect environment?"

"Turn the heating up," seemed to be the most popular suggestion, and one with which Louise would happily comply. Poor Jim was trapped inside a heated room with no ventilation and no water, breathing the same recycled air. The class crowded around to watch their human test subject. The more he coughed the less oxygen there was pumping around his body. The question soon became did he suffocate from the lack of oxygen in the environment or in his body. That was lesson two for the class.

After a week of self-pity and purchasing every cough syrup on the market Jim was on the mend. He'd managed to go to work throughout but housework was beyond all possibility, not that he was a great contributor anyway. Louise kept a clean and tidy house, it wouldn't have won any awards, you couldn't see your face in highly polished surfaces, but it was functionally clean. Louise was a busy lady. If Jim had wanted a stay-at-home wife, he should have got a better job or chosen a different wife. A place for everything and everything in its place was Louise's motto, and it even held true when dusting, which she did over and around the object. Also, if Jim moved an item, she'd know – the dust line would be disturbed. Louise didn't have OCD, well maybe just a little, she liked things done her way. "Crazy" Jim would call her, which she took as a twisted term of endearment for she'd always been a little crazy, loopy bat-shit crazy not crazy-stab-stab-crazy. She prided herself on being different from the herd and danced to her own tune, which was defiantly one that nobody else could hear. Jim struggled to accept this side of his wife. He'd had a conservative upbringing and remained inside the box his whole life, whereas Louise's family definitely lived life running around the outside of the box.

45

Louise woke up feeling exhausted. She'd had a dreamless full night's sleep but felt as if she'd slept on a bed of nails. Walking down the stairs she experienced a dizzy spell and had to grab hold of the bannister to prevent herself from tumbling down the hard wooden staircase. Louise managed a few mouthfuls of cereal before dragging herself to work. Maybe she'd caught the bug after being Jim's nurse maid. Louise struggled through her shifts at work, neglected the housework and produced meals for one, her appetite had packed it's bags and left, leaving no return date. She was surviving on toast and water. She hadn't been right for the best part of a month but with Jim being ill, the grandchildren to babysit and shifts at work she just thought she was over worked and underappreciated.

A trip to the GP reassured Louse that she wasn't dying from the dreaded lurgy. However, the newly qualified doctor couldn't provide a diagnosis so took what felt like half her body's worth of blood and reprimanded Louise for not coming to the surgery earlier.

The results were back, Louise needed more tests, but they had detected a treatable iron deficiency. Louise took a prescription of super-strength iron tablets daily and forced down a disgusting diet of leafy greens and pulses. She was happy with the increase of meat but devastated at the reduction of dairy. After a week she felt her body was displaying withdrawal signs from the lack of chocolate which she easily remedied with a bar of Galaxy. She felt much better after the sugar rush, it didn't last and by nine o'clock she was falling asleep on the sofa. Jim expressed his concern that Louise was doing too much, but concern was all he did express for he didn't pick up the hoover or the frying pan, those were still jobs for Louise.

The results were back, and Louise had been called in for a consultation. The baby-faced GP informed Louise that her results indicated that, despite her best efforts, her iron count was still below the recommended level and she would have to persist with a green diet. In addition, she was told she was suffering from a mild case of myalgic encephalomyelitis, explaining the dizziness and fatigue. With no cure or prescribed treatment, she would have to manage the condition. Jim could hardly disguise his pleasure that a professional had conquered with his opinion, Louise was over-working herself towards an early grave.

As the days got warmer and the sun shone brighter Louise's mood became darker. She tried to shine through the haze, but her positivity was failing her and caring for the grandkids was becoming a battle, one that she would fight until its conclusion. Work had been understanding and allowed for flexible hours, so Louise could complete a shift and provide Jim with a cooked meal before being collapsing on the sofa. Her mind was as drained as her body leaving her without the energy to even daydream. Jim had been left alive and well for far too long.

Since the death of his mother Jim's approach to mortality had changed. The sudden death of his father had taken him by surprise and shaken him, but he had recovered. The ill health of his mother had made him angry with the world at the cruelty it was capable of, yet her death had been a grateful release for them all. However, his own brush with death had made him question the purpose of life and re-evaluate where he was going. Not that he changed anything he did, where he went or where he was going. Unlike Louise, Jim didn't fear death, he didn't welcome it, but he had accepted the inevitability of life.

Though Louise bumped off her husband of a regular basis in her mind she hadn't really contemplated losing him. Even on the trips to hospital as Jim fought for his life she didn't seriously entertain spending her senior years alone. Nobody ever thought the worst would happen to them. Life insurance and wills had been in place since the children arrived on the scene so there was no financial hang-up if one partner exited the union via heaven.

What would the Wilsons do without each other?

Would they remarry or lead a life of celibacy? Louise was sure they would both find new partners for their twilight years, besides Jim already had Mrs Henderson. There were a few potential candidates at work, maybe she should start laying some ground work in the warehouse, ready to find herself a new suitor. Jim would never admit that he had given the slightest thought to either divorce or death, which he had. He knew he had a willing applicant in Heather next door. Not that he would be letting Louise into that secret, but as long as his meals were cooked, and he was serviced in the bedroom he'd be reasonably happy, although he would prefer the woman he chosen to marry.

Louise found it doubtful that Jim's sexual orientation would shift, and Jim would fervently agree. Louise had the odd drunken fumble in college with other women but nothing beyond adolescent experimentation. She didn't plan on embarking on a gay relationship should she find herself single, but she didn't discount the possibility. Louise was happy to give most things a go, at least once. Except hard drugs or anything sexually degrading or illicitly illegal or morally wrong.

Would their new partners be younger or older? Louise fancied the idea of being a cougar over a bunny boiler, besides she'd always preferred cats over rabbits. If she bagged herself a younger model she should see the grave first and avoid the heartache of losing a loved one, assuming she got over Jim's death. At a few years older Jim wouldn't benefit from dating Mrs Henderson, but he'd also be too idle to put the effort into finding and dating someone else. Jim would enjoy being chased, that's how Louise snared him, but wouldn't be an active player in the game. Jim would love to find himself in the role of gigolo. He liked to think he would earn an extravagant lifestyle, but Louise worried he'd end up homeless. They both came to independent conclusions that they were best off as the dysfunctional couple they were.

46

Louise and Ellen had planned a girlie shopping trip to the newly opened multiplex. The hotly anticipated development was almost the size of a whole village and came straight from the architectural designers responsible for creating theme parks. It even had trams to get you around as well as a North and South entrance. A cinema, arcades, play areas and even a mini-casino tempted you from the last remaining pounds that the hundreds of retail outlets had not teased from your wallet. There were bars, restaurants, international cuisines and tea shops. There were butchers and bakers but not a candlestick maker, but plenty of home décor stores that could sell you one. You could spend a whole week there and still find something to do. It was over-whelming. There were even pop-up health clinics situated in the furthest corners of the car park, which in itself had been zoned into coloured areas. Not that Louise would remember what zone she was in. She'd started taking a photo on her phone so that she could confidently return with her shopping instead of aimlessly wandering around, looking lost. More than once she'd swear her car had been stolen, only to find it exactly where she'd left it.

Six and a half hours later Louise, Ellen and Sophia, who was used for her buggy more than her company, returned to the car.

"Nooo, my car." screamed Louise. She dropped her shopping bags and ran the remaining few feet to inspect her beloved automobile. The driver's side was a jagged mess of dents and scrapes with a trail of suspicious red paint that ran from the bonnet to bumper. There was no note of explanation, of insurance details or even an apology. This wasn't a little fender-bender but a case of GBH. The front wheel arch was twisted at a dangerously sharp angle. They loaded the shopping into the car and headed back to the complex to report the incident and await the recovery vehicle. Louise was told they would look into the matter, however, the signs on every post warning that 'vehicles at left at the owners risk' resolved them of any responsibility. Louise pictured Jim holding his breath waiting for them to get back to him, it was not a pretty sight.

Women plus a small child meant that they were a priority. The rugged mechanic took one look at poor old Clarence and declared the German motor unfit to drive. Within forty minutes of the call Louise, Ellen, Sophia and Clarence were loaded onto the recovery truck and were on their way home.

The BMW sat mournfully on the drive as its fate was discussed. Louise wanted it mended but Jim insisted that any repair would outweigh the value by far, Louise knew he was right. It was about time she let it go, Jim would be damned if she was going to pull off the same stunt she did to get Clarence repaired last time. She had a small hire car in the interim, there was no way Jim was lending her the keys for the Esprit. One of Louise's flaws was that she became attached to inanimate objects. The source of many rows was Louise's tendency to hoard and her collections drove Jim round the bend. To Louise they contained memories or stirred feelings that made her happy, to her they represent love, so she loved them. Jim outwardly portrayed the desire for minimalism, yet his private spaces were chaotic and messy.

Louise looked longingly at Clarence as she climbed into the temporary solution to her vehicle predicament. She was not relishing the long day of meetings and staff appraisals ahead of her.

After a nightmare day - two sackings, one disciplinary, four warnings and a promotion – Louise left scorch marks as she left the store. The pop rock tones of Cher had eased the journey home, but all Louise wanted was a bath and bed.

Louise bumped up the lane. She gasped in shock as the tree line gave way to reveal at startling surprise. She looked in horror at the empty driveway. Where Clarence had glumly sat this morning was now a vacant space, just the paved drive and a clear view of the house.

"Where the hell is my car?" screamed Louise at the universe.

Jim wasn't answering his phone and he hadn't left a note.

Louise was furious. She paced around the house, trying Jim a few more times. She was too unsettled, not knowing what had happened to Clarence, to concentrate on anything. Louise hoped that Jim had taken her treasured car to the garage, but she feared he had taken him to be euthanised.

Tea hadn't been started by the time Jim came sheepishly through the door, considerably later than scheduled. Jim was met by his wife, arms crossed, foot tapping, eyebrows raised, and mouth pinched. He was carrying a bunch of flowers AND a box of chocolates, which, as Louise knew, did not spell good news.

"Where's my car?" demanded Louise.

Jim handed Louise her gifts with a wishful smile. "I thought you deserved a treat." replied Jim, taking off his coat.

"My car?" Louise enquired as her eyebrows raise even higher.

"How was work today? Did the appraisals go well?" asked Jim innocently.

"It was fine, usual crap. Thanks for the flowers. Where's my car?" fired back Louise.

"You're welcome Honey. Have you already eaten?" Jim was starting to sweat.

"My car Jim. What have you done with my car?" The heat was beginning to rise as Louise ground her teeth. She still wasn't feeling at full strength yet and Jim was wearing her out.

"We'll talk about that later. Shall I go out and get us something?" said Jim changing the subject.

Louise mentally counted to ten before she replied. He had something to hide, he has either having an affair or he had done some despicable to Clarence. "Listen to me Jim. Tell me. Now. Where is my car?"

Jim was already backing away as he carefully prepared his answer. "The car was a rot box for crying out loud Louise. The bloody thing was an eyesore. It had done God knows how many miles, was costing more every year to patch it up. You were never going to get rid of it Louise".

"IT'S MY CAR." roared Louise. "What have you done to Clarence?"

"It's a car," stated Jim "and it's gone."

"Sorry." he begrudgingly uttered after what felt like an eternity of stony silence. Louise shooting daggers at Jim who resembled a boy caught with his hand in the cookie jar.

After further death stares and snarled comments about ownership and rights Jim retired to his study and Louise to the bathroom, both hungry and miserable. Louise's tears dissolved in the hot water of the shower. She was emotionally and physically exhausted. Louise sobbed to herself as she drifted off to sleep, no consolation for the loss of her car, and the freedom that went with it.

In Louise's mind Jim accompanied Clarence on his final journey, in the boot. Louise waved goodbye and blew a kiss as Clarence was lifted into the air, suspended by a gigantic magnet and deposited inside the car crusher. The sound made Louise wince as metal compacted on itself. Clarence protesting as its metal skeleton was twisted and bent like a contortionist. Jim's screams were lost to the scraping of metal. Louise looked despondently at the cube of metal. It could make an abstract art installation on the drive, but Louise left her beloveds to a rusty graveyard. The trickles of blood that would eventually make their way through the maze of twisted metal would be lost against the copper patches of rust. Like a film with alternate endings Jim's crushing defeat was played out with various solutions. Broken Jim's from the factory were sent to the industrial hydraulic press department to be reformed into shredded material that was used as packaging by companies.

Jumping back to the middle ages Jim was accused of treason and was sentenced to a public execution, he was to suffer the fate of being crushed. The executioner would either crush his skull in a specially designed device or his chest would be weighted until his ribs cracked and his organs were compressed like rotten tomatoes. Fast forwarding fifteen centuries to the present and Louise pictured Jim walking innocently down the street. Before he reaches his destination, an ill-devised pulley system transporting a grand piano to the tenth floor of a hotel snaps. The calls to "watch out" lost from the height of the building. Jim strode along the pavement without a care in the world, a strange whistle in the wind and a shadow forming over him should have altered him to his impending death. It did not, and Jim was squashed, like an ant under a heavy boot.

The temperature was frosty inside and outside the Wilson household for a few days. Louise ignoring Jim's attempts to make contact and Jim feeling guilty and exasperated in equal measure. Louise was tolerating Jim. Still smarting from the loss of Clarence the equilibrium at home had improved from deadly to hostile with talks to downgrade the threat to severe. A surprise visit from Frank and the kids, after hearing about the shopping trip from hell, caused a temporary ceasefire. Louise, under the persuasion of her eldest, allowed Jim to take the mantle as head of the house and take her 'shopping' for a new car. He'd seen loads of bargains on eBay and was in his element showing her all the economic little run-arounds she could choose from. "Yes, that's an option" or "Let me think about it" became the easiest reply.

Eventually they agreed on a compromise, Jim's choice of shopping outlet, Louise's choice of transport. They had arranged to go and see a car the next day. Louise decided that the pictures were certainly taken from the sellers unique perspective and she remained carless.

Jim reignited the war by releasing a nerve agent, otherwise known as his feet. Louise crinkled her nose in response to the odious scent. She didn't actually vocalise her offended sense, but Jim knew the problem was his man size tootsies. Jim's response was to narrow his eyes at his wife. Fuming, but stubborn, Louise shoved her thumb and index finger up her nostrils to further emphasis her disgust. "It's not my fault." complained Jim in his own defence before stomping off to wash his feet. Louise was furious. It wasn't her fault Jim's feet stank. Cleaning up the trail of sweaty footprints Louise muttered over the foul imprints of her husband and waited for Jim to return, they still had a car to find.

47

Although Louise liked to dream up ways for Jim to kick the bucket she never really considered that he would. Well, not until he was an old man. She had thought about it when Jim was causing her strife but only ever as fantasies to make her feel better, the same way she dreamed of running off to America and marrying a famous Hollywood star. In her current mood she seriously considered the implications of being widowed, after the initial heartbreak had healed.

They would be financially stable. The mortgage was paid, and Jim's life insurance would give Louise the capital for a trouble-free old age. There were certainly advantages, she could do what she wanted when she wanted, and she'd only have to cook if she wanted to. She might find a new partner and experience that flutter of excitement in their presence or have more than one gentleman caller. The children could move back home, there'd be room and no objections, and Louise suspected no takers. Louise never denied that she liked her own company, but she did get fed up with herself and Jim offered an attractive alternative.

Without Jim Louise would be lonely. No matter how much time the couple tried to spend apart, Louse would miss Jim, and she would miss him terribly.

Jim's mood was still as consistently unpredictable as a teenager's. One minute he was angry at the world and everyone in it, the next at the injustices blasted from the news stations and finally at his personal demons. His family suffered the brunt of his frustrations and faced a future with a man that looked and talked the same as their beloved Jim but was emotionally and behaviourally a stranger. Jim struggled the most. He had made a great recovery. The majority didn't survive the surgery, and many were left with cognitive delays, but Jim had retained his memories, skills and strength, but had lost what little patience and empathy he had. He couldn't help himself, he knew he was being cruel or unreasonable yet couldn't stop his reactions. There was so much of the original Jim that he found it hard to fathom the new, but not improved, version. He found himself thinking or acting irrationally over minor upsets and his tolerance level for other people was at an all-time low.

Jim wasn't deliberately lazy or thoughtless, it seemed an innate trait that would never change. He was brought up in a totalitarian household and had rebelled in his adult years. Louise had assumed that Jim would grow out of his broodily alluring ways, he did not. Louise had enabled to him by washing his clothes, making his dinner and generally cleaning up after him in a desperate bid to impress and prove herself to be marriage material. This continued when they had children and when their children had children. Louise had inadvertently made a rod for her own back, which she tried her damnedest to break or bend.

Louise hadn't slept well. The unease and anger between the married couple was playing on her mind and saddening her heart. Louise hated falling out with people she loved, hated to feel alone in their company. Ignoring the sleeping mass of manhood next to her Louise got up. She would wait for Jim to wake before stripping the bed. Wrapping herself up in fluffy fabric she softly padded down the hallway, her footsteps silent on the wooden floorboards. She was determined to be happy, to rise above Jim's moods and find enjoyment every day.

The mess that Jim had left in the living room suggested that he anticipated getting up first, a contest he rarely won. The state of the place crushed Louise's positive intentions. It looked like he'd had a party. There were sweet and crisp wrappers littered across the floor, slippers abandoned, and empty beer cans balanced in a precarious re-enactment of the leaning tower of Pisa. Louise eat her breakfast after returning the room to her preferred state. Jim was up, she'd heard the springs on the bed moan in protest and the floorboards creak as Jim shuffled around the co-inhabited bedroom.

Louise trudged up the stairs to retrieve the dirty laundry. "Did you forget where the bin was last night?" asked Louise, unable to resist the question she didn't want an answer for. She pulled the sheets from the bed and stripped the pillows of their cases. She knew that it would wind Jim up, to be pulled up on his mess but did it anyway. Jim grunted a reply, unwilling to engage in his wife's spiteful interaction.

Hot from rushing around Louise discarded her dressing gown and scooped up t-shirts and yesterday's underwear muttering that Jim never does it and that she was fed up of doing everything. Louise was laden down with washing, she could barely see over the pile and it weighed heavy in her arms. Louise marched across the hall with a face like thunder. She was usually careful placing her feet at the top of the stairs, she didn't want to fall. She'd slipped a few Christmases back on the final few steps, carrying armfuls of presents and it had left her shaken with a bruise the size of plate. It hadn't stopped her running around the house in her socks though and she'd had several near misses since.

Annoyed, she took the approach to the stairs at speed and was negotiating the first step of her descent when Jim walked behind her. Jim had been struggling lately to control his emotions. He was angry at himself and the universe for having the aneurysm but was bottling everything up. His work was stressing him out, he missed his mum, feared his own mortality and the tension over the stupid car was driving him insane. Jim found it hard to talk about his feelings, always had, even as a child. Louise thought it was intriguing and sexy at first, a puzzle to solve, but over the years it became tedious and exasperating. In a moment of madness Jim did something that would make him question the man he had become.

For no reason other than not being able to help himself Jim pushed Louise, catching her square between the shoulder blades. He regretted it the instant he had done it but, despite time seeming to move in slow motion, he was unable to reverse his actions.

It wasn't a hard push, it was more of a nudge. However, with one foot suspended and cradling the bundle of clothes, the unexpected pressure from behind forced Louise to lose her balance. Instinctively Louise threw the washing into the air as she hurtled forward. Her hands desperately grabbed at the bannisters as they span fast, her nails scratching the wood in a frantic bid to find leverage. Louise's cries echoed to the bone crunching noise of her body hitting the exposed beams of the wooden stairs.

Jim looked on in horror, eyes wide, a scream caught in his throat. His outstretched arms lead to empty hands, his attempt to save his wife too slow. Jim winched at the sound of Louise's head hitting the hardwood floor. A pillow case fluttered down and came to rest over Louise's twisted legs.

Jim didn't move.

Louise didn't move.

Silence.

Even the clocks seemed to have stopped ticking.

It was over in a flash. The fall itself happened before Louise had time to process what was happening, the few remaining seconds were filled with fear, terror, confusion and pain before everything went black. This was no daydream. There was no reset button, no resurrection stone, no second coming.

Louise was stone cold dead.

48

Jim stared in disbelief, telepathically urging his wife to get up. Louise did not move. It was several minutes before Jim's body and mind caught up to his actions and he was flooded with the sudden realisation that Louise may actually be hurt. He refused to consider that he had killed her.

"Louise." Jim shouted in the hope she would respond. "Louise. Love." he tried again. He began to run to his wife's aid but after a few steps he stopped, only a single sock disturbed. It was as if Jim was being held back by an invisible hand as his brain ran through the possible outcomes. If Louise was alive she would kill him when she was able, or divorce him, or stay with him but make his life a living hell. If she was dead he could go to prison as a murderer, and if he didn't who would make his tea and clean the house? Either way his life was going to change, forever.

Jim picked his way prudently downstairs, careful not to disturb any of the washing and risk being labelled a killer. But first he had to know if her heart was still beating.

Louise's body was twisted at an unnatural angle. Her legs were still on the stairs, the left leg hanging floppily over her right. She was lying face down, her overweight belly exposed by the ruffled and raised fabric of her pyjama top. Louise's arms were outstretched in a failed attempt to save herself, her left wrist shattered in the fall. Louise's head was turned to the side, her eyes staring blankly at the kitchen door and her neck limp from the snapped vertebrae.

Jim knelt next to his dead spouse and tentatively held two fingers against her neck, searching for a pulse. He tried several places but the only throbbing he could feel was the beating of his own heart.

He had to think. To get away from Louise's lifeless yet accusing eyes.

Jim headed over to Mrs Henderson's on the pretence of enquiring if she needed any jobs doing and that he was seeking sanctuary from Louise's nagging, a regular occurrence. It would get him out of the house and give him time to consider his next cause of action. And it would give him a much needed alibi. Heather Henderson set about making a cup of tea and inventing jobs that Jim could help her with. Heather made polite small talk, asked about the family and if Louise had found a car she liked yet. Jim was happy to tell her that Louise was on the war path about the car and that he'd left her stripping the beds and storming around the house like a woman possessed. "I should come and live with you Heather." joked Jim.

"I'd look after you Jim dear." blushed Heather, wishing that Jim was serious.

"Why don't you come back with me and I can show you a few of the cars I've found. Maybe between us we can convince 'er indoors to get a little run around." suggested Jim hopefully. Excited at the joint collaboration Mrs Henderson jumped at the chance. Jim had an underhanded motive for inviting her back to theirs, together they could 'discover' Louise's body. Jim offered his arm to steady his unwitting accomplish on the uneven stones and held his front door open for her to enter in his ultimate show of chivalry and deception. Heather let out a shrill scream at the sight of Louise's lifeless body at the bottom of the stairs.

"What is it?" faked Jim, sounding concerned.

Poor Mrs Henderson stood shaking in the doorway as Jim rushed to his wife's side, almost slipping on a felled item of clothing.

Jim urgently uttered his wife's name and gently felt for the pulse he knew wasn't there. "Louise. Louise, can you hear me?" asked Jim, caressing his wife's still warm head.

Jim looked pleadingly at Mrs Henderson in an Oscar worthy performance. "I'll call an ambulance Jim." replied Heather soothingly, shuffling into the hallway and picking up the house phone. To Jim's mind's eye his house looked like a scene from a sex movie gone wrong, there were bedsheets and clothes flung over the stairs, but the star was fully clothed, and quite dead. Heather calmly detailed the scene to the operator, describing the position that Louise's body laid and that she couldn't detect a heartbeat. "The ambulance is in the way Jim." informed Heather.

At a loss as to what to do she put the kettle on. Jim could do with a good brew to calm his nerves she surmised.

Jim was pacing the hallway, his head in his hands. Every few laps he would squat beside Louise and gently shake her shoulders, whispering her name and willing her to wake up.

A gentle tapping on the open front door announced the arrival of help which was swift in coming and conduct. A quick check of the pulse confirmed that Louise was not breathing and, after repositioning her unresponsive body on the floor they commenced with CPR. The rapid response team worked in unison in their efforts to preserve life. A call to head office had an ambulance dispatched to support their colleagues, who called for reinforcements from the police. Jim only needed the fire brigade and coast guard to turn up to complete the set. A tiring paramedic was performing chest compressions whist their green suited colleague directed Jim and Heather away from the drama. As he was guided into the kitchen Jim heard a very faint crack followed by an equally faint "shit". He didn't know a lot about medicine but instinctively knew that one of his wife's ribs had succumbed to the pressure. It was a noise that would stay with him until he drew his final breath.

Sirens altered them to the arrival of the police, and with it Jim's future.

After establishing the facts of the case, a scene log was set up and more phone calls made. It was the police constables job to keep the area as sterile as he could, avoid cross-contamination and preserve any evidence, all of which was needed for a successful prosecution. Jim and Heather were quizzed over the course of events; who had discovered the body, when, what they had done, or not done, what they had touched and where they had been. All the while paramedics knelt over Louise in a vain attempt to bring her back from the dead. Unable to certify the death the dedicated professionals carried on with the charade until Louise's doctor could attend and they could leave, and officially hand the case over to the police.

A disagreement ensued, with the GP confirming Louise had visited him very recently and was indeed suffering from a condition that could have caused her to fall so was confident to certify her death, but the cautionary police officer was reluctant to release the body. The blameless doctor was quizzed like a leading gang member, confirming the medical diagnosis and treatments with the sceptical investigator. There was no blood or other obvious signs of trauma and technically it was Mrs Henderson who had discovered the body, though Jim was confirmed as the last person to see her alive.

The officer couldn't be one hundred percent sure that he wasn't looking at a murder scene and could make a tragic accident worse by arresting an innocent man. On first inspection it did look like a disastrous misfortune. He was in a quandary. It didn't look like any crime scene he'd been to in his lengthy career and Jim looked suitably grief stricken and shocked. The officer had painstakingly recorded every scrap of evidence should he need to present his findings to the coroner's office and called the incident in, with a request that his contemporaries in CID join him.

The circus was about to get busier with two suits arriving on the scene. They looked at Louise, spoke quietly with their colleague and re-questioned Jim and Heather. A heated discussion between the cross-section of officers followed with pointing, shaking of heads and shrugging of shoulders. The two suited CID personnel bid farewell to the two potential suspects leaving them in the hands of the responding officer.

The next visitor came to take Louise on one of her final journeys. A plain white transit style van with the words 'private ambulance' embossed on the doors blocked the lane, the Wilson driveway to full to accommodate another vehicle. Heather comforted Jim who was sobbing gently as he watched his wife being wheeled out of his life forever. "At least I don't have to deal with a new car now." thought Jim to himself.

Jim and Heather watched the van as it tentatively drove back down the lane. Mrs Henderson hoped that Louise was strapped down otherwise she'd be bouncing around the back. In their grief they almost forgot that the police officer was still present. "Would you like a cup of tea dear?" offered Heather as she refilled the kettle.

"Um. No thank you ma'am I'm afraid I'm going to have to ask you both to accompany me to the station". An eerie silence fell on the room as the Killer and his unknowing accomplish processed what the officer had said.

"But, but…." stammered Mrs Henderson whilst Jim stared in disbelief at the officer.

"My wife's just died." he reasoned. For a split second of insanity Jim considered fleeing. He thought better of it looking at the arsenal of crime preventing paraphernalia hanging off the officers utility vest. Much of the black equipment camouflaged against the charcoal coloured uniform but the visible yellow handle of his taser was a stark warning of his intention. Also, the officer was not a small chap and looked like he could take Jim down without even trying. And running would definitely confirm his guilt.

"I'll head home now Jim, I'll pop back later." tried Heather, shuffling towards the door.

"Ma'am." said the officer civilly, "Ma'am, there's been a death, you can't just leave the scene".

"Don't' be silly. Anyone can see what happened." answered Heather continuing towards the door.

"Yes, ma'am but I need to fully investigate so you, and Mr Wilson, will have to come with me."

"I've never committed a crime in my life." announced Heather, appalled at the accusations.

The officer turned to Jim, his hand hovering over the handcuffs.

"Jim Wilson. I am arresting you on the suspicion of the murder of Louise Wilson. You do not have to say anything, but it may harm your defence if you do not mention when questioned something which you later rely on in court. Anything you do say may be given in evidence. Do you understand?" rattled off the officer. Dumbfounded Jim nodded.

The officer turned to Jim's neighbour and repeated the statement. "No, no I don't young man. I came in and she was lying there. End off. I'm not going to the station." replied Heather defiantly.

"It's procedure ma'am and I have formally arrested you, so you, and Mr Wilson, will be coming with me." confirmed the officer.

"I'd like to see you try." challenged Heather.

"As you wish ma'am." said the officer approaching Heather with the handcuffs. "That's not necessary officer." interrupted Jim. "Don't make me cuff you too sir." responded the constable. Jim backed away, pleading with Heather to comply with the officers demands. She didn't, and her hands were bound in connecting metal bracelets. Jim was permitted to leave a bowl of food out for the cat and lock the house before being transported to the station where he would be charged or acquitted.

49

Jim was seeing a different side to Mrs Henderson who sat stubbornly alongside him in the back of the squad car. The sweet lady that lived next door had a rebellious streak. The car was one of the classic Vauxhall Astra's with fluorescent markings, the constabularies insignia and an unusual aroma that was neither pleasant or odious. There wasn't a lot of leg room in the back, but Jim deduced that they weren't bothered about providing luxury and comfort to the criminal element of society. He had expected the dash to be fitted with state of the art technology, intricate recording and communication devices or some other kind of Inspector gadget style panel filled with specialist crime fighting tools, but it was no different to a standard family vehicle.

On Mrs Henderson's request the handcuffs were removed, and she followed Jim obediently into the station. Owing to Heathers reluctance to cooperate she was first in front of the custody Sargent. Jim had been too distracted to ask the officer his name, couldn't even recall his badge number. PC Newbury outlined the circumstances of each arrest and no health concerns were recorded. The pair both refused legal advice and were placed in separate cells whilst Newbury carried out his investigation. Background checks on the property came up negative as did the history of any criminal behaviour, with the exception of Heather who had two minor misdemeanours from her life as a young woman. She failed to disclose them and blamed it on her age, and the fact that she was never formally charged, and they happened so long ago. On one occasion she drove a car eight meters, without insurance and the other time she was caught being drunk and disorderly after a graduation party.

Jim was first in the hot seat. He was happy to be out of the depressing cold cell but still felt nauseous as he was led to an interview room. Jim was directed to sit in the chair facing the door. PC Newbury was accompanied by a gentleman he introduced as DC Monroe. Jim was expecting a one way mirror, the characteristic tape recorder and bolted down furniture but the tiny room had bare dirty walls painted a pastel green, a small table and the interview was digitally recorded. The only way in or out was through the door they'd just come through. Newbury again outlined the reason for Jim's arrest. He asked Jim to explain to him what had happened preceding the events that resulted in the death of his wife, Louise Jane Wilson. Jim had been rehearsing in the cell, going over and over his story, making sure he didn't trip himself up.

He told them all about his aneurysm, how Louise cares for him but that he gets a little down sometimes when Louise was in one of her funny moods. He explained about the car and why she was upset and that he had left her rushing about doing the washing and went to see

Heather for a little while, a common habit. Most of it was true, he only missed out a detail here and there and he was genuinely mourning over the loss of his wife. Newbury asked a handful more probing questions before suspending the interview to corroborate a few details. DC Monroe remained silent for the entire interview. Jim was led back to his cell. He shuddered as the door closed with a loud metallic clink. Jim sat on the hard bench staring blindly at the white tiled wall wondering if they had bought his version of events.

Mrs Henderson was next into the same interview room, with the same interviewing officers. PC Newbury again outlined the reason for her arrest, taking the time to reiterate that had she not protested she would not have handcuffed. He asked her about Jim's visits and what happened earlier that day. Heather confirmed everything she could that Jim had said and was quick to his defence over questions about the married couples relationship.

"Well dear, she was an accident waiting to happen, rushing here, there and everywhere. If you keep juggling you're bound to drop something sooner or later aren't you. Such a waste." she sighed

"She was a lovely maid though, good as gold, do anything for you she would." Mrs Henderson happily informed the officers. "Oh, poor Jim." she gasped dramatically, "Whatever is he going to do now?" Heather quite enjoyed being interviewed, she had nothing to hide, unlike Jim.

"Right. Yes. Well, thank you Mrs Henderson." said PC Newbury "I am suspending the interview. I'd like to check a few details. If you can come with me Mrs Henderson I will return you to your cell."

"If you must dear. Can DC Quiet take me instead?" enquired Heather hopefully.

"No." replied Newbury and led Heather back to her cell.

With one final perspective to glean PC Newbury made the decision to contact the Wilson children. The only motive he had for Jim was Louise's life insurance policy, taken out half a lifetime ago. The house was paid off, they both worked, had a perfect credit score and ample savings. It seemed they had an average relationship, married for decades, no infidelities, no allegations, just an ordinary well-off middle class mid-life couple.   The only motive he could find for Heather was that she may be attracted to Jim and saw Louise as a threat. He couldn't seem to fathom a way in which Heather had got unseen into the Wilsons house, pushed Louise down the stairs and returned before Jim noticed that she was missing. Both the suspects stories matched. He considered that they were in on it together, were having an affair, that they, or Jim, or Heather had killed Louise and they had fabricated the whole scenario to avoid capture and be free to start a relationship. Even if Heather did like Jim in more than a neighbourly way he had detected no hidden feelings on Jim's behalf. He had watched them interacting closely at the house, but Jim acted accordingly, like a shell-shocked, bewildered husband.

As Ellen lived close he made a personal trip to inform her of the passing of her mother and the arrest of her father. Naturally she was devasted. Norman made the officer a cup of tea whilst Ellen facetimed her brother and the siblings grieved over the loss of the beloved mum.

They each said they wouldn't have been surprised if it was Louise in custody for killing Jim, but both stood as character witnesses that their father was a nice guy who loved his wife and the only thing he was guilty of is not being an active or attentive husband. Jim was straight laced and dependable and had never done nothing illegal, the kids doubted he'd even ever taken a drag on a spliff as a teenager.

After seven hours in custody Jim and Heather were released without charge, pending further investigation. "Don't leave the country." warned Newbury as they left. A tearful Ellen was waiting in reception to take them home. Newbury had no hard evidence, but he'd requested a post mortem to determine any undiagnosed medical cause for the fall.

All that could be heard on the way home were that of the occupants breathing and other vehicles on the road. Jim sat in the car for several minutes staring at his front door. Ellen and Heather left him alone and went inside. The only evidence that anything dreadful had happened was the washing littering the stairs. They solemnly picked up the discarded laundry, removing the evidence of Jim's betrayal.

Mrs Henderson resumed Louise's role as matriarch and rifled through the stocked fridge. Jim hadn't eaten all day, he may be wounded but he still needed to eat. Ellen found it strange seeing another woman in her mother's place but as she'd known Mrs H since they'd moved there, and she provided a familiar comfort. She was glad she was taking charge.

Jim knew he couldn't stay outside forever. He'd loved Louise, with all his heart. He hadn't meant to kill her. But he had and now had had to deal with the consequences. He wasn't about to let his family lose a father and grandfather too. Mustering all his courage Jim bravery entered the house he had shared with his partner of a lifetime. He couldn't help but stare at the spot where Louise had fallen. The bare step was as it had been millions of times before, as if nothing had happened. The smell of food drew his stomach toward the kitchen. He hadn't realised he was hungry until his tummy rumbled in protest at the forced abstinence. The food was tasteless, but his digestive system was satisfied. Each found solace in their own company, remembering Louise in their own way. Mrs Henderson retuned home and Jim went to bed. Ellen stayed in her old room.

With eyes blurred by tears Jim climbed the stairs, taking time to pause on each step. An immediate consequence of his actions was a martial bed with no sheets and no wife. He spent the night in the spare room.

50

Jim woke feeling groggy. He momentarily frowned at finding himself in the spare room and for a split second forgot what had happened yesterday. A blink of his eyes dropped all vestiges of sleep and the realisation of what he had done stunk in. He felt as if he'd been punched in the stomach. Jim came downstairs to the smell of coffee and both his children talking in hushed tones in the kitchen. Frank had arrived early in the morning.

With a police investigation and the likelihood of an autopsy hanging over their heads the Wilsons were held in a grief limbo.

The phone was in constant use. When they weren't taking calls of condolences they were making them to inform family and friends of their tragic loss. Fran had reacted to the news of her sister's death by losing herself in a bottle and Joan was inconsolable at out-living her eldest child. Ellen assured her nan and aunt that they should remain where they are for the time being, but Joan insisted on being there for Jim, after all both Frank and Ellen had young families and working partners to consider. Jim half-heartedly protested at his mother-in-law coming but was secretly pleased that he wouldn't have to be in the house on his own. He wasn't ready yet to face the reality he had created.

The whole house was a reminder of the life that he had taken. Louise's personality stamped into every room, with the exception of his study, that had been a Louise-free zone. Her smiling face shone out from family portraits on the walls, her ornaments stood as testament to her love of things and her clothes hung limply from the clothes horse, never to be worn again. What was he going to do with all her stuff? When should he touch it? Jim was overwhelmed with indecision. It was easy when his mother passed, the retirement home had packed her sentimental personal belongings into boxes for Jim to collect and the rest had been distributed around the residents. Mary had a will and as the only living heir Jim received a lump sum once the paperwork had been completed. He had only to arrange the funeral. Her possessions sat untouched and boxed in the garage. Jim had a tendency to avoid what he didn't wish to be involved in, and keeping memories boxed and hidden were his way of coping. Out of sight, out of mind.

Jim was anxious to hear from PC Newbury. He needed to know one way or the other the outcome of the investigation. PC Newbury was not ready to contact Mr Wilson. He had submitted his report and was waiting on the autopsy. The morgue had a backlog, but despite Newbury's urgency, Louise's case was not considered priority and she was held in a queue.

The quietness in the Wilson house was deafening. Jim thought he craved solitude but now he had it he wanted only for the love and life that Louise brought to the household. He had to admit that he was lost without her, he felt like a bird with no wings or a wagon with three wheels. They'd been apart before, when Louise went away with the girls but knowing that they would never be together again made Jim feel cold inside, that daylight would never again shine upon his world.

Mrs Henderson came round, sporting a puffy face and red eyes from crying and holding a steaming pot of casserole. "You need to eat." mothered Heather as Jim falsely informed her he wasn't hungry.

By early evening Jim had a houseful. Heather hadn't left after bringing him dinner, Joan had arrived, bringing with her an estranged aunt that Jim had no idea even existed and the kids were back. Louise's life was remembered, and her greatness toasted over dozens of bottles of red and white wine. When the wine ran dry Jim cracked open a bottle of Cognac that lived at the back of the cupboard, the evidence a thick layer of undisturbed dust. Jim cared little that he slept on a sheet-less bed, he was so drunk he could have slept in a rose bed and not given two hoots.

Hammering on the door and the ringing of the bell woke those in residence at the Wilson house. PC Newbury had come to deliver his verdict, in person. Never one to be rushed, Jim pulled the pillow over his head to try and block out the day as Ellen went to answer the door to their eager visitor. Ellen, spritely despite having a blood alcohol level that would probably put her over the limit, invited the officer inside. Newbury was offered refreshments, which he declined, whilst Ellen went in search of her father.

An apprehensive Jim walked dismally down the stairs and greeted the officer. PC Newbury's neutral expression gave no indication as to the outcome of his visit. Ellen positioned herself by the wardrobe of her old room. As a child she had discovered that a vent connected the two floors, and if she was quite, she could hear a faint echo of the conversations downstairs, as long as they weren't whispering and stayed near the south side wall.

"Mr Wilson. How have you been?" enquired Newbury.

"Um, well. Um. As you'd expect." replied Jim. He couldn't very well reply that he was fine, and the brass band marching around his head prevented him from being any more convincing. He excused himself to get a drink as his mouth was dry and his tongue felt swollen, the officer refusing for a second time.

"The purpose of my visit, Mr Wilson, is to update you on the investigation concerning the death of your wife." Newbury left a dramatic pause before continuing, gauging Jim's response which was neither one of worry nor fear. "I have completed my enquires and spoken at length with the coroner." Stated PC Newbury, the tension building in the silence between his statements.

"Have you had a call from the coroner's office Mr Wilson?" asked the officer, clearly aware that Jim had not.

"Um. No." answered Jim, adding "Should I?"

Ignoring Jim's question, the officer carried on, opening the file he had under his arm and showing Jim several pieces of paper. Jim thought he detected a note of disappointment as the officer tactfully read the report compiled by the pathologist in charge of examining Louise's body for signs of foul play. They had found none.

The autopsy confirmed that Louise's injuries were consistent with a fall. They could find no obvious signs of additional trauma or a medical reason for her death other than the characteristics of her diagnosed condition which could have contributed to her becoming unsteady on her feet. Jim felt the officer did not believe him and that he wasn't convinced of the conclusion. Jim was glad that PC Newbury was fighting for justice on behalf of his wife but desperately hoped, for his own sake, that he officer could not prove any of his allegations. He couldn't.

The coroner recorded a verdict of accidental death. The crown prosecution service would not entertain a conviction as there was not enough evidence to bring about a successful prosecution.

Jim had got away with murder.

With Jim off the hook for his wife's murder he was free to organise a fitting farewell. Jim made an appointment with the small family run funeral directors that had buried his mother and father. Accompanied by his daughter, Jim and Ellen looked through brochures of caskets, organised the flowers and discussed the bespoke pricing for the preparation, ceremony and disposal of Louise's body. Jim wasn't adverse to saving a few quid by retrieving his wife's corpse himself, but Ellen insisted that their mother would have a dignified ride in the back of a purpose made vehicle and not the boot of the family car. Not that they had a family car right now, as Clarence was a rusting cube of metal, and he wouldn't get Louise in the boot of his Lotus, there was barely the room to cram a toddler let alone a fully grown woman.

Louise had her funeral music selected, her wishes expressed over the years, but she never made the final decision to go six-feet under or be blown away in the wind. Being warm was so important to Louise they decided a cremation was a fitting option. Ellen suggested that Louise would have liked something a bit different, an eco-coffin or one of those modern customised or pictorial cardboard caskets. Jim settled on a traditional style coffin with hardwood veneer and a rosetan crepe interior. His belief were funerals weren't for the dead, they were for the living and what was the point in spending thousands on something that could only be used once then burnt to a crisp or left to rot. A spattering of simple floral displays using Louise's favourite flowers would accompany her to the service with a request for family flowers only but donations to the local animal sanctuary would be happily received in Louise's honour.

Jim contemplated visiting his wife as she lay at rest in the fridges at the funeral parlour but there was nothing he could do or say to change the situation. Besides, all he could think of to say was "sorry" and that would raise questions he hoped he'd already convincingly answered. He was struggling to hide from Louise's dead reproachful eyes that stalked his waking thoughts and haunted his dreams, so he didn't need a cold grey reminder of the crime he had committed. Fortunately, the sympathetic funeral director dismissed his attitude as a response to grief, after all everyone handles it differently.

51

The day of Louise's funeral loomed largely for Jim. Everything he had known during his adult life was over. His supporter, his lover, his sounding post, gone. Work had been fantastic, his boss, a fellow widower had granted him compassionate leave without hesitation and for as long as he needed. To be honest Jim was raring to get back to work, he was quite bored at home, mopping around and eager to put the whole sorry mess behind him. Jim couldn't help feeling a little guilty over the sympathy he'd been getting, he really didn't deserve it.

Joan, and the mysterious aunt Mabel, who it turned out wasn't strictly related but had been unofficially adopted as a surrogate family member before Louise was even born, stayed with Jim to "keep him company and help him adjust". Jim appreciated the gesture.

The day of the funeral Jim woke uncharacteristically early. For the first time since Louise had died he broke down in floods of tears. His body shook with the force of emotion pouring out of him. His whole being yearned to hold the woman he had chosen to spend his life with. At that moment he would have given anything to touch her skin, to hear her voice again.

There was a gentle tapping on the door. "I'm here when you're ready Jim." He heard Joan's delicate footsteps retreat.

Jim looked at the suit hanging on the back of the door. "I'll put it on later." he thought to himself. Jim faced a torturous morning of waiting around. Family arrived in dribs and drabs until the house was full of sad faces. Ellen had requested that everyone wear a bright top in memory of Louise, to commemorate her positive personality. Jim's shirt was green.

At ten past one the doorbell rang. It was time. Two limousines were parked in the lane. A middle aged gentleman in a tailored black suit smiled kindly at Jim and gestured towards the waiting cars. He helped Joan into the first limousine while Frank and Ellen loaded their entourage into the second. Jim locked up and assisted aunt Mabel to the car. The sun glared off the polished sleek noir exterior of the funeral possession, casting rays of reflected light in all directions.

As they neared the end of the lane Jim could see the hearse, patiently waiting to take the Wilsons on their final journey together as a family united. The mood was sombre, Jim's eyes were locked on Louise's coffin like a snipper. Joan stifled the tears that were threatening to fall.

As they pulled up outside the crematorium Joan smiled at the colourful turnout. Jim steadied the sensation of panic that was starting to grip him. He took deep breaths to calm his racing heartbeat. Jim allowed Ellen and Frank to go first, giving him a barrier between himself and unwanted words of sympathy. He just wanted it to be over. He'd settled the invoice in full, leaving a cheque in a sealed envelope on the seat as he'd left the car.

Silence fell as Louise's casket was lifted into the air and carried into the non-descript brick building. Jim, arm-in-arm with Joan, led the assembled mourners inside. The room filled with the sound of shuffling of feet, hushed whispers and gentle sobs. As the final person was seated the reverend began her speech. She thanked everyone for coming to pay their final respects and gave a rendition of all the best parts of Louise's life. Jim sat motionless throughout the service, only a faint acknowledgement of admiration when his children spoke of their mothers strengths and love. Before Jim was ready the service was drawing to a close. He didn't want to say goodbye.

The angelic voice singing *Hallelujah* took Louise from her family forever, her coffin slowly disappearing from view. The service concluded, and Jim numbly led their family and friends through the memorial garden and back to the car park. Anybody that wished could return to the White Oak Inn for a wake.

Jim woke up the next morning, laying diagonally across the bed unable to recall much after arriving at the pub.

Another consequence he thought to himself, he got the bed all to himself. Jim tried to get up but found his mind more willing than his body. He flopped around like a beached whale but mustered little progress, eventually giving up and conceding that he was probably still drunk from yesterday. He could hear activity downstairs but had no desire to be part of it. He must have fallen back to sleep as he woke again, this time feeling a little more human. He blinked at the stinging daylight, his eyes and head adjusting to a new day. The first real day without Louise. The first day he had to go-it alone and forge a new start. It would be just his luck if she came back to haunt him.

It was midday before Jim ventured downstairs. He was distracted from staring at the spot where Louise had come to land by Jared shouting "Anda. Anda. Anda". He smiled at his grandson, he looked just like Frank did at that age, all cheeky smiles and mischief. Jim knew that he would survive this, that his children would survive it. They would hurt, for a while but Louise had instilled in them the strength of character to be fighters, to rise above adversity and to laugh and love with all their hearts.

By nightfall the kids had returned to their lives with Joan and aunt Mabel departing the next day.

Ellen called every day, was a constant presence in her dads life and Frank when he remembered.

Jim was back to work within the week. Colleagues he'd never spoken to before nodded at him and wished him well, but none eyed him with suspicion though he'd obviously been the subject of the office gossip. The only difference to Jim's working day was that his shirts were unironed, and his lunches now came from the garage on the way to work but when he got home he did feel the loneliness of an empty house. The cats had all but moved in next door as Heather at least remembered to feed them and Jim was a regular visitor, much to the encouragement of Mrs Henderson. The novelty that his new found freedom brought was starting to wear off. He was really missing the food and sex that he'd taken for granted and was seriously contemplating what he was going to do for the next thirty years. Jim thought of himself as a bit of a loner but now he was without company he was finding that he didn't want to be alone.

Jim had collected Louise's ashes from the funeral directors. The family gathered at one of the trails that Louise used to drag them to as children. They each took a handful of remains and scattered them in the wind. Jim was surprised to find the texture gravelly, he had expected it to be smooth, as soft as Louise's skin. Jim whispered a final goodbye as he allowed the sandy mixture to blow across the landscape.

The final chapter had closed on his relationship with Louise Wilson. There would now only be anniversaries that would be remembered and commiserated. With Ellen's help Jim sorted through Louise's belongings, donating anything that Jim had no use for and passing treasured items into the care of her heirs. Over time Jim slowly removed the items that had given him cause to moan and groan over the years. He boxed the annoying collections and décor in favour of empty space and nothingness.

Ellen gave birth to another beautiful baby girl that she named Eloise, but the joy was diminished without her mother to share it with her. What pained Ellen the most was that she never got to tell her mum she was pregnant. She was waiting just a few more weeks and it broke her heart knowing that her little girl would never know her name sake. Louise had been so integral in those early years with Sophia, she didn't know how she'd manage, but she would. She loved her dad, but he'd never been a hands-on grandparent like Louise. Also, he'd been going about the business of moving on. It aggrieved her, but she wanted her dad to find happiness, not to replace her mum but to not be alone.

The relationship between the two long-term neighbours had blossomed into something beyond friendship. They were not exclusively a couple, yet. Friends with benefits the younger generation would call it. It was much to the pleasure of the scarlet Mrs Henderson who had a carefully constructed plan of attack to seduce her widowed neighbour. After all, she'd been dreaming for years of ways to dispose of Louise so that she could get her hands on her man.

THE END

N.Joy

Nickie is a cat-loving married mum of two who was born and bred in Bideford, a pretty little town in North Devon. With a love of books from a young age and a passion for writing stories Nickie's debut novel, Jill, won a Gold award.

She writes under her maiden name of Joy and hopes that you will 'enjoy' her work.

For more information visit her website @

www.nljdesigns.co.uk or find her on social media.

N.Joy

This is the book Louise is reading on page 16.

Jill

By NJOY

In the autumn of 1888 terror stalked the streets of Whitechapel.

'Jack the Ripper' was never caught.

Follow a surprising suspect as she weaves her mayhem into a tapestry of blood and lies in a twist on one of Britain's most notorious unsolved murders.

What if Jack was a Jill ?

www.nljdesigns.co.uk

Available in paperback & Kindle on Amazon

N.Joy

Check out what Louise is reading on page 214.

IF ONE DRAGON BURNED THE CITY OF NIVERSAI
TO THE GROUND IN A SINGLE NIGHT, HOW
WOULD WE FARE IF A HUNDRED BESIEGED OUR
WORLD?

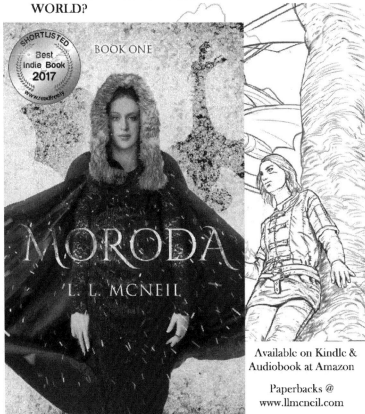

Available on Kindle &
Audiobook at Amazon

Paperbacks @
www.llmcneil.com

Book 1 is the novel that Louise is reading on page 283.

N.Joy

Printed in Poland
by Amazon Fulfillment
Poland Sp. z o.o., Wrocław